Prairie Skies Series

Under Moonlit Skies

CYNTHIA ROEMER

MANTLE ROCK
PUBLISHING LLC
MantleRockPublishingLLC.com

Published by Mantle Rock Publishing LLC
2879 Palma Road
Benton, KY 42025
http://mantlerockpublishingllc.com

Printed in the United States of America

ISBN 978-1-945094-98-9

Cover by Diane Turpin at dianeturpindesigns.com

All Scripture is taken from the King James Version.

*"For the Lord seeth not as man seeth for man looketh on the outward appearance,
but the Lord looketh on the heart."*
1 Samuel 16:7 KJV

To the One who gives me grace and purpose.

And to my husband.
Thanks for wishing upon a star
that moonlit night so many years ago.

Endorsements

Trapped between the weight of obligation and the haunting pull of conviction, Under Moonlit Skies brings to life the beauty that is found when two hearts yield control to the plans of a loving Creator. Full of intrigue, adventure, and romance, this story is sure to leave an indelible mark on your heart.

—Tara Johnson, Award-winning author
of *Engraved on the Heart*

Cynthia Roemer has the unique ability to bring the adventure of the 1800s prairie to life as she unfolds another authentic story in the Prairie Sky series. Her characters stay with you long after the book is finished, which made reading Under Moonlit Skies feel like visiting old friends!

—Misty M. Beller, USA Today Bestselling Author
of *Hope's Highest Mountain*

Acknowledgments

I'm so grateful for each of you who've contributed to the writing of *Under Moonlit Skies.*

Thanks to my husband, Marvin, for your patience and understanding as I spent countless hours at the computer, turning the scenes and characters in my head into a viable story. I'm so grateful for your love and support. May our next twenty-five years be even more special than our first.

Thanks to my sons, Glenn and Evan, for all of your technical support and helping me make sense of things when I didn't know up from down. I love you both dearly!

Thanks to my parents, Alvin and Florence Smith, for instilling within me a love for the Lord and for being so supportive of my writing through the years. Thanks also to my sisters, Lisa Cannon and Renae Ernst and their families for being so kind in your efforts to lend a helping hand.

Thanks to my friends and Beta readers, Savanna Kaiser and Cara Grandle, for all your wonderful counsel, support, and much needed pep-talks. You two are truly a gift from the Lord. When we connected at the ACFW back in 2014, we never could have guessed what a special bond the Lord had in store for us. God bless you both as we continue our writing journeys together.

I'm so grateful for my Launch Team members for taking time out to read, review, and help spread the word about *Under Moonlit Skies*. Thank you for your commitment to my writing and your kind encouragement.

Thanks to my critique partner and fellow author, Pam Meyers, for reading through my story ahead of time and pointing out areas that needed tweaked. Also I'm grateful to Pam, as well as Crystal Caudill and the staff at the Cincinnati Public Library, for lending me their expertise regarding the history of Cincinnati. I am indebted to you for your knowledge and insights.

Special thanks to gifted authors Tara Johnson and Misty M. Beller for their sweet endorsements for *Under Moonlit Skies*. I can't tell you how I appreciate you taking time out of your busy schedules to read my novel and write such splendid comments about it. Thank you so much!

Thanks to the staff at Mantle Rock Publishing: Jerry and Kathy Cretsinger for giving me this opportunity to fulfill a lifelong dream and all your work in publishing my Prairie Sky Series, Diane Cretsinger Turpin for her beautiful cover art and typesetting, and Pam Harris for helping weed out unnecessary words and punctuation.

Most of all, I'm indebted to the Lord for taking this country girl's dream of one day being published and bringing it to fruition in His time. May You receive the glory and honor in all I write for without Your inspiration, my stories are but words on a page.

God bless you, dear readers, for finding my novels amid the sea of books out there. May you be blessed beyond measure in reading this Prairie Sky Series. You are the ones that make the rigors of writing worthwhile.

PART I
BEGINNINGS

Chapter One

Avery (Circle J) Ranch ~ Illinois, May 1859

"PUSH!"

The midwife's firm directive brought Esther Stanton to a sharp halt several paces from the bed where her sister, Charlotte, lay with knees bent, a sheet draped over her lower body. Teeth gritted, she breathed a labored groan and bore down hard, her crimson hair damp with sweat.

Esther tugged off her travel gloves and closed the gap between them. She'd missed the birth of Rachel, her sister's firstborn. It appeared she'd arrived just in time to witness the second child's coming.

Charlotte expelled an exhausted breath and sank back on the bed. Her gaze flicked to where Esther was standing, and a weary grin touched her lips. "You came."

"Course I did." Warmth flowed through Esther at the appreciative glint in her sister's eyes. The nearly four years apart seemed to melt away as they took each other in. Gone was the spoiled, sassy older sister of their growing up years. Instead, Charlotte's emerald eyes exuded genuine warmth and caring.

Esther slid a chair to the bedside and clasped her sister's hand. "And none too soon, it appears."

Through shallow breaths, Charlotte managed a slight nod, her smile fading. Pain stabbed at the back of Esther's hand as her sister's fingernails dug into her skin. With her free hand, Esther wrung out a damp cloth and dabbed the beads of sweat blistering Charlotte's forehead.

Obviously bone weary from what must have been hours of labor, Charlotte drew in a determined breath then curled forward in another grueling effort.

"You're almost there. Keep pushing!" Mrs. Brimmer urged from the foot of the bed. The midwife had aged considerably since Esther had last seen her. Would she have the stamina to aid the delivery?

Numbness shot through Esther's hand as Charlotte loosened her hold and lay back, gasping for air, in yet another failed attempt. The poor dear looked exhausted.

Pacing boot steps sounded outside the door. Charlotte's husband, Chad, had been more fidgety than a fly on a windowpane when Esther arrived. Waiting seemed nearly as taxing as giving birth. But judging by the tension on Charlotte's face, not quite so much.

Esther leaned forward, desperate for some encouraging words to spur her sister on. "You're doing fine, Sis. It'll all be worth it when you hold the baby in your arms."

Charlotte gave a soft chuckle as though sensing her reward was imminent. How beautiful she looked with her wavy, red hair draped loose about her shoulders. Agony mingled with joy in her eyes. No regrets, only determination and hope streamed from her.

A few more toilsome moments and the misery would be all but forgotten.

With a painstaking yell, Charlotte heaved her upper body forward, her hold on Esther's hand tightening once again. Esther mouthed a silent prayer as Charlotte's groan intensified, then quieted. A baby's vibrant cry sounded, drawing Esther's gaze to the foot of the bed.

Mrs. Brimmer's eyes danced. "It's a boy!"

Esther leaned to give her exhausted sister a kiss on the forehead. "How wonderful. A girl and now a boy."

Moisture pooled in Charlotte's eyes as she slumped back onto the bed, her expression wavering between fatigue and joy. Still breathless, she stretched out her arms. "May I hold him?"

The midwife beamed as she dabbed a cloth over the infant's face and handed him to Charlotte.

Heavy footsteps shuffled to a halt outside the door then returned to pacing. Mrs. Brimmer paused her cleaning and cast a weary glance at Esther. "You'd best let Chad in before he wears a hole in the floorboards."

Chuckling, Esther hurried over and lifted the latch. As she eased the door open, Chad's eyes searched hers. She smiled and widened the door. "You've a fine, healthy son."

Chad released the breath he'd been holding, a hint of a grin touching his lips. As he stepped into the room, his eyes fled to Charlotte and the bundle now clutched in her arms. He moved to her side and brushed a hand over her damp cheek.

The love in her sister's weary eyes for husband and child blossomed as Chad leaned to kiss her. Feeling intrusive, Esther eased toward the doorway. As she backed away, something brushed against her skirt. Glancing down, she saw young Rachel toddling by, her gaze fixated on her infant brother. "Baby?"

A boy of ten or eleven strode in after her and scooped her up in his arms, his voice apologetic. "Sorry."

Though nearly a foot taller than when Esther had last seen him, she recognized the lad as Chad and Charlotte's adopted son, Johnny, who seemed to be thriving under their care.

The young girl in his arms squirmed for freedom, her loud protests echoing through the small bedroom. Esther smothered a grin. With hair the same crimson shade as her mother's, the youngster seemed to have a temper to match.

Looking exasperated, Johnny hugged her tighter and backed toward the door.

Chad grinned and motioned for them to come. As Johnny released his hold, the child's squalls erupted into giggles. She tottered to the bedside, her eyes still glued to the infant in her mother's arms.

Esther paused in the doorway and drew a contented breath. There'd been a time she couldn't have imagined her older sister a mother. She'd been so spoiled and self-centered growing up. Now, here she was, a happy wife and mother to three vibrant children.

Slipping from the room, Esther laid her gloves and travel bag aside and glanced around the small cabin, intent on making good her stay. While the children were occupied, she'd tidy up the place, starting with the clutter of dishes scattered about. Even with the added bedroom, the cabin seemed swallowed up by the growing family. Or had she become so accustomed to the largeness of city houses that the log home seemed dwarfed in comparison?

She rolled up her sleeves and put a pot of water over the fire to heat. Gathering up the cups and silverware, she carried them over to the metal wash pan and gazed out the window. Sight of the open prairie stirred a longing in her she hadn't experienced for some time. So accustomed to being surrounded by buildings and people instead of grassland and trees, she'd forgotten how beautiful the open landscape could be.

Laughter and voices flowed from the bedroom. Esther crossed her arms and leaned against the windowsill with a sigh. In Cincinnati, she had polish and culture, every advantage a person could wish for. But somehow, Charlotte seemed to have found something much richer and deeper, the blessings of love and family.

Esther tried to picture Lawrence Del Ray working the land or living within the confines of a tiny log cabin. The very idea made her chuckle. More than likely, he'd not put in a full day of manual labor his entire life. He was so different from the man she'd envisioned marrying. Could she endure being wife to such a rigid, business-minded man?

She gnawed at her lip, a sudden tightness in her middle. If Mother had anything to say about it, she most definitely would.

STEWART BRANT LEANED FORWARD in his saddle, gazing over the prairie landscape dotted with cattle. No doubt he'd found what he'd been searching for. The neighboring homesteader's directions had landed him smack-dab in the middle of Chad Avery's cattle ranch. Stew's lips lifted in a sideways grin. Judging by the stocky herd, well-tended fence, and homey cabin, his friend was thriving.

A tap of his heels set his paint gelding, Scout, into a slow walk. Long weeks of travel had them both eager for a good rest. If he had Avery pegged right, this might prove a welcome oasis before continuing home to Missouri.

The door to the cabin opened, and a woman emerged toting a dish pan full of water. She heaved its contents over the side of the porch rail then stood gazing out over the prairie, seemingly unaware of his approach. As he neared, the woman's fetching features became more apparent—her golden locks, delicate profile, and shapely figure. Stew released a slow breath. This lovely lady put his old sweetheart, Delta, to shame.

He wagged his head side to side. If this were truly Chad's place, things had definitely gone in his favor the past four years. Why, when Stew'd first met him, Chad barely had a penny to his name, only a handful of cattle, and no girl to call his own. Now, here he was bursting with blessings. A twinge of envy trickled through Stew. What had *he* to show for the past four years? Nothing but a saddle-sore body, a tuckered-out horse, and a broken heart.

The woman pivoted toward him, jumping slightly at his

approach. He tipped his hat to her. "Sorry to startle you, ma'am. Would you by chance be Mrs. Chad Avery?"

Her hazel eyes perused him, her expression cautious. Straight from a cattle drive, he must look a sight. And smell even worse. "Mrs. Avery is inside. I'm her sister."

Stew leaned back in the saddle, unable to hold back a grin. "Say now, that's good news."

The young woman's stunned expression pleaded for explanation.

With a slight cough, he trimmed back his smile. "I mean, it's good Chad's found himself a wife. Last I saw him he was pretty hard up."

She lowered the empty dish pan to her side. "And when was that, Mister…"

"Stewart Brant. Stew, to my friends." His gaze drifted to her left hand in search of a gold band, but the way her fingers were turned made it impossible to see. He pulled his attention back to her face. "I uh…we ran a cattle drive together a few years back."

Her expression softened. "Life has changed quite a bit for him since then. Not only is he married, but he's just become father to his third child."

The first inclination Stew had that his jaw had dropped was the presence of a fly landing on his lip. He snapped his mouth shut and shooed the pesky insect away, still trying to fathom the news. A wife and three children within four years? The woman's soft chuckle gave clue to how silly he looked. He cleared the dryness from his throat. "He's been busy."

The young lady's cheeks pinked, and Stew glanced down at the saddle horn, his palms growing clammy. What an impression he was making. He really should stop thinking out loud. Good sense told him he'd do well to rein Scout around and head home to Missouri before he made more of a fool of himself. But he'd come this far to see his friend. He couldn't let a few thoughtless words deter him.

"Would you like me to tell him you're here?"

Stew's eyes lifted. Given the mess he was making of this first encounter with this lovely lady, it was a wonder she hadn't sent him on his way. But the gentle tone in her voice and the sincerity in her eyes gave him something to cling to. "I'd be obliged."

With a nod, she started toward the cabin door.

"I—I didn't catch your name." Stew called after her.

Pausing, she turned to face him, not quite meeting his gaze. "Esther. Esther Stanton."

Stew tugged at the rim of his hat. "Pleased to meet you, Mrs. Stanton."

She squinted up at him against the sunlight. "It's Miss Stanton."

Then she *wasn't* married. The welcome news trickled through Stew like fresh spring water. His lips spread in a wide grin. "Glad to know you, *Miss* Stanton."

A shy smile touched her lips as she turned to go.

He drew in a long breath. Esther. Hadn't his ma read a story to him in the Bible about a queen named Esther? The name suited this Esther well. Her alluring presence lingered even after she'd disappeared inside the cabin.

A sobering thought sliced through him. The last time he'd been so enamored with a woman, he'd gotten his heart stomped on. He'd not entertained the thought of lending his affections to another since.

Until now.

Dismounting, Stew ran a hand down Scout's neck, tightness pulling at his chest. He cast a glance to where Esther had stood on the porch, envisioning her golden hair and fawn-like eyes flecked with green. Something told him she was the sort of gal that could mend his broken heart and make him forget Miss Delta Fanning ever existed.

Chapter Two

"Stew!" Chad bounded down the porch steps and stuck a hand out in greeting, a warm smile spilling over his face.

Stew stretched out his palm, grateful he'd made the effort to locate his friend. "How are you, Avery?"

"Couldn't be finer." Chad gave Stew's hand a hearty shake. "What brings you way out here?"

"On my way home from a cattle drive. Thought it was about time I look you up."

Chad clapped him on the back. "Glad you did. You still running cows for Pete Callaway?"

"Yep. Goin' on six years now." Just the sound of that many years in the saddle made his bones ache. At twenty-three, he'd be an old man before his time if he kept it up.

With a click of his tongue, Chad shook his head. "Don't know that I'd have the gumption to keep at it that long."

"If I had good reason to quit, I'd be done with it in a heartbeat."

Chad knit his brow. "If memory serves me, you had a gal back in Missouri you were pretty sweet on."

"That didn't turn out so well, I'm afraid." Stew hung his head, working his fingers up and down the leather reins. Three long years had passed since he'd returned home to find Miss Delta in the arms of another. The thought of it still burned in his chest.

Brief silence followed Chad's breathy exhale. "Sorry to hear it."

Ignoring the wave of tension in his gut, Stew pasted on a grin. "Ah, it's over and done with. But I hear tell you've been a might more productive."

A hint of a smile seeped onto Chad's face. "The Lord's been good. Come on in and meet the family."

Stew looped Scout's reins over the railing and followed his friend up the porch steps. Slipping his hat off, he ducked through the doorway. As he stepped inside, his gaze darted to Miss Stanton seated in a rocker before the fireplace. The fact that she had her back to him allowed the liberty of drinking in her presence a bit longer than he otherwise would have. With her fancy dress and golden curls, she looked more a lady of leisure than a product of the prairie. Did she live nearby, or had she traveled to get here? She'd stated she wasn't married, but was she promised to someone? Betrothed even?

So many questions, ones he had no right to ask. Such a fine lady was certain to have a beau of some sort. And even if she wasn't spoken for, she was much too refined for the likes of him.

The curly-headed child being bounced on her knee stopped giggling and peered over at him. Miss Stanton turned, putting an end to his stares. Chad strolled over and whisked the young girl from Miss Stanton's lap. "This here's my daughter, Rachel."

Hair red as firelight, the youngster resumed her giggling as Chad tossed her over his head and caught her. "Up until a few hours ago, she was our youngest. Now she'll have to share her momma with baby Michael." He wrapped Rachel in his arm and nodded toward Miss Stanton. "I believe you've already met my wife's sister, Esther."

Stew met her gentle gaze with a nod. "A pleasure."

He shot her an awkward smile, gleaning a faint one in return. If Chad's wife was anything like her sister, he'd done well.

Chad gave his daughter a kiss on the forehead and returned her to Miss Stanton's lap. "She's been kind enough to agree to stay with us a few weeks till Charlotte's back on her feet. I'd just get underfoot."

Stew arched a brow. Beauty *and* a kind heart. Miss Stanton would certainly make a fetching wife for some lucky fellow.

The cabin door pushed open, revealing a blond-haired boy poised in the doorway, a fishing pole draped over his shoulder and a string of fish in hand. The scrappy-looking youngster looked to be about ten or eleven, too young to be a hired hand and too old to belong to Chad's family.

Chad nodded in the boy's direction. "That's our oldest boy, Johnny."

Stew shifted his gaze from the boy to Chad, eyes wide.

That he was cursed to have a face which shed light on his inner thoughts was apparent in Chad's hearty laugh. "Not to worry. Charlotte and I came by him honest. We adopted him."

Stew gave a relieved chuckle and nodded toward the boy. "He's quite the fisherman."

"The best." Pride told in Chad's voice. It was plain he thought as much of the boy as if he were his own flesh. He gestured toward Stew. "Johnny, this is Stewart Brant, an old buddy of mine from the cattle drive I told you about."

The boy lowered his wooden fishing pole, his eyes sparking. "A real cattle drover?"

"I reckon." It humored Stew to see the boy's excitement, like he was some sort of hero.

Johnny leaned his pole against the wall and picked up the bucket inside the door. "You'll stay t' supper, won't ya? I'd like to hear what it's like to work a cattle drive."

Stew scratched his stubbled chin. "I reckon that's up to your folks. I don't want to intrude."

The boy turned his gaze on Chad. "He's not intruding, is he? There are plenty of fish."

Chad clapped Stew on the shoulder. "You're more than welcome to stay. Charlotte would never forgive me if I didn't introduce you."

Stew stole a glance in Esther's direction. He had to admit the thought of getting to know her better, as well as Chad's family, was appealing. At last, he shrugged. "I would like to see your spread before I go, so long as Miss Stanton doesn't mind another mouth to feed."

She met his gaze, a hint of red touching her cheeks. "It's no bother at all, Mr. Brant."

Stew surrendered to the smile playing at his lips. This lovely young lady had just welcomed him to supper, and he wasn't about to let the opportunity pass. He called over his shoulder at Johnny, eyes still trained on Esther. "Well, Johnny, get your knife. You and I have some fish to clean."

CHARLOTTE'S EYES blinked open as Esther entered the bedroom, a bowl of soup in hand. "I thought you could use some nourishment."

"Thank you." The babe lay tucked in the nook of Charlotte's arm, swaddled in a linen cloth, his complexion less red than it had been just after birth. A soft smile edged across her face as she leaned to kiss his forehead. "Isn't he beautiful?"

Esther set the bowl on the night table and eased into the oak chair beside the bed. "How could he be anything else?" She stroked a finger down his cheek. So soft. So precious. A new life bursting with possibilities.

"Would you like to hold him?"

Her sister's request produced a strange sort of longing inside

Esther, mingled with a bit of apprehension. She'd had little opportunity to hold an infant. At least one so tiny.

Charlotte gave a soft chuckle. "He won't break."

Warmth shrouded Esther's palms as she slid her hands beneath him. He stirred ever so slightly, the faintest of sounds escaping his throat. Could he sense her inexperience? She cradled him in her arms, surprised at how light he felt. No heavier than a tin of sugar. She shifted for a better hold, and his tiny features pinched. Would he cry so easily?

Sitting forward in the chair, she swayed side to side as she'd seen young mothers so often do. His eyelids flickered then squeezed tighter, his breaths becoming steadier.

Charlotte pulled herself to a sitting position. "There, you see? Nothing to it."

Esther sensed herself relax, her nod more for her own reassurance than Charlotte's. If she were to be any use to her sister, she'd best rid herself of such insecurities. She gazed into Michael's tiny face, a bit of both his parents displayed in his features. Chad's strong jaw and small ears, Charlotte's dainty nose and long lashes. His smidgen of hair had a lighter hue than his older sister's, hinting it might favor Chad's sandy brown rather than Charlotte's crimson.

Charlotte smothered a yawn and reached for the bowl of soup. "Was someone here? I thought I heard a man's voice earlier."

The memory of Mr. Brant's ready smile and lingering gaze stirred a rush of unwelcome heat in Esther's cheeks. Strange a man she'd just met could induce such a reaction. Only once had she blushed where Lawrence was concerned, when he'd asked to call on her amid a roomful of people. But that was a matter of embarrassment. Mr. Brant had merely smiled and shown enthusiasm at being welcomed to stay.

Uncertain she could look her sister in the eye, Esther fixed her gaze on the babe in her arms. "A friend of Chad's stopped in. A Mr. Stewart Brant."

"Stewart Brant?" That the name was unfamiliar to Charlotte

was plain by her hushed tone and puzzled expression. "I don't recall the name. Did they say how they were acquainted?"

"Mr. Brant said they met some years ago on a cattle drive."

Charlotte's expression eased, and she gave a slow nod as though it finally made sense. "I recall Chad mentioning a young fellow named Stew."

"Yes. That's him."

With a sigh, Charlotte scooped up a spoonful of soup, looking tired in body and spirit. "What a day for someone to stop by. Has he left?"

Esther stopped swaying, questioning if she'd been wrong in consenting for him to stay. "Chad's invited him to supper. He's showing him around the place just now."

Charlotte paused in mid bite, a slight grin working its way onto her lips. "I should have guessed as much. And Rachel and Johnny?"

"With them, I'm afraid. I tried to get Rachel down for a nap but…"

Charlotte held out a palm. "No need to explain. She has her father's love for the outdoors and my willful spirit."

The two of them shared a knowing grin. It hadn't taken long for Esther to realize the truth of her sister's words. Young Rachel was a vibrant youngster reminiscent of Charlotte in her early years. How fitting that she should have a daughter of her own making.

Baby Michael stirred and let out a whimper which quickly erupted into a squall.

"He's hungry." Charlotte set her nearly untouched bowl of soup on the stand and reached for him. Holding him in one arm, she worked to unfasten her nightgown. "What sort of fellow is this Mr. Brant?"

Esther leaned to place a cloth over the nursing infant. How should she answer? She knew so little about Chad's friend other than he was tall and lean and had a smile that could melt a December snow. He wasn't particularly handsome, at least not in comparison to Lawrence's striking good looks. And yet, Mr. Brant had a presence about him that was refreshingly genuine and unassuming.

Something Lawrence most definitely did *not* possess.

She swept a wisp of hair from Charlotte's forehead. "Much like Chad, I suppose. Full of adventure and hopes and dreams for the future."

Charlotte pursed her lips. "Such a description makes me sorry I'll likely not have the chance to meet him."

With a nod, Esther slid her hand away. Though she couldn't very well admit it, a part of her was pleased she'd met Stewart Brant.

And left her wishing he'd not be leaving quite so soon.

"WELL, WHAT DO YOU THINK?"

Stew panned the wide prairie and the large cluster of Hereford cattle grazing in its midst. "You've got yourself quite a spread. Healthy stock. Plenty of room to grow."

Chad hoisted Rachel onto his shoulders, his gaze fixed on his herd. "I figure by next year I'll have over seventy head, and the following year a hundred."

The excitement in his friend's voice was as satisfying to Stew as if the cattle were his own. "A sizeable herd. You should be proud."

"How many head do you run on your drives, Mr. Brant?" Johnny's question oozed with enthusiasm.

"A couple thousand, most generally. Sometimes more."

The boy's eyes widened. "I can't imagine so many cows all bunched together."

Stew crossed his arms. "It's quite a sight to see, till you get accustomed to it."

Chad reached to straighten his hat. "It's all Johnny and I can do to keep up with what we've got, what with branding, field work, and choring. Charlotte's always saying I'm too strapped for time to enjoy it."

A moment of silence passed between them, then Chad cast Stew a sideways glance. "Just how eager are you to get back to Missouri?"

It would have been easy for Stew to admit that after meeting Miss Stanton, he wasn't nearly so eager. Pushing the thought aside, he hooked his thumbs in his pants pockets. "Nothing pressing. Why?"

Chad arched a brow. "'Cause if you're willing, I may just have a reason for you to stay on a spell."

Chapter Three

STEW LEANED back in his chair, rubbing a hand over his belly. "That's as fine a meal as I've tasted in a long while. Got old Cookie's grub beat."

Chad groaned. "That's certain. My tongue's still burning from his chili."

Miss Stanton seemed to brush the compliments aside, despite the splash of pink in her cheeks. She wiped crumbs from Rachel's face and hands. "There's plenty more."

Stew stuck out a palm. "None for me, thanks."

She held the platter of fish out to Chad, then Johnny. When both declined, she slid Rachel from her lap and started to rise. "Then perhaps Charlotte will want some. She's hardly eaten since I arrived."

"I'll take it." Chad pushed back from the table with the eagerness of a lovesick school boy.

Miss Stanton settled back on her chair and allowed him to take the platter, a questioning glint in her eyes.

Without a word, Chad made his way to the closed bedroom door, leaving Stew with the notion his friend was up to more than offering his wife a bite to eat. After his mention of Stew staying on, Chad had clammed up tighter than a snapping turtle. Whatever he had in mind, it was likely he would want to run the idea past his wife first. The thought of working alongside Chad was more than inviting, especially given the possibility of getting better acquainted with Miss Stanton.

Alone with her now, but for the two youngsters, Stew shifted in his seat, struggling for something worthwhile to say. A rush of heat worked its way into his cheeks. He was more adept to being around cattle than women, and this pretty gal had his tongue tied in knots. The walnut-sized lump in his throat convinced him it was safer to steer the conversation at the boy.

"So, Johnny, besides fishing and cattle, what's a fella your age do way out here?"

With a shrug, Johnny finished off his last bite of biscuit. "Mostly chorin' and school work." He lowered his voice and leaned toward Stew. "I'd just as soon skip the schoolin', but Miss Charlotte says I gotta."

Stew chuckled. "Well now, I can see both sides on that issue. I wasn't much on schooling myself, but it does come in handy." In fact, he'd barely finished the fourth grade before being stolen away to help out on the farm.

Something he wasn't about to admit in present company.

"Where do you hail from, Mr. Brant?"

The soft-spoken words returned the lump to Stew's throat. He took a hard swallow. "A little town called Taylor Springs, Missouri."

"Is that where you're headed?" piped Johnny.

"Those were my plans. Unless I find a reason to stay." Stew ventured a glance at Miss Stanton, his gaze finding hers just long enough to catch the rosy glow of her cheeks. Had he unwittingly made her assume he referred to her? Not that staying on her account was an unpleasant thought. Esther being unaware of Chad's offer, he could understand the mistake. It seemed he had a way of blundering where this pretty lady was concerned.

She stood and gathered up the dishes. "Have you kinfolk back in Taylor Springs?"

"Yes, ma'am, I do." He paused, curious if she was fishing to find out if he was attached to anyone the way he had her. Shifting in his chair, he gave a slight cough. "My folks and eight brothers and sisters of which I'm the oldest."

"Nine children?" Once again Johnny's eyes widened.

With a nod, Stew leaned back in his chair. "One of the reasons I left home. My folks had a lot of mouths to feed. At seventeen, I figured it was time to strike out on my own and give them one less to worry about."

"Is that when you started herding cattle?"

"Yep. Started out as wrangler, lookin' after the spare horses, and worked my way up to swing man."

The door to the bedroom creaked open, and Chad emerged, the plate of fish not much barer than when he'd entered. He glanced at Stew, a smile on his lips, leaving little doubt as to the outcome of the short, private conversation. Silence blanketed the group in the brief moment it took Chad to cross the room. He set the plate down and placed a hand on Stew's shoulder. "For weeks, Charlotte's been urging me to hire someone to help out around here. I'd like that someone to be you, if you're willing. How 'bout it?"

A myriad of uncertainties rippled through Stew. Was he ready to settle in one place after roaming the countryside these past few years? Or would he tire of the routine and get itchy feet, longing to venture off to bigger and better things?

Once again his gaze veered toward Miss Stanton. Her rounded eyes searched his. Was she as eager to become more acquainted with him as he was her?

His muddled mind cleared. What had he to lose in staying?

Nothing. And possibly much to gain.

His lips spread in a wide grin. "I think I'd like that."

SHE'D DONE IT AGAIN. Blushed under Mr. Brant's gaze.

Esther ran the brush through her hair a bit too vigorously and cringed at the tug on her scalp. With a huff, she dropped her hands to her lap. Why had he looked to her in making his decision to stay? If he thought to win her affections, his hopes were unfounded. In a matter of weeks she'd be gone, back to her life in Cincinnati.

And Lawrence.

Setting the brush aside, she glanced out the loft window. A faint glow of lantern light illuminated the barn interior. Johnny had willingly joined Mr. Brant in the barn, leaving her and Rachel the privacy of the loft. Chad, too, had graciously offered to bed down in the straw a couple of nights to allow Charlotte and baby Michael better rest in the solitude of the downstairs bedroom.

Esther breathed in the cool night air. The vast sky beckoned to her, its shimmering starlight much brighter here than in the city where gaslights dotted the streets. The rasp of insects droned at her through the open window. How she'd missed the prairie. Even under cloak of darkness, its beauty wasn't hidden.

Heaviness swept over her. In the years since she'd left, not a day had passed that she hadn't longed to return. Yet for her mother's sake, she'd made Cincinnati her home. And though, in the months and years away, her new life had grown easier, in her heart, she would always belong to the prairie.

The light in the barn extinguished, and she edged back from the window. She slid her hands down her long hair, separating it into three sections. With practiced ease, she worked them into an over-the-shoulder braid, her mind still wishing for what may never be. Now that Mother had remarried, would it be so wrong to leave her? With a houseful of maids and servants and a husband to occupy, would she be so terribly missed?

With a soft sigh, Esther tied off her braid and eased onto the corner of the bed, young Rachel's steady breaths sounding out a cadence behind her. Of course she'd be missed. Mother would be heartbroken to have both of her daughters so far away. Charlotte had been the headstrong one who'd refused to leave. To please her mother, Esther had done what had been expected. As she would continue to do.

Her lot was cast. There would be no other life for her.

A baby's muffled cry sounded from the far side of the cabin. Esther glanced at Rachel sleeping soundly. Perhaps she should be certain Charlotte didn't need anything before retiring. She tucked the covers tighter around Rachel then started down the loft ladder.

Red-hot embers glowed in the fireplace, lighting her way through the darkened cabin. Soft noises drifted from within the bedroom. She paused outside the door and tapped on it lightly.

"Come in."

Esther peeked in at Charlotte seated upright in bed, the baby at her covered breast. "How's he doing?"

Her sister smiled through a yawn. "He can't seem to get enough of eating. I don't recall Rachel being half so greedy for a meal."

"Perhaps boys have heartier appetites, as men do." The puncheon floorboards cooled Esther's feet as she stepped to her sister's bedside. "Can I get you anything?"

With a quick glance down at the nursing infant, Charlotte softened her voice. "Could you slide the cradle a bit closer? He's nearly asleep."

A gentle tug on the oak cradle brought it within inches of the bed. Charlotte strained to lower Michael in, obviously still sore from birthing.

"Here. Let me." Esther slid her hands under the tiny babe, pausing a moment to take in his features before laying him in the cradle. She covered him with a thin blanket and smiled at Charlotte. "He's precious."

A brief moment of silence fell between them before Charlotte spoke. "I've missed you, Esther. I'm so glad you're here."

The endearing tone warmed Esther. Her sister's words were not shallow ones. It had taken their father's untimely passing and years of maturity and separation to bring them to this point. She placed a hand on Charlotte's arm. "Not half so much as I am."

Charlotte's brow creased. "I always hoped you and Ma would come back. Now that she's remarried, I don't suppose she, at least, will ever return."

With a shake of her head, Esther leaned over in a whisper. "Not likely, and she prefers to be called Mother now."

Charlotte stifled a giggle. "Does she really?"

"I'm afraid she's become rather stuffy. City living seems to agree with her, especially now that she's married a wealthy businessman."

Charlotte scrunched her nose. "What's he like, this William Leifer?"

Esther drew in a long breath and shrugged. "He's nice enough. Nothing like Pa though." She paused, her lips lifting in a grin. "Pa would get a huge chuckle out of seeing Mother all gussied up and hifalutin' like she's become."

"As would I." Charlotte rubbed a hand over her still swollen abdomen. "Too bad she couldn't have come with you."

"Oh, but she does plan to come for a short visit before we head back to Cincinnati."

"Then I'll have the chance to judge for myself how she's changed." A mischievous grin spilled over Charlotte's face. "But I dare say I'll call her Ma, not Mother."

Esther knew all too well the spirited gleam in her sister's eyes, one that wouldn't be reckoned with. She smothered a grin. "I'm just thankful to have you and your little ones all to myself for the time being."

Truth be told, she had already begun to dread the day her mother would come to usher her back.

Chapter Four

"So you're Stew."

"Yes, ma'am." With a tip of his hat, Stew sized up his friend's wife. Nearly as lovely as her sister, but with fiery red hair, Mrs. Avery had a look in her eyes that told him he'd best watch his step else she'd let him know just what she thought.

She rocked forward in the porch rocker, squinting against the midday sun, her day-old baby nestled in her arms. "Chad tells me you've a lot of experience with cattle."

"Been around 'em most of my life."

His answer seemed to satisfy her for she gave a curt nod. "Well, you've come at a good time. I've been pestering Chad for weeks to find someone to help with the herd. Among other things."

She slid Chad a sly smile, and he shifted his gaze to Stew, a knowing look in his eyes. "By other things, I believe she's referring to the promise I made to dig a well."

Stew nodded, brushing the dust from his pant legs. "A well would be a right nice addition to the place."

Mrs. Avery's lips curved in a satisfied grin. "I think I'm gonna like you, Mr. Brant."

Chad arched a brow and elbowed Stew. "See what happens

once you marry? They learn real quick how to sweet-talk you into just about anything."

A generous laugh sounded from Mrs. Avery. Striding onto the porch, Chad stooped to plant a gentle kiss on her lips. "Good to see you up and about." He touched a finger to the sleeping infant's face. "How's my boy doing?"

"Couldn't be better."

The couple shared a loving smile, the homey scene stirring a longing inside Stew. For years he'd been content to live the care-free life of a cowboy. No obligations. No real place to call home. Accountable to no one, save his boss. He came and went as he pleased. But since his arrival yesterday, something within him had shifted, like evening shadows giving way to morning light. He could blame it on the Averys' hospitality or Chad's willingness to provide him a steady job. But more than likely, it had something to do with a certain fair-haired maiden whom he had a hankering to know better.

The door to the cabin swung open, and young Rachel burst out, followed by Miss Stanton. "Time da eat." The young girl's untrained voice cut through the stillness.

Removing his hat, Stew ran a hand through his hair. Judging by the unsettled feeling in his stomach when Miss Esther glanced his way, his intuition had been correct. She had plenty to do with his eagerness to stay.

Up until now, he'd had little chance to speak with her alone or find out much about her.

Hopefully, that would soon change.

"LET ME HELP YOU WITH THOSE."

The weight of Esther's water buckets lessened, and she turned to see Stewart Brant coming up beside her. She managed a shy smile. "Thank you, Mr. Brant."

"Call me Stew. And may I call you Miss Esther?"

She ventured a glance his way. "If you like."

His tall frame towered over her several inches, the tip of her head barely clipping his shoulder. Comfortable silence blanketed them as they strode toward the cabin. A jingling noise drew her attention to the silver disks protruding from the back of his boots.

Stew slowed his pace, following her gaze. "Those are spurs. I use them to guide my horse when my hands are busy."

"You don't jab them into the horse?" The words came out more statement than question.

He fell back into step, a slight grin lining his lips. "Not really. A little pressure and Scout turns quicker than you can flip a coin."

"Scout. Is that your horse?"

He gave a firm nod. "Best cattle horse ever was."

His slight southern drawl hung in the air like the sweet scent of wildflowers. So different from the clipped, refined voices she was accustomed to hearing. Much about this pleasant, young man intrigued her.

When they reached the cabin, Stew hefted the water buckets onto the porch. Esther paused at the bottom step and turned to face him. "Thank you. That was very kind of you...Stew."

The name tumbled awkwardly from her lips, but yielded a broad smile from her companion. "My pleasure."

Esther started to climb the steps, but something in Stew's pale blue eyes and friendly demeanor held her in place. She clasped a hand to the porch rail, searching for words. "I—I can see why my sister longs for a well. With two youngsters to bathe and a newborn to diaper, it calls for a lot of hauling of water."

"Chad mentioned we'll be starting on it real soon. Don't know as it'll be done in time to benefit you though. How long will you be stayin'?"

"A few weeks. Long enough for Charlotte to regain her strength."

With a slow nod, Stew propped his boot on the porch step, "Well, I'm sure you'll stop in now and again. You live far?"

His hopeful expression made her hesitant. "Oh, it's a ways."

His eyes crimped ever so slightly. "Where abouts is it? Maybe I've heard of it."

"I'm almost certain you have." Part of her dreaded telling him. For whatever reason, Stewart Brant had taken a liking to her, and she hated to disappoint him. And yet, she longed to see his response when she bared the truth. She cringed. "I live in Cincinnati."

Just as she'd suspected, his expressive, blue eyes widened to twice their normal size. He swallowed. "As in Cincinnati, *Ohio?*"

"Yes." A pang of regret washed through her as his gaze fell away. How she wished she could have told him she lived two miles away or five, or even ten. Instead, her response had ruined any chances of getting to know him further. But then, perhaps it was for the best. If they should become close, it could only end in grief. It was best he knew the truth before any sort of fondness could develop between them.

He swept a hand through his wavy, brown hair and donned his hat. "Well, I'd best get back to work. If you need help carrying more water, just let me know."

His eyes lost their spark as he turned to go. Esther stared after him, her chest pinching. Here was a man who'd most likely give the shirt off his back to help someone, and she'd crushed him. In their short acquaintance, she'd taken him for a man of strength and virtue, and quite possibly a God-fearing one as well. Though not overflowing with Lawrence's attractiveness, Stew seemed much more thoughtful and down-to-earth.

More the man she'd envisioned for herself.

With a sigh, she reached for one of the buckets. Like it or not, her life was in Cincinnati, and his was here. Wishful thinking couldn't change that. What might have been and what was were two very different things.

STEW LEANED back on his bedroll, twirling a piece of straw between his fingertips. It was good he'd found out Miss Esther was out of reach. Deep-down he'd known it all along. Even if she had been from around here, she was too fine a lady to take up with his sort.

"You're awful quiet tonight. Didn't think you'd wear out so easy like Johnny there."

Stew glanced over at the young boy asleep on his blanket, Chad's gentle tease doing little to improve his sullen mood. Tossing the bit of straw aside, Stew tugged at his boots. "Just wondering why things seem to fit and then they don't."

A soft chuckle sounded from Chad as he lay back on his straw bed. "You'll have to explain that one."

Stew wavered, unsure he wanted to expose his inner thoughts regarding Esther. Yet, mulling over his regrets was eating away at him. He blew out a breath. "Why is it, when you find someone you think you could spend the rest of your days with, you find it can never be?"

Chad clasped his hands behind his head. "You still mooning over that gal back in Missouri?"

"No. Someone more recent." He cleared his throat. "Someone I've just become acquainted with."

Chad craned his neck, his expression brightening. "Who, Esther?"

Immediately, Stew regretted his more than obvious hint. After all, what was the use? She'd soon be gone. "It doesn't matter. Forget I brought it up."

A roguish grin crossed Chad's face. "Well now, I don't know. The good Lord has a way of working the seemingly impossible."

Stew shook his head. "She lives hundreds of miles away. Her life's in the city, and my roots are here."

"Her roots are here too. She's only been away four years. How do you know she wouldn't be willing to return, given the right reason?"

A flame of hope ignited within Stew. Was it possible? Was there a chance he could persuade Esther to leave her life in the city? Given the fact they'd only known each other for a day, it seemed presumptuous to even consider. But they had a few weeks —time enough to get to know each other. Could she come to think enough of him to stay?

Lord willing, he meant to find out.

Chapter Five

ESTHER FLEXED HER FINGERS, staring down at the bucket of milk tucked beneath old Nell. My, but she was out of practice. It had taken her twice as long as it should have. Her hands hadn't felt this stiff and cramped since she was but a young girl milking for the first time. She gave Nell a pat on the rump and lifted the bucket from beneath her. Standing, she drew in a breath. How she'd missed the peacefulness of a barn with its scent of hay and livestock. Chores she'd dreaded as a girl now brought her a deep sense of satisfaction.

She stepped outside and drank in the vitality of the prairie. These past couple of days had brought her more pleasure than anything the city could offer. She had to admit she'd enjoyed some pleasant times in Cincinnati, strolling along the banks of the Ohio River and taking in the sites. She'd even enjoyed her evenings with Lawrence, when he wasn't enthralled in talk of business with her stepfather or droning on about his successes.

Even so, the prairie would forever hold a special place in her heart.

"Aunt Esther."

Esther slowed her pace and turned toward the approaching boy, unaccustomed to being addressed as aunt.

Johnny trotted up beside her, a basket of eggs in hand. "Would you mind taking these to the cabin? They're startin' on the well, and I wanna help."

She followed Johnny's gaze several yards east of the cabin where Chad and Stew stood, short-handled shovels and pick in hand. With a grin, she took the basket of eggs. "All right, Johnny."

"Thanks." With that, he scurried toward the men, who seemed engrossed in what they were doing.

Unable to resist the urge to have a look, Esther set the milk bucket and egg basket on the porch, pausing outside the cabin window long enough to ensure all was peaceable before strolling to where the men were digging. Having abandoned their shovels, they'd removed a tire band from an old wagon wheel and were situating it on the ground.

"What's that for?" Johnny spoke what Esther begged to ask.

Chad shifted the metal band a few inches to better align it with the cabin then sat back on his haunches. "We'll use it as a guide for digging so we get our hole rounded."

Esther edged closer. "How deep do you suppose you'll have to dig?"

Her question pried Stew's attention from the imaginary hole. "Ten or fifteen feet if we're lucky. More if we're not."

Chad leaned over and placed a hand on Johnny's shoulder, his brow pinched. "You stay clear of this area when we're not around, do ya hear?"

"Yes'r."

"And make sure Rachel doesn't get anywhere near it."

Johnny gave a firm nod and then his eyes brightened. "But can I help dig while it's shallow?"

Stew handed him a shovel. "Have at it, son. Shovel all you want. We'll get our fill before we're through."

Esther clasped her arms behind her back as the three set to

work. The task ahead wasn't an easy one. Had Stew stumbled into more than he'd bargained for? Yet, he seemed in his element, chopping chunks of earth away with his pick while Chad and Johnny hauled it away with their shovels. He'd come just at the right time, as though the Lord had sent him.

An infant's shrill cry sounded from within the cabin, reminding Esther of her duties. As she turned to go, Stew called, "Make plenty of those fine victuals of yours, Miss Esther. By noontime, we'll be hungrier than a pack of wolves in winter."

She glanced over her shoulder long enough to glimpse his wide smile. His eyes sparkled, every trace of yesterday's sadness erased. She nodded, returning a shy grin. Had she misread his interest in her? Perhaps he was merely the friendly sort who took an interest in whomever he met.

A touch of disappointment trickled through her as she continued toward the cabin. It was for the best. There was no room for any sort of fondness between them. And yet, a part of her couldn't let go of the thought that the Lord had brought Stew here for her sake as well as Chad's.

STEW SHIFTED IN HIS CHAIR, taking a peek out the cabin window. Another half-hour and darkness would settle over the prairie. He wiped clammy hands on his trousers. If he didn't act soon, the household would be heading to bed. His gaze fled to Esther seated beside her sister in the far corner of the room. Oblivious to his stare, she seemed content to watch the sleeping babe snuggled in her arms. Would she resent him for interrupting?

Still, with only a few weeks to win her over, there was no time to lose.

As he started to speak, a small hand gripped his arm. Young Rachel smiled up at him then disappeared behind his chair. When she reappeared, he gave her nose a gentle tweak. The curly-haired youngster hid a second time then burst into view. She stared up at him, patting his forearm and leaning in closer as if to dare him to tweak her nose again. Instead, Stew reached to tickle her tummy, and her giggles vibrated through the small cabin.

"Looks as if Rachel's found a new playmate." Chad's humored voice sounded from over by the hearth. "You should feel honored. She doesn't cotton to just anyone."

Stew looked up to see everyone's eyes on him and wielded a bashful smile.

"Rachel, quit pestering Mr. Brant." Mrs. Avery scolded the youngster who responded with a soft moan and a scowl. "She gets giddy when she's tired. I'm so sorry."

"Not a problem. I'm used to young'uns."

She gave a low sigh. "I don't relish the thought of trying to corral her to bed."

"I'll get her." Esther passed baby Michael to her sister and started after Rachel.

Knowing what was coming, the youngster started to flee. Stew grabbed her and scooped her up in his arm, giving her belly another soft tickle. Her frown turned to a smile as he stood and cradled her in the nook of his arm. His eyes met Esther's, and he cleared his throat to steady his voice. "Actually, I was thinking of taking a walk and wondered if you'd join me?"

Esther blinked, staring up at him. "Oh, well I—I should get Rachel to bed."

"That'll be my job tonight." Chad sauntered over and lifted Rachel from Stew's arms. "Now, go enjoy the evening."

Stew caught his friend's quick wink and smothered a grin. Chad knowing his secret had its benefits.

Esther cast a glance at her sister who readily waved her toward the door. As she turned her gaze on him, Stew tried to temper the rapid beating of his heart. "Ready?"

With a timid nod, she stepped toward the door. He moved to

open it, feeling like an awkward school boy asking his teacher for a dance. Was he ready for this?

Lifting her shawl from the peg by the door, she wrapped it around her shoulders and stepped into the night. With a sideways glance back at Chad, Stew followed her out. He touched a hand to her elbow as they downed the porch steps then pulled it away, fearful she might think him forward.

They strolled through the yard and out past the corral, serenaded by the steady cadence of crickets and frogs. Stew peered into the amber glow of the western sky, struggling to make sense of the jumble of thoughts clouding his mind. Should he try to impress her with his knowledge of cattle? No. She was no starry-eyed boy like Johnny. Maybe he could feign a knowledge of city life. After all, he'd been to the outskirts of Chicago numerous times. But only to the stockyards and a restaurant or cheap hotel.

He drew in a long breath, suddenly realizing he had little to offer this beautiful woman at his side. Yet, he refused to pretend to be someone he wasn't. Miss Delta had alluded on more than one occasion she wished him more dashing and clever. If Esther couldn't be satisfied with the man he was, it was best to find out sooner rather than later.

"Nice evening."

Her feminine voice jarred him from his reverie. "Sure is." He wet his lips, struggling for words. "I hope you didn't mind me asking you."

"Oh, no. It's good to get out. I love this time of evening." She flashed a pleasant smile.

They fell into easy stride, watching the cattle graze on a distant hillside and an owl swoop from a treetop in search of prey. Stew tugged on a grass stem and snapped it into pieces, feeling more at ease in the familiar setting of the outdoors. "What would you be doing about now if you were back in Cincinnati?"

She gave a soft chuckle. "Probably gazing out the window

wishing I could stroll through the countryside and watch the sunset."

Stew slowed his pace and glanced her way. "You're not happy in the city?"

"I've learned to be content." She clasped her hands behind her and stared at the hem of her dress. "But it'll never be home to me. Not like here."

Her words sparked a glimmer of hope within him. "You…uh… ever consider moving back?"

"I hope to someday, when my mother no longer needs me."

He was tempted to ask how long that would be but thought better of it. "Is she hard up, your mother?"

Esther chuckled. "Hardly. Just this past year, she married a wealthy businessman."

"Well then, she's well taken care of."

Her expression turned sullen. "Mother's needs are emotional ones. She was heartbroken when my father was killed in a logging accident and Charlotte chose to stay behind. I went because she needed me. Still does."

"But she's doing without you now."

Esther stopped walking and turned to face him. "For a short time and only because she knew how badly I wanted to be here for Charlotte. If I left for good, she'd be devastated."

Her words should have snuffed out any thoughts Stew had of persuading her to stay, but something in her eyes kept his hope alive.

Chapter Six

"LET ME DO THAT." Esther pried the broom from her sister's hands and set to work sweeping up the mess of crumbs left from the noon meal.

Charlotte's hands flew to her hips. "Honestly, Esther, I'm not helpless."

"It's only been a few days. I don't want you to overdo."

"I'm feeling much stronger. Surely I can manage a few chores."

Esther paused her sweeping. "Don't be in too big of hurry to get better, or there'll be no need for me to stay."

Charlotte raised a brow. "You have a point."

The two of them shared a chuckle as Esther swept the crumbs onto the porch.

Rachel laid down her cloth doll and trotted toward the open door. "Outside?"

Esther caught her by the back of her frock, jolting her to a stop. "Hold up there little one."

The youngster gave a loud squeal and squirmed for freedom. Esther cast a pleading look at her sister, wishing she had Stew's charm with her little niece. But then, he was always having fun with her, and she was always putting a stop to it.

Charlotte motioned toward the doorway in defeat. "Let her go, just be sure she doesn't get in the way of their digging."

As Esther released her hold, Rachel's smile returned, and she toddled outside. Their dog, Rubie rose from her spot on the porch and greeted her with a lick. The young girl giggled and swiped at her dampened cheek. Looping her arms around the red and white border collie's neck, she bobbed up and down several times before scooting down the porch steps.

Esther closed the cabin door and took to sweeping the porch while keeping a watchful eye on Rachel. A glance to where the men were working assured slow but steady progress with the well. Only Stew's head was visible as he shoveled out dirt from within the deepening hole.

The midday sun beamed overhead, the strain of the work telling on both Johnny and Chad's expressions. As soon as Rachel was down for her nap, Esther would offer them a canteen of fresh water from the stream. She'd turned but a moment to sweep the far corner, when she heard Rubie sound a warning bark. Esther spied Rachel scurrying toward the men and released an exasperated groan. "Rachel, stop!"

The youngster giggled and kept running as though having fun at Esther's expense.

Hiking her skirt, Esther dropped her broom and took off after her.

Chad caught her first and scooped her up in his arms. "And just where do you think you're going?"

Esther rushed over, drawing a hand to her chest as she attempted to catch her breath. "I'm sorry. I turned for a moment, and she was gone."

"She's a sly one, all right." Chad shifted Rachel to one side, a wry grin edging onto his lips. "Takes after her mother."

The tension in Esther's muscles eased at his good-natured

response. He didn't seem the slightest bit annoyed at her over the mishap.

Rachel craned her neck, pointing to where Stew was shoveling. "Hole?"

Chad stepped closer to let her peek down it. She clung tighter to his shirt, her green eyes widening. "Yep. Papa and Uncle Stew are digging a well for Mama."

"Down? Hole?"

Stew paused his shoveling and lifted his hat to wipe sweat from his brow. "You don't want t' come in here, Sweet Pea. It's too deep for little tykes like you."

Chad swept a sweaty curl from Rachel's forehead. "That's right, sweetie. You keep away from here."

Her lip puckered as he passed her to Esther. "I'll bring you some fresh water as soon as she's down for her nap."

"No! No nap."

Realizing her mistake, Esther's shoulders sagged. She certainly had a lot to learn where children were concerned. The child squirmed in her arms until she was forced to heave her over her shoulder like a sack of potatoes.

Stew's humored smile rippled through her. He tossed her a wink, his spry whistle cutting through Rachael's protests as he set to work. He seemed to be enjoying her conundrum.

Turning toward the cabin, Esther wasn't sure whether to laugh or cry. One thing was certain, little Rachel most definitely had her mother's youthful tendencies.

"You'll attend church with us tomorrow morning, won't you, Stew?"

At Charlotte's inquiry, Stew stopped bouncing the giggling Rachel on his knee. It had been years since he'd attended a formal church service. Not that he didn't have a reverence for the

Almighty, but being on so many cattle drives had conditioned him to a life on the go with little time to nurture his spiritual well-being.

He slid the child to the floor, sensing not only Charlotte's eyes upon him but Esther's as well. "I 'spect I could, though I don't know as I have anything fit to wear. It's been a while."

Chad set his armload of wood in the kindling box and brushed his hands together. "You're too long-legged for my trousers, but I'm sure I've a shirt I can loan you."

Stew nodded. This new life of his required more than a set of new clothing, His whole perspective was changing. This family had welcomed him in like one of their own. For that he was grateful. But he couldn't help wondering what his decision to stay would come to? He couldn't live out of Chad's barn the rest of his days. If he could convince Esther to stay—which didn't seem likely—he had nothing to offer but the clothes on his back. A steady job would bring income and a sense of stability, but little else.

For the first time in his life, he was looking toward the future. Up until now, he'd had little reason to settle in one place. Now, he'd like nothing more than to make a home for himself and one day, a wife. He'd thought Miss Delta was the one for him, but deep down he'd known she hadn't loved him. Not really. She'd loved his wit and the money he brought home from cattle drives. Not him.

Esther was different. Special. Though he'd known her less than a week, when he was with her, it felt right. Good. Like rain on the heels of a drought or new-fallen snow on Christmas morning.

Maybe God was the missing piece in this new life of his, the One he needed to lean on for guidance, wisdom, and a future. He'd neglected his faith since he'd left home. Maybe if he got himself right with God, everything else would fall in place.

STEW'S EYES bulged at sight of Esther strolling toward him in her blue satin dress, Bible in hand. He fumbled with Scout's reins, unable to pry his eyes from her. If she'd been beautiful before, she was breathtaking now.

Which made him feel even plainer in his borrowed shirt and dusty trousers.

A slight grin touched her lips as she approached the wagon where Chad and the two older children awaited. "Charlotte will be here shortly."

Fearful his expression was too telling, Stew dropped his gaze to his shined boots. At least something about him looked somewhat polished.

"Are you riding?"

At Esther's question, his eyes lifted. "I'm sort of partial to the sway of a saddle over the jolt of a wagon bed."

Her gaze swept past him and then back again. "I agree." She took a step toward Chad seated on the wagon bench. "Is Willow still ridable?"

He seemed to waver. "Uh…Charlotte takes her out now and then, yes."

"If it's not too much trouble, I'd like to ride her to church service."

Once again, Stew sensed his eyes widen. "You ride?"

Esther's mouth twisted. "Well, I admit it's been a while. But I used to."

"I can ride," Johnny piped from the wagon bed.

"You sit still. I'll get her bridle." Chad set the reins aside and started to climb from the wagon.

Stew shook his head. "No sense you soiling your Sunday clothes. If she's not skittish, just tell me where you keep it, and I'll saddle her."

"Inside the barn door, to the right."

Stew returned with the bridle just as Chad was helping Charlotte onto the wagon seat with the baby. Though her bonnet hid much of her face, something about the set of her jaw as her gaze settled on Esther caused him to slow his pace. "You can't be serious. In that fine dress? Besides, it's five miles into town, and you've not ridden in years."

Esther rested her hands on her hips. "It can't be much worse than the jostle of a wagon."

Charlotte glanced at Chad, whose expression seemed to say he was staying out of it. Releasing a long breath, she shrugged. "Well, it's your backside."

Stew caught Esther's eye and smothered a grin, then cleared his throat. "You folks go on. No sense in us making you late."

Charlotte stared down at him from atop the wagon, a layer of distrust in her eyes.

Looping the bridle over his shoulder, he stepped closer and squinted up at her. "I'll take good care of her."

The babe in her arms whimpered, and she joggled him, doing her best to keep him shaded from the sun. At last, her features relaxed, and she gave a conceding nod.

"We'll see you there then," Chad said as he took up the reins. He smacked them across the horses' backs, and the team lurched forward along the trail toward town.

Esther stepped up beside Stew and pointed toward the pasture. "That's Willow, over there. I'd better go with you. She may be flighty toward a stranger." Glancing down at her dress, she chuckled. "Though, in these clothes, she may take me for a stranger as well."

Stew hesitated. "You'll spoil that fine dress of yours traipsing around out there."

"I'll manage." She hiked her skirt up over her boots and started forward.

He cast her a sideways glance, touching a hand to her arm to steady her as he fell into pace beside her. "You look mighty pretty, Miss Esther."

"Thank you, Stew."

His name seemed to come easier to her now. If nothing else, they'd become friends. His stomach clenched. Maybe that's where they needed to leave it.

The marbled roan mare raised her head at their approach and took a few steps back but didn't offer to run. Esther touched a hand to Stew's forearm. "Let me go first."

He hung back, allowing her to edge closer to Willow. The mare nickered and bobbed her head up and down at Esther's approach. "Easy, girl. You remember me, don't you?" She spoke in soft tones, easing forward until she was close enough to clasp her mane. She gave Willow a pat on the neck then flashed Stew a warm smile.

He drank in the pleasant scene, his chest tightening. Here was a woman he could spend the rest of his days with, loving, protecting, sharing life with.

If only he had the chance.

Chapter Seven

"HELLO, BECKY."

Esther's cousin's eyes sparked with recognition as Esther greeted her and Pastor Brody at the back of the church building. Having arrived late, she and Stew had slipped onto the back bench unnoticed.

"Esther?" Becky took her by the hands, surveying her from head to toe. "Just look at you! I hardly recognize you. Not at all the pigtailed girl from when I last saw you. You're so elegant."

The years apart seemed to melt away as Esther leaned into her cousin's warm embrace. So much had changed since they were young girls drawn together through tragedy. And yet, their bond of friendship seemed to span time and circumstances, like a precious jewel that never lost its shine.

Moisture glistened in Becky's eyes as she pulled away. "It's so good to see you. I'm sorry I wasn't up to joining Matthew when he met you at the stage."

Esther gave Becky's fingers a gentle squeeze, her gaze flicking to her cousin's rounded belly. "I can well understand why you wouldn't want to venture the bumpy ride in your condition. I'm so happy for you."

"Thank you." Pressing a hand to her abdomen, Becky smiled up at the pastor. "We're very blessed." Her gaze returned to Esther. "I only wish you could be here when my time comes in the fall. How long will you be staying?"

"Only a few weeks, I'm afraid."

With a gentle smile, Becky tipped her head to the side. "Well, you must steal away some time to spend with me before you leave."

"I will, most assuredly."

Stew pressed closer, and Esther pivoted toward him. "Oh. Becky, Pastor Brody, this is Stewart Brant, a friend of Chad's from his cattle drive days. He's just been hired on at the Circle J."

Stew nodded to Becky then stretched his palm out toward Pastor Brody. "Glad to meet you. Wonderful sermon, preacher. Best I've heard in a good, long while."

Esther caught Stew's quick wink and held back a grin, certain it was the *only* sermon he'd heard in a long while.

Pastor Brody gave his hand a shake, a smile crossing his face. "Thank you, Mr. Brant. We'll be seeing more of you then, I take it?"

"Count on it."

The pastor nodded. "Good. At least we've gained one of you. I fear we've lost Esther to the wonderments of the city."

She forced a smile. "For the time being anyway."

Stew's expression sobered as he donned his hat. "Nice meeting you, pastor, Mrs. Brody." He touched a hand to Esther's elbow, ushering her forward.

She waved back at them then glanced at Stew, longing to know what his sudden hurry was. But the disturbed look on his face beckoned her to silence. Chad and Charlotte were still inside swarmed, no doubt, by adoring onlookers showering compliments on their new baby.

Stew helped her onto Willow, his demeanor suddenly elusive, distant. Was he angry with her? If so, for what reason? Taking up

Willow's reins, her mind played over what had been said. Pastor Brody had only exchanged pleasantries with Stew, had even shown joy at the knowledge he'd be staying. It wasn't until he'd made mention of losing her to the city she'd noticed the change.

She cast Stew a sidelong glance as he swung his leg over Scout. This was the second time he'd grown sullen at the mention of her leaving. They'd only been acquainted a matter of days. Why should he care if she stayed or went?

Her throat tightened as she tapped her heels into Willow's flanks. The thought of no longer having Stewart Brant in her life initiated an unwelcome emptiness inside her. They'd found a kinship, a comfortableness, like they'd known each other since childhood. And yet, she couldn't bring herself to ask what she longed to know most.

If he truly wished her to stay.

"So, were you jesting about Pastor Brody's sermon or in earnest?"

Esther's playful question pulled Stew from his heavy thoughts. He tried to muster a clever response but failed. "He's a fine speaker."

The moment of quiet that followed pricked at him like a stubborn splinter. Did Esther sense what was wrong?

"His wife, Becky, is my cousin." Her voice sounded strained, as if she were grasping for something optimistic to say.

"I gathered that." Stew churned inwardly. The terse conversation was so unlike their ride in when they'd chattered like a couple of crows.

They fell to silence, the creak of leather and steady clop of hooves filling the void. At this rate, it would be a long trip back. Must he spend what precious little time he and Esther had pining away? There was still time. More than once she'd hinted she was less than thrilled with city life.

He lifted his eyes to the cobalt sky above. He'd been slack in his relationship with the Lord far too long. But, how did one rekindle faith that had lain stagnant for years? Praying seemed a good place to start. *Lord, I—*

"Have you forgotten me?"

Stew tightened his grip on the reins, his shoulders tensing. So engrossed in his thoughts, it took a moment for him to realize the voice had hailed from his companion and not the heavens.

At last, he shook his head. "I haven't forgotten you." Much the opposite. He cleared his throat. "I was…praying."

"Oh. I'm sorry." Her voice softened. "Then faith is important to you."

He lifted a brow, keeping his eyes on the path ahead. "Let's just say I'm working at it."

She pulled her horse closer, making it impossible to ignore the splash of blue from her fanned out dress. "Are you ready to tell me what's troubling you? Or are you keeping it between yourself and the Lord?"

The gentle appeal pierced his soul, breaking down the barrier he'd erected between them. "Something the pastor said."

"About the shepherd leaving his ninety-nine sheep to find the lost lamb?"

He snickered. "No. Though I could probably qualify for a lost lamb."

"What then?"

Her eyes seemed to bore into him, tugging at his deepest thoughts. With a defeated sigh, he pushed his hat higher on his forehead. "What he said as we were leaving, about you being lost to the city."

When she didn't respond, he stole a glance at her, noting the upturn of her lips. Was she pleased by his concern, or did she find him humorous? Heaviness flooded his chest. This was one time he had no intention of being funny.

At last, she spoke, her words little more than a whisper. "You don't want me to leave?"

He shrugged. "Sort of grown used to your company. Won't be the same if you go."

She touched a hand to his arm, its warmth surging through him like a branding iron. He met her gaze, relieved there was no hint of laughter in her eyes. Only tenderness. "I enjoy your company as well."

Stew's lips tugged in a grin. Suddenly he knew just where his prayers should begin. What was most heavy on his heart.

Esther.

Chapter Eight

ESTHER TRIED to hide her discomfort, but yesterday's ride into church had her wishing she'd chosen to ease her way back into a saddle instead of plunging in so vigorously. She tried her best to keep pace with Stew—his long legs much spryer than hers—but her sore thighs and backside beckoned her to slow down.

He glanced her way, brows creased. "Somethin' wrong?"

"No, no. Just a bit tired tonight."

"Would you like to head back?"

They'd barely been gone from the cabin five minutes. Their evening walks had become a ritual over the past week, one she enjoyed immensely. She had no intention of letting a sore backside spoil their stroll. "If we could just slow down a tad, I'll be fine." She fought back a cringe but knew by Stew's humored grin, she'd been unsuccessful.

"You saddle sore?"

She slowed her pace. There was no use denying it. He above anyone could recognize the symptoms. "A little."

More than a little. A lot!

He gave her arm a light squeeze. "Do you want to sit and rest a bit?"

"Trust me. Sitting is the last thing I need."

At that, he threw back his head in laughter. "Guess you should have heeded your sister's warning."

"I suppose. But I did enjoy the ride."

He matched her slower steps. "If it's any consolation, the next time won't be as bad."

"That's a comfort."

An owl hooted from a nearby tree and was answered back by one in the distance. Esther breathed in the night air, loving how the setting sun's tawny rays cast a golden glow over the grassy slopes. How she'd missed the simple pleasures of the prairie, the sounds, the openness, the beauty.

Lawrence understood none of these things. His thoughts seemed consumed by business ventures, financial affairs, and accompanying her to the theater and stuffy ballrooms. How refreshing it was just to listen to the nightlife and stroll through the miles of untouched prairie with someone who appreciated it.

Stew bent low and pressed a hand to the small of her back, pointing toward a grove of trees. "Look. Over there." Though he kept his voice hushed, enthusiasm seemed to ooze from within him.

Esther followed his gaze to a doe nibbling grass, golden in the sunlight, twin fawns at her heels. She smiled over at Stew, suddenly conscious of his nearness, his touch. His eyes remained trained on the deer, a childlike expression on his face. There was no pretense with Stew. He was who he was, a simple man with a heart as golden as the sunlit plains.

At last, he turned to her, a wide smile illuminating his face. "Bet ya don't see sights like that in the city."

"I'm afraid not." Sadness crept in to dampen her joy. Her time here was short-lived. Each treasured moment would soon be only a memory. Already, Charlotte had regained much of her strength. Soon there would be no further need for Esther to stay. The Lord knew her heart. He also knew what was best. If she was meant to return to Cincinnati, it must be His will. But that didn't mean she couldn't delight in visiting. Perhaps her mother's trip here would be delayed, allowing more time to enjoy Charlotte's family, old friends, the prairie.

And Stew.

STEW TUGGED Scout to a halt beside Chad's buckskin, taking in the ramshackle cabin overlaid with weeds and broken mortar. "What's this place?"

Chad sat forward in his saddle. "This is where I lived before Charlotte and I married."

Stew pursed his lips. "I'd say you've bettered yourself in more ways than one."

"It needs work, a great deal of chinking and daubing, and timbers repaired in spots, but I've replaced a lot of the shingles and some of the floorboards."

With a slow nod, Stew stared at his friend. Did he want help fixing up the place? For what purpose? They'd not even finished digging the well. It seemed an odd time to take on another weighty project.

The disgruntled look on Chad's face hinted Stew had missed something. At last, Chad pushed his hat back with his thumb. "Well, you can't sleep in our barn forever."

"You want me to live here?" Stew hoped he didn't sound ungrateful. Just the opposite. He didn't feel right moving into a cabin that belonged to the Averys and calling it his.

"If you're staying on, you'll need a place to live. This place is no palace, but it beats bedding down on a straw floor with live-stock. Consider it part of your wages for as long as you're here."

Dismounting, Stew looked the cabin over in more detail. His friend was right. The place looked a shambles. But he'd seen worse. Anything was better than the cheap hotels and hard ground he'd spent the majority of his nights on these past few years. He'd never had a place to call his own.

Chad gestured toward the cabin. "'Course you'll need some furnishings, and I know it won't be as handy as living at the Circle J. But it's only a mile away. And you're welcome to continue to eat your meals and spend as much time with us as you choose."

Stew nodded then tramped through the tangle of weeds surrounding the cabin. He stepped onto the porch—littered with mouse trails, dirt, and dried leaves—and tugged at the latch string. A stale, ashy smell wafted out as the door creaked open, revealing an empty cabin coated with dust and soot. Streams of sunlight shone through cracks in the poorly chinked walls. It would take a lot of work, but not nearly so much as building a new one.

A vision of him carrying Esther over the threshold into a fully furnished room, gleaming with the soft glow of lantern light and a warm fire, filled his senses. Was this the start of an answer to his prayers?

He turned to Chad with a wide grin. "It'll do just fine."

"You've gotta flick your wrist like this, then let it fly." Stew's voice carried from the yard inside the cabin. Esther dried her dishwater-soaked hands on her apron and peered out the open window in time to see him twirl a circle of rope over his head. He let it go and the rope sailed through the air and landed around a grass-stuffed feed sack atop the split-rail fence. The achievement set off a shout of approval from Johnny and Rachel.

"Just what are they up to out there?" Charlotte called from the far side of the cabin, her hands busy pinning a cloth diaper on a cooing Michael.

A smile tugged at Esther's lips. "It appears Stew's demonstrating how to rope a cow."

Charlotte shook her head. "After a full day's work digging and tending cattle, you'd think they'd be too tuckered for such."

"Stew never seems to tire." Esther leaned against the windowsill, toying with the thin, beige and white curtain hanging at its edge. "The children have certainly taken a liking to him." She sensed Charlotte's eyes boring into her from across the room.

"You seem to have warmed to him as well."

Heat flamed in Esther's cheeks at her sister's comment. Would she deny it? How could she? For more than a week now, she and Stew had enjoyed nightly strolls, and each time she returned almost as giddy as Rachel after being bounced on his knee. Stew had a way of making her enjoy life. It was hard not to grow fond of someone who made your heart happy.

With a sigh, she let go of the curtain and spun toward her sister. "I suppose I have."

Charlotte lifted Michael, fully changed and swaddled. A subtle grin pricked the corners of her mouth. "I'm certain he's every bit as partial to you. If not more so."

Esther suppressed a smile. "Do you think so?"

"Yes, indeed. Better watch yourself, or he'll snatch you away from the city and keep you here forever."

Esther's pulse quickened, her hopes soaring then dying away. Moving away from the window, she slumped down in a chair, shoulders drooping. "Mother would never approve. She has her sights set on me marrying Lawrence Del Ray and living close by to tend to her in her older years."

Taking a seat at the table beside her, Charlotte cuddled young Michael against her. "Oh, so you already have a beau."

With a sigh, Esther ran a finger over the rough grain of the oak table. "If you can call him that. Truth be told, Mother has more affection for him than I have."

"Have you told her as much?"

"I've tried. But she only says, 'Lawrence is dashingly hand-some, wealthy, and jovial, what else could a woman want?'"

Charlotte chuckled at the mimicking tone in her voice. "And is he?"

Esther shrugged. "He is quite handsome and well-to-do, but I find him more prudish than jovial, always spouting off his ambitions and achievements."

Michael let out a whimper, and Charlotte patted his back. "Have you told Stew of him?"

"What would it accomplish? In a matter of weeks, I'll be back in Cincinnati, and Stew will be here. I'd rather enjoy the time I have here free of such hindrances."

A girl's muffled scream sounded from outside the open window, followed by men's excited voices. Esther's eyes locked with Charlotte's. Heart pounding, Esther jumped to her feet and flung the door open.

Charlotte skirted past and downed the porch steps, Michael clutched in her arms. "What happened?"

Chad and Stew gave no answer as they sprinted past. Johnny stood peering down the well hole, face ashen.

When she realized Rachel was nowhere to be seen, Esther clapped a hand to her mouth. The boards atop the well were in disarray, the hole partially exposed.

At Charlotte's shriek, Esther whispered a prayer and followed her out into the yard.

There was no need to be told what had happened.

Rachel had fallen.

Chapter Nine

STEW'S long legs carried him to the well hole several paces ahead of Chad. He tossed aside the remaining boards weighted down by rocks and knelt beside it, his heart at his throat. How had the youngster managed to wander off and move the boards without any of them noticing? One moment she was there. The next she was crying out. They'd been so wrapped up in their lassoing, she'd slipped away unnoticed.

Their carelessness could have cost her her life.

Or had it?

Chad skidded up beside him and peered down into the near eight-foot hole, the peril in his father's heart telling on his grief-stricken face. "Rachel?"

His frantic call yielded only silence.

Stew leaned over the hole, boxed in by sturdy sideboards. The deepening shadows of evening made it difficult to see past the first couple feet. He eased back on his haunches, meeting his friend's stunned gaze. "We need some light."

Chad's jaw flinched, and he called over his shoulder. "Bring a lantern!"

Moments later, Esther appeared, lantern in hand, her face stoic.

She handed Chad the light then moved to where Charlotte stood with the baby, eyes closed, head tipped downward. If ever there was a time to pray, this was it.

Stew eased back to give his friend room. Leaning forward, Chad held the lantern over the hole, peering deep within. "I see her!" His expression shifted from relief to concern. "She's not moving. Rachel!"

A whimper sounded behind Stew, followed by Charlotte's frantic cry. "Rachel!"

He closed his eyes, his breaths shallow, chiding himself for having distracted Chad and Johnny from their job of watching Rachel. If anything happened to her, he'd not forgive himself. *Lord, please don't let this child suffer for our mistake.*

A soft moan sounded from within the hole. Chad held out his arm. "Shhh!

The group fell silent, listening.

Another moan.

He lowered the lantern, and his shoulders lifted. "She's moving!"

Shouts of joy and relief erupted from Charlotte, Esther, and Johnny. Chad motioned them to quiet. "Rachel, honey, are you all right?"

A muffled cry drifted from within the hole. "Fall down."

"Yes, I know, sweetie. Can you stand?"

Another barrage of whimpers sounded. "Uh huh. Out, Papa. Hurt."

Chad's gaze fled to the posts straddling the hole and the rope wound around the roller. He swiped a hand through his hair and peered over at Stew. "Lower me down on the bucket with the windlass."

Stew shook his head. "Too risky. If the rope broke, she'd be crushed." He fingered the lasso in his hands. "Wait. I have an idea."

He bent over the hole, barely able to make out the tiny figure below as Chad again held out the lantern. "Hey, Sweet Pea. It's Uncle Stew. Hows about you and me playing a game?"

There was a pause in her whimpering but no reply. He made a loop a little smaller than the opening with his lasso and held it over the hole. "See the rope, Rachel?"

A sniffle. "Uh huh."

He tensed at Charlotte's nervous sobs behind him. *Lord, I'd be much obliged if You'd see this youngster to safety.* He swallowed, willing himself to concentrate. "All right, Sweet Pea, I want you to stand as still as you can. I'm gonna send this rope down and lasso you the way I did that fake cow of ours on the fence post. Hold steady now. I'm sending it down."

With a lick of his lips, Chad gave Stew a reassuring nod. He eased the rope down until it hit against something solid. "Do you have the rope, Rachel?"

"Mm hum."

"Good. Now, loop it around you and slide it under your arms."

A faint rustling could be heard within the hole. "Ow! Mama?"

Charlotte edged closer, her voice shaky. "Hang on, sweetie. Do what Mr. Brant tells you."

Shifting the lantern from one hand to the other, Chad wiped sweat from his brow.

Stew gave a soft tug on the rope. There was substance. "Ready, Rachel?"

She sputtered then whined. "Want out."

"We're gonna get you out. Hold tight." Stew looped the end of the lasso over the windlass roller log and pulled the rope taut. With a reassuring glance back at Charlotte and Esther, he tugged on the rope. The girl's slight frame made it easy to keep a steady hand-over-hand pace. Long seconds ticked by, an air of anticipation shrouding the group. As she neared the surface, Chad's face beamed. He reached his arm down. "Grab hold, Rachel."

The rope slackened in Stew's hands as Chad pulled the youngster up and into his embrace, showering her with kisses. Charlotte passed young Michael to Esther and ran a hand through Rachel's unruly hair. "Are you all right, sweetie?"

With a nod, Rachel reached for her mother. Charlotte took her in her arms, hugging her tight. She glanced at Stew, her eyes moist with tears. "Thank you."

He mustered a weak grin then leaned against the windlass, a wave of nausea rippling through him. The incident could have ended much differently had the hole been deeper or her fall more severe. He shuddered to think what might have been.

Rachel reached out a soiled hand to him, her lower lip extended. Blood trickled from three of her knuckles. Cuts and bruises lined her face and hands, and her frock was torn beyond repair. But her movements seemed unhindered and every bone intact. Taking her hand in his, he gave it a soft kiss and tossed her a wink. "You stay away from that hole from now on, Sweet Pea, you hear?"

She gave a pouty nod then nestled against her mother.

Stew caught Esther's tearful gaze behind Charlotte, a tender smile streaming from her face, one that hinted she hailed him a hero.

He was no hero.

He lifted his eyes heavenward, to the tufts of clouds shining pink with the fading glow of the sun. No. He wasn't a hero.

But something told him he'd just become reacquainted with Someone who was.

ESTHER HIKED HER SKIRT, clutching the bundle of freshly baked corn muffins and tin of ham and beans tighter as she hopped across the small stream. She twisted her ankle in her landing, unaccustomed to trekking across the prairie in her heeled boots. How soft she'd grown these past years in the city. When she was younger, she had run over the prairie barefoot the entire summer, the bottoms of her feet so calloused they could withstand most any sort of terrain. Though the thought of ridding her feet of their trappings sounded inviting, she'd grown too old for such and her feet much too tender.

The heat of the afternoon sun soaked through her bonnet, warming her head. It seemed a bit muggier than when she'd started out. Had she ridden Willow, she could have arrived much sooner, and yet the mile-long trek to the cabin where Stew was staying gave her time to gather her thoughts. Yesterday's excitement had them all a bit weary and frazzled. She wanted to be certain Stew was faring well. Thankfully, Charlotte and the two young ones had lain down to rest, allowing her time to steal away.

As she topped the hill, the old Randall place came into view. Her heart leapt to her throat at sight of Stew thwacking horseweeds taller than him from around the cabin. Even on a Saturday, he was hard at work, utilizing what time he had to transform the neglected homestead into a viable home. She glanced at the dilapidated cabin and cringed. If its interior looked as shabby as the exterior, there was much to be done to make the place livable. Would he accept her help?

With a deep breath, she continued on, formulating how to explain her unannounced visit. Would he find her intrusive? She clutched her bundle of food tighter to her chest, knowing she could never share the entire truth—that she missed him, that the day seemed bland without his colorful presence. Instead, she would find some nobler reason for coming, one she hoped he wouldn't see through.

Coming up behind him, she resisted the temptation to startle him. So intent on his work, he showed no sign of knowing she was anywhere near. She took in his muscled frame once more before voicing a quiet hello.

He stopped whacking and stood erect. As he spun toward her, his vivid expression vacillated between surprise and pleasure. "Miss Esther. Where'd you come from?"

She held out her bundle, all her contrived reasons for coming forgotten. "Charlotte sent me with some supper for you. Figured you'd most likely not take time to make any yourself."

"She figured right. Be sure to thank her for me."

Stew's eyes locked onto hers, the slight upturn of the corners of his mouth making her wonder if he guessed the truth, that the visit had been entirely her idea.

She let her gaze drift to the cabin, hoping the heat of the day would mask the glow in her cheeks. "N-nice of Chad to let you stay here."

Stew turned to face the cabin and leaned on his hoe. "Not much to look at, but it's a roof over my head. I'm not sure which is in worse shape the outside or the inside."

Keeping her gaze fixed on the ramshackle cabin, Esther cleared the lump from her throat. "I won't be needed for a couple of hours if you'd like some help."

Out of the corner of her eye, she could see his head snap toward her. "That's mighty nice of you, but I can't ask you to do that."

"You didn't ask. I volunteered." She ventured a glance in his direction and witnessed a grin creeping onto his lips.

"Well then, I reckon that's an offer I can't refuse."

She returned a shy smile before starting up the porch steps. "I'll just put this food inside and get to work."

"I warn you. It's not a pretty sight," he called after her.

She chuckled. "I'm sure it's nothing I haven't seen before."

With a tug of the latch-string, she pushed open the door. Musty air drifted out, and she held back a cough. She stepped inside, taken aback by the sheer emptiness of the place. No furnishings of any kind, only a few utensils resting on the hearth and a few pieces of clothing lying about. Dusty streams of sunlight shone through holes in the poorly chinked walls. In the corners, bits of dried leaves and debris lay strewn about, remnants from years of disuse and, given the spattering of droppings lying about, home to numerous rodents. She scrunched her nose at the thought.

Setting the food atop the mantel, she drew a decided breath. It would take days or weeks, not hours, to remedy such a mess. All she'd have time for was to give the place a thorough sweeping. She tugged her sleeves up to her elbows, thankful she'd worn her least favored dress. She rested her hands on her hips and took another glance around the filthy cabin. Not a broom or cleaning rag to be had.

Striding over to the doorway, she stuck out her head. "Have you a broom?"

Stew paused his hacking. "No, ma'am, I haven't."

Her shoulders sagged. There went sweeping. "How about a bucket of water and some rags?"

"That I can manage." With a good-natured grin, he dropped his hoe and strode toward the barn.

Esther smiled to herself, amazed at his boundless energy. How was it he never seemed to tire? Rarely had she seen him without his ready smile and cheery disposition. How different he and Lawrence were. Lawrence's demeanor was as tedious as a long winter, while Stew carried with him the essence of spring, fresh and bursting with life.

What she wouldn't give to have more time to enjoy him.

Chapter Ten

STEW TUGGED at his new shirt collar, the ribbon tie confining. He hoped the Lord appreciated his sacrifice. At least he looked more like he belonged in a church building than the last time. Esther's smile hinted she approved or else was humored by his discomfort.

The hymn came to a close, and the congregation was prompted to its seats. From the far side of Esther, young Rachel leaned forward and grinned up at him, seeming much more at ease with his presence than when he'd first arrived. He tossed her a wink, and her smile deepened before she hid her face in Esther's sleeve. How grateful he was the youngster had only suffered minor cuts and bruises from her fall. If he'd been treated well by the Avery family before, now they doted on him like he was made of pure gold.

Esther's affections, too, seemed to have deepened. He'd sensed it in yesterday's unexpected visit, in her tone of voice and her eagerness to help. Yet, was her regard for him enough to alter her plans? Each passing day was one less they'd spend together. His nightly prayers gravitated toward Esther, urging the Lord to let her stay. It wasn't right, he knew, to hound the Lord with such a selfish plea, and yet it seemed his best hope.

His only hope.

The last couple of weeks had been like something out of a dream. As if the Lord had given him a fresh start and suddenly decided to shower him with blessings. The question was, would the dream last?

The room quieted as Pastor Brody took his place at the front. After an initial greeting, they were asked to turn to the book of Ephesians. Esther took her Bible in hand then glanced his way. She leaned toward him, her voice a soft whisper. "Have you forgotten your Bible?"

He bent toward her, his mouth close to her ear. "Don't have one."

Esther stared up at him, her expression a blend of remorse and disbelief. He lifted his shoulders in a self-conscious shrug, suddenly wishing he'd taken opportunity to purchase one at some point. He'd never owned a Bible of his own. Instead, he'd listened to it read from the pulpit or by his parents on wintry evenings around the fireplace.

Reading had never been his strong suit. Hopefully the Lord would forgive him that.

And hopefully Esther wouldn't hold it against him either.

"THAT'S THE LAST OF IT." Esther finished wringing out Rachel's dress then tossed it in the basket of wet clothes to be hung. Monday wash day seemed to come all too soon. She set the wash-board aside and stood, pressing her hands to her lower back. Yesterday's ride to church service had again left her a bit saddle sore, though nothing compared to the previous week.

"Good." Charlotte paused from pinning up damp diaper cloths. A grin spread over her face as she glanced from Rachel playing at her feet to Esther. "Sore again, are you?"

Esther straightened. "Just a bit."

"Another week or two riding to church and you'll be as at home in the saddle as Chad and Stew."

Heaviness pulled at Esther's chest. Another week or two and she'd be gone. Back to her blissfully boring life passing the time with needlework, entertaining guests, and attending dull plays that did little to stir the imagination. In the two weeks she'd been here, she'd felt more vibrant and alive than in years. Here she could be herself, the person God had created her to be.

In months to come, would this all seem like a distant dream?

The sound of horse hooves coming up behind caused her to turn. Stew tugged his paint to a stop beside her, his familiar lanky frame seated tall in the saddle. She tried to stem the rush of heat rising in her cheeks at his pointed stare. With a tip of his hat, he shifted his gaze to Charlotte and Rachel. "Mornin', ladies."

Rachel smiled and waved, her attachment to him evident on her glowing face.

Charlotte cocked her hands to her hips, squinting up at him. "Good morning, Stew. How's that cabin suiting you?"

"Can't complain. I'm obliged to you for the living quarters."

Charlotte let out a chuckle. "If you can call it that. I'm certain Chad will lend you a hand fixing up the place when he has time."

"Already had some good help." His gaze darted to Esther, the words of praise setting her face aflame once again.

"Have you, now?" The uptick in Charlotte's voice, along with her raised brows, only added to Esther's discomfort.

She cleared her throat in attempt to rid her voice of defensiveness. "Nothing much. I only cleaned a bit on the floorboards."

Stew fingered the reins in his hands, an awkward expression edging onto his face. By mid-morning he and Chad were usually hard at work digging the well or working with the cattle. Esther noticed Willow tethered behind his horse, saddled and ready, and her heartbeat quickened. Did he intend to ask her on a ride? Saddle sore or not, she'd not decline. She took a step toward him, willing herself to let go of the hope. "Was there something you needed?"

Clearing his throat, he leaned forward in his saddle. "Chad and Johnny are making a trip into town for supplies. Chad asked if I'd search for a missing cow that may have calved overnight. I wondered if you wanted to ride along?"

Esther resisted the urge to shout a resonant "yes!" Instead she clasped her hands behind her back and worked to extinguish her blossoming grin. "I'd love to, but we haven't yet finished with the wash."

"Don't let that stop you. Go on. Enjoy yourself." Charlotte's enthusiastic reply hinted of more than casual approval.

Esther shot her a curious glance. "Are you sure?"

"Of course. All that's left is to hang them on the line. Michael's napping. Rachel and I'll be just fine."

Esther bit at her lip, glancing up at Stew. "All right, then. I'd be glad to."

With a satisfied nod, he held out Willow's reins.

She took them, thrilled at both the unexpected time alone with him and the adventure of searching out the newborn calf. Sliding the reins over Willow's head, she gave the horse a pat on the neck. She'd come to relish riding. As a girl, she'd rarely ridden for pleasure. Now, alongside Stew, it seemed a pure delight.

As she mounted, Stew veered his horse to the north then turned to Charlotte. "I'll have her back in a couple hours. Hopefully the cow and calf as well."

She brushed a stray strand of hair from her forehead and smiled. "I'll count on it."

He peered over his shoulder at Esther. "Ready?"

She nodded and tied on her bonnet then reined Willow up beside him. "Where should we begin?"

"I've a few places in mind." He gestured toward the distant timber. "I figure over there's a good place to start."

With a wave to Charlotte and Rachel, Esther tapped her heels into Willow's flanks. A meadowlark's sweet song pealed overhead as they rode. Lifting her face to the sky, she let the sun's warmth caress her cheeks. She'd not realized how beautiful the day was. Had she been too engrossed in her work to notice?

She slid a glance in Stew's direction. Or was it her companion that made the day more inviting?

He reined his horse closer. "You're looking more at home in the saddle."

She patted Willow's neck, a daring thought crowding out good sense. "Enough so I think Willow and I can take you and your paint in a race."

Stew's lips lifted in a sideways grin. "Oh, you think so?"

"I do." Esther gave a brisk nod, her heart pumping faster. She must be mad. Was she truly going to race this cowboy who'd likely spent more time in the saddle than out of it? Willow had always been fast on her hooves, but she and Esther were both out of practice.

Stew arched a brow. "You're sure? I wouldn't want to face your sister and tell her you'd broken your leg coming off her horse in a race."

Esther cast a hesitant glance back toward the cabin. If she was thrown or injured, she'd not hear the end of it from Charlotte. And what a tizzy Mother would throw when she arrived.

Brushing aside her jitters, she tossed Stew a playful smile. "I'll chance it."

He held her gaze, jaw flinching, as though weighing her abilities against her determination. At last, he tugged his horse to a stop and stared out ahead of them. "See that grove of trees up ahead? First one to reach it wins. Scout and I will even give you a head start."

"Not necessary." Esther leaned low in the saddle and tightened her grip on the reins. "But if you insist." With a chuckle, she kicked her heels into Willow's flanks and clicked her tongue. The roan mare lurched forward, leaving Stew in her wake. Willow's easy canter quickly deepened into a full gallop. Esther clutched her mane, melting into the rhythm of her gait.

Not daring a look behind, she kept her gaze fixed on the grove of trees in the distance. The stiff breeze peeled back her bonnet, exposing her face to the sun's bright rays and tousling her hair. There was something invigorating about racing over the open prairie, the wind in her face. She drew in a breath, ignoring the soreness in her thighs. For the moment, she was free of cares, free of what the future held.

She sensed more than heard Stew's paint approaching to her right. Venturing a glance over her shoulder, she caught sight of him atop his horse, seeming to revel in the pursuit. With what seemed like easy strides, Scout inched past Willow. Stew looked her way, tipped his hat, and flashed a taunting grin.

Pressing her heels into Willow's sides, Esther urged her faster. With each jolting stride, the mare's breathing grew heavier. Would she have the stamina to keep up this pace? With less than a hundred yards to go, it seemed impossible for Willow to reach the grove of trees ahead of Scout. Yet, as they drew closer, she found herself gaining ground. She bent forward, molding her body to Willow's until they moved as one.

A few more strides and the horses would be neck and neck. Then, for whatever reason, as they neared the grove of trees, Scout slowed, allowing Willow to pull ahead and finish first.

Esther tugged on the reins, her exhilaration mingling with annoyance. A hollow victory.

He'd let her win.

Stew pulled Scout to a stop beside her. Removing his hat, he bowed low. "Why, Miss Esther. In all my days, I've not seen a finer piece of riding."

She tilted her head, eyes narrowing. "Oh, come now. You gave me the win. Why did you hold back?"

Straightening, he set his hat back on his head, a mischievous gleam in his eyes. "My mama taught me a lady always comes first."

Esther opened her mouth to speak then closed it, fighting back a grin. She shook her head, her angst dissolving. "Your mother is a wise woman."

He wiggled his brows. "That she is."

Sweat streamed down Willow's neck and chest, her breaths heavy. Esther patted her, the mare's damp hair coating her fingers. "Poor Willow. I fear I've pushed her too hard."

"Scout's a bit winded as well. Do you mind walking a bit?"

"Not at all."

Looping his leg over Scout, Stew slid to the ground. "There's a creek not far from here where the horses can drink."

She pointed eastward. "Over that way. I used to wade in it on occasion with my cousin Becky and her younger sister when we were young."

Strong hands encircled her waist as she started to dismount. Her breath caught at Stew's unexpected touch. He set her gently on the ground, his pale blue eyes perusing her undoubtedly flushed face. "Is that so?"

She swallowed, certain he could hear the beating of her heart. Many a young man had glanced her way, but none with such fondness or tenderness. It did strange things to her insides. Taking a step back, she pried her eyes from his and smoothed her crumpled dress. "Yes. We thought it great fun. If we stood very still, the tadpoles would swim right up to us."

She sensed his eyes still upon her. He closed the gap between them, cupping a hand to her chin. "That adventurous girl is still tucked inside you. The city hasn't driven it from you yet."

She flashed a mischievous grin. "I'll see that it doesn't."

He brushed the back of his fingers against her cheek. "Promise?"

Warmth trickled through her at his tenderness. She stared up at him, every fiber of her being longing to return his touch with one of her own. Instead, she nodded. "I promise."

His face brightened as he edged closer, his voice soft and low. "That's a promise I'd help you keep, if you stay."

She bit her lip, his declaration choking off her words. He'd not mentioned her leaving since their ride home from church service that first Sunday. Now, it seemed to hang between them like a murky fog, each day drawing it closer.

At the slight shake of her head, he drew his hand away and eased back, squinting out into the prairie. He exhaled a long breath. "Welp, we'd best see to the horses."

With a nod, Esther tugged at Willow's reins, feeling every inch a coward. Too timid to voice her misgivings or how fond she'd become of Stew, her silence, it seemed, had spoken the opposite. On wobbly legs, she walked alongside him, the swishing of their boots in the tall grass loud against the silence, his pained expression mirroring her own tortured spirit.

She swallowed down the dryness in her throat. If he only knew how much she wished to stay.

The midday sun's warmth soaked through Esther's bonnet, yielding dampness to her forehead. She swept a hand over her brow and slid a glance at her silent companion. What could she say to lighten his mood?

Just up ahead, the timber-lined creek seemed an oasis in an arid desert. As they reached its shade, she slid off her bonnet. "My, but it's warm. I believe I'll wade in for a drink right along with the horses."

Instead of his usual ready smile, Stew's expression sparked of melancholy. Retrieving his canteen from his saddle, he held it out to her.

She took a long swig and handed it back. "Thank you."

Not quite meeting her gaze, he pressed the canteen to his own lips, their moment of closeness shattered like broken glass.

While the horses drank, Esther leaned against a tree trunk and peered out across the prairie. The acres of tall grass stretched out ahead of her like a vast sea, swaying in the gentle breeze. "The missing cow and calf could be anywhere. We could search for hours and not find them."

"Oh, I don't know. Seems we've about found them already."

"What do you mean?"

He nodded toward a small cove in the trees to the east. Barely visible amid the prairie grass stood a single Hereford cow, grazing along the tree-line. Esther snapped her head toward Stew, her mouth agape. "How did you know she'd be here?"

He shrugged, reaching to tighten Scout's cinch. "Been keepin' an eye on her of late. This was one of the spots she frequented."

Esther strained for a better look. "But I don't see a calf with her."

"It's most likely hidden in the grass somewhere. Find the calf, and the cow will follow."

Esther propped her hands on her hips, a smile tugging at her lips. "You certainly know cattle, Stewart Brant."

He lowered the stirrup, his expression softening. "It's my business to know them."

Mounting, he motioned her to follow. "Let's ride closer and see if we can spot it. Look for a downed area where the grass is laid back."

Once atop Willow, Esther fanned out several yards to the left of where Stew rode and perused the grass for a place where the young calf might be sleeping. Several minutes passed with nothing but a rabbit and a startled covey of quail to show for their efforts. The mother cow lifted her head at their approach, giving a low bawl.

"I found it." Stew's welcome words rippled through Esther like summer rain. He dismounted, strolled forward several paces, then bent to pick up the calf.

Esther reined Willow closer, still unable to see the calf or much of Stew concealed by the thick grass. A faint shaking sound gave her cause to stop and listen. "Stew? Is anything wrong?"

"Stay back." She tensed at his hushed, pithy tone.

He seemed frozen in place. Why wasn't he moving?

The sound intensified, pulling at the recesses of her mind.

She'd heard that sound before when she was very young. The shaking noise followed by the deafening roar of her father's gun.

With a sudden intake of breath, she clapped a hand to her mouth, the blood draining from her face.

A rattler.

Chapter Eleven

STEW CROUCHED with his arms under the newborn calf not daring to move or even breathe. The rattling sound confirmed the snake's sinister intentions. Out of the corner of his eye, Stew saw its vibrating tail and its head poised, ready to strike at the slightest movement. A hundred thoughts pummeled his mind. At the forefront, Esther's well-being. Would she heed his warning not to approach? What would happen if he were bitten? Would he die here in her arms?

His rifle was of no use to him tied to his saddle. Would Esther know how to use it? Even if she did, it was likely the snake would strike before she could load it. His best bet was to remain still and hope the snake wouldn't deem him a threat.

Scout sounded a jittery nicker from behind, causing the calf to squirm in Stew's arms. Sweat trickled down his temples and onto his cheeks. The mother cow's concerned bawl brought the calf to its feet. As the weight of the calf lessened, the rattlesnake lunged at Stew, and he leapt away with all the force he could muster. Esther's scream rang in his ears as he landed several feet from where he'd started.

A warm sting pierced his left leg just above his ankle. He looked down to see the rattler clinging to the top of his boot.

Prying the snake loose, he flung it by its tail, gritting his teeth against the pain in his leg.

Esther rushed to his side, breathless, her hazel eyes tainted with worry. "Are you all right?"

Ignoring the query, he struggled to loosen his boot. Already he could feel his leg beginning to swell. "Help me get it off."

She pulled at the boot, her face blanching. As it slid off in her hands, she gasped at the dark spot on his sock just above his ankle. "He's drawn blood."

Stew peeled off his sock to assess the bloody wound. "It's not deep."

Only one of the fangs had truly punctured the skin, yet enough poison had found its way in to darken the area around it. Without the boot's protection, he hated to think how deep the fangs might have penetrated.

A death sentence, more than likely.

"Your foot is swelling. We have to get you to Doc Pruitt."

Stew sank back on his elbow, the pain excruciating. His toes began to tingle, a sure sign the poison was spreading. "There's no time."

"But you need help."

"I know what to do." Slipping his knife from its sheath, he held it out to her. "Cut a slit through the wound and drudge out as much of the poison as you can."

Realizing the urgency of the matter, to her credit, she didn't hesitate.

He lay back, grinding his teeth against the burn as he stared into the blueness of the sky. A string of puffy, white clouds proved a welcome distraction amid the sharp pain that sliced through him at the touch of the blade to his skin. A moan escaped him, and he clutched his hands to his knees, wishing for something to bite down on.

Esther drew her hand away. "I'm sorry."

"Go on. It has to be done." His voice sounded gritty, strained. Sweat dampened his forehead and neck as he again felt the scrape of the knife in the wound. Heaviness clawed at his chest, the intensity of the pain numbing his senses. Would he be able to keep his wits about him or sink into fitful unconsciousness?

Esther peered at him, her expression a blend of nausea and relief. "It's done, but the bleeding has worsened."

He loosened his bandanna, swallowing down the dryness in his throat. "Here. Tie this over the wound."

Her fingers quivered as she took it from him and fastened it around his leg.

With shallow breaths, Stew reached out his hand. "Help me to Scout."

Her hazel eyes widened. "Should you be moved?"

"The wound will need better cleaned and cauterized. My cabin's not far. You can tend to it better there."

She helped him to his feet and slid his arm around her shoulders. Under other circumstances, Stew would have relished her nearness. But for now, he was simply thankful she was with him.

WITH SHAKY HANDS and a prayer on her tongue, Esther pressed the hot knife to Stew's wound to flesh out the remainder of the poison. With a loud groan, his body tensed then went limp. She drew in a jagged breath, tears welling in her eyes. "Please, Lord, no."

The whispered words seemed to echo in the silence of the cabin. She studied his chest for movement. Its steady rise and fall assured her he'd merely passed out. Closing her eyes, she breathed a silent thank you to God then pressed a trembling hand to her mouth. "I can't do it."

It must be done.

Like a splash of dew in the dry of summer, Stew's words eased her uncertainty. She brushed a tear from her cheek and again touched the knife to his swollen foot. With nothing to numb the pain, his unconsciousness proved a blessing as she worked to cauterize the wound. The rank smell of blood and rotting flesh nearly gagged her. In the short time that had passed, the infected area had enlarged to the size of a walnut. How thankful she was the Lord had spared him from a full dose of venom. Had his boot not protected him, the outcome could have been much worse. Even now, the swelling in his leg was fierce.

A mucus-like substance, along with a trickle of blood, poured from the wound as she dug deeper into the blackened flesh. Cringing, she dabbed it away with a dampened rag then doused the soiled cloth in a tub of water warmed over the fire. She scraped along the outer edges of the bite wound with the knife. Stew had said it was important to get every bit of the rotted skin, else the poison would continue to eat away at him.

Finally, satisfied she'd removed the last of the infected skin, she rinsed the area one last time then washed her hands in a pan of fresh water. Ripping a section from the hem of her dress, she dipped it in warm water and smeared a generous dab of lard and salt at its center in hopes of drawing out any remaining poison. As she wrapped the poultice around Stew's shin, the muscles in his leg began to twitch. A rush of apprehension flooded through her. Had she been diligent enough in cleaning the wound? Would it be enough?

She moved to his head and knelt beside him. But for the creases above the bridge of his nose, his face lacked expression. She brushed a strand of hair from his temple, his brown waves the color of oak leaves in the fall. Such a gentle, caring man she'd not known since her pa. Stew reminded her of her father, the sort to lend a hand wherever needed, generous to a fault. He'd proven that in helping Chad and young Rachel. In saving her, he'd become a hero of sorts, and yet would be the first to deny the claim.

A smidgen of guilt wedged its way into her thoughts. Dare she think so highly of him? His faith was mediocre at best. He'd gone years without so much as opening a Bible or attending church service. Would he ever know what it meant to truly love the Lord?

She wiped sweat from his brow. There was no denying that his vivacious personality had woven its way into her heart. How uncanny that he lay here now so devoid of life.

Bowing her head, she closed her eyes and placed a hand on his arm. "Lord, I thank You for your protection and ask that Your healing touch be upon Stew. He's a good man. Please don't let life slip from him before he has the chance to know what it means to give his heart fully to You."

Movement beneath her fingertips startled her, and her eyes shot open. Stew's eyelids fluttered, stirring hope within her. "Stew?"

His eyes opened and flicked from one end of the cabin to the other, finally settling on Esther.

She touched a hand to his forehead. "How are you feeling?"

His face pinched. "Well, I'm alive. Death wouldn't hurt this much."

A weak smile tugged at her lips. "I'm glad of that. That you're alive, I mean."

He wet his lips, his voice but a whisper. "So thirsty."

Esther stood, looking for some sort of drinking vessel. A tin cup rested on the hearth. She dipped it in the water bucket and brought it to Stew. Placing a hand under his head, she held the half-filled cup to his parched lips. After a couple of swallows, he lay back, winded. He strained to see his swollen leg. "You've wrapped it? Guess I must have dropped off."

"Passed out, you mean." She set the tin cup aside. "I did my best to clean the wound. I just hope it's enough."

"Thank you." He drew in a sharp breath. "Thank you for being brave."

A nervous chuckle welled in her throat. "Brave? I was terrified the entire time."

His cheek flinched, his pale blue eyes fixed on hers. "You've done all anyone could do."

Moisture pooled in her eyes. "But you're still so weak, and your foot is swollen to twice its normal size. It wouldn't take more than a couple of hours to retrieve Doc Pruitt. Let me..."

"No." He clasped her wrist, tension in his jaw.

The worry in his eyes surprised her. Was she truly such a comfort to him? Or was he fearful he'd be left to die alone?

He moved his hand atop hers, the warmth of his touch trickling through her like fresh spring water. "Stay with me."

She gnawed at her lip. Charlotte would grow anxious over the delay in their return. Would they guess something had happened? Perhaps Chad would come looking for them and go for the doctor.

With a decided breath, she nodded. "All right. I'll stay."

BANG! Bang! Bang!

The thunderous pounding on the cabin door startled Esther from a light sleep. She lifted her head from the timbered wall and glanced out the window. Elongated shadows hinted evening had settled in. She started to rise then realized Stew's fingers remained latched onto hers. He stirred as she slipped her hand from his and draped his arm gently across his chest.

Another impatient rap on the door brought her to her feet. "Stew? Esther? Open up in there!"

It was Chad's voice, though his tone held an edginess she'd not heard before. The horses outside lent to the fact that she and Stew were there. She'd not given thought to appearances when she'd brought Stew to his cabin. Surely Chad wouldn't suspect anything was amiss.

She crossed the cabin, her boots clipping against the recently scrubbed floorboards. Lifting the latch, she eased the door open. Chad pushed through, his stern expression begging for explanation. "What goes on here? Charlotte's beside herself with worry."

At sight of him, the emotions Esther had pent up inside exploded into unwanted tears. "It's Stew. He's been bitten by a rattlesnake."

Chad's eyes widened, his gaze shifting to the corner of the cabin where Stew lay motionless. Quick strides carried him to his friend's side. Raw emotions played on his face as he assessed Stew's swollen leg. "When did it happen?"

"Midday." Esther swiped a tear from her cheek, her tone apologetic. "I'm sorry to cause you and Charlotte worry, but I couldn't leave him."

Chad peeled back the poultice, grimacing at the sight of the wound. "You did right. He'd likely not have survived otherwise."

"Do you think he'll be all right?"

Touching the back of his hand to Stew's brow, Chad released a long breath. "Time will tell." He stood, tipping his hat back on his head. "Keep him comfortable as best you can. If he wakes, offer him some broth. That is if you can find anything of substance around here."

Esther nodded and followed him to the door. "What are you going to do?"

"I'll swing by home to let Charlotte know what's happened, then fetch Doc Pruitt."

Renewed hope surged in her chest. The Lord had seen fit to let Stew survive this long, surely He'd see him through until the doctor arrived. She followed Chad onto the rickety porch. "Godspeed."

With a quick nod, he mounted his horse. Veering him toward the Circle J, Chad tapped his heels against his horse's flanks and sped away.

Esther pressed a hand to her chest as she watched him go. She turned her moist eyes heavenward, the sky a rich amber hue against the glow of the receding sun. *Lord, speed his way and keep Stew in your care until he returns.*

Chapter Twelve

ESTHER RUBBED a dampened cloth over Stew's forehead and down his neck. He was burning up. At her touch, a moan escaped him, and he writhed back and forth, his quiet rest having deteriorated into fitful twitches. He'd awakened long enough for her to offer him a bit of broth made of venison stock and wild onions, all she could find among his meager supplies. Then, he'd slipped back into confused slumber.

It pained her to see him in such agony. *Please, Lord, see him through.*

The minutes ticked by in dubious monotony. She bided her time searching the cabin for ways to make herself useful and tending to Stew, all the while praying he would live to see another day.

She lit a lantern, its orangey glow chasing away the darkness that had invaded the small cabin. Drawn by the scent of broth and the lantern's flame, numerous flies found their way inside the cabin and to Stew's wounded leg. She shooed them away, unnerved by the blueness of his foot. If he did survive, would his foot have to be taken?

Sitting beside him, she touched a hand to his toes. Their coolness stood in stark contrast to the heat emanating from his upper body. With careful strokes, she massaged his toes then worked her way down to the arch of his foot. If she could only get the blood flowing again.

The sound of approaching horses sent her scurrying to the open cabin window. She peered into the dark night, eyes searching. As two horsemen rode up outside the cabin, she mouthed a word of thanks to the Almighty. The buckskin assured one was Chad. The other, no doubt, was Doc Pruitt.

With renewed vigor, she swung open the cabin door and ushered them inside. Without a word, Doc Pruitt swept past her to Stew. One glance at his wound and the elderly doctor heaved a low sigh. Reaching in his bag, he took out his stethoscope. As he lifted Stew's shirt, Esther turned and edged her way to the far corner of the cabin.

Chad stepped inside, meeting her gaze. "How's he doing?"

"Hard to tell." She ventured a look back at the doctor, her heart at her throat. "Do you think he'll be all right?"

Doc Pruitt removed the stethoscope from his ears, lowered Stew's shirt, and sat back on his haunches. "Thanks to your resourcefulness, he stands a good chance. His pulse is a bit weak, but he's young and strong." He peered down at Stew's leg. "It's his foot I'm concerned about. The color isn't good. It's not getting adequate blood flow."

Chad stepped closer, tension in his jaw. "Will you have to take it?"

A whimper welled in Esther's throat, and she bit her lip to still it.

The doctor examined Stew's foot more closely. "I think it might be wise."

"No!" Esther's blunt appeal surprised even her. Who was she to tell a doctor his business? And in no way did she wish to endanger Stew. But to think of him maimed and crippled the rest of his days was more than she could bear. More than she thought *he* could bear. He was so full of vitality. To strip him of his spirit seemed cruel.

But if it would save his life, how could she oppose it?

She inched closer. "What if we could get the circulation going again through massage?"

Doc Pruitt extended his bottom lip and tipped his head side to side. "There's a chance it could be saved." He wagged his finger at her. "But only a chance, mind you."

She gave a brisk nod, her hope swelling. Nothing was too difficult for the Lord. "I'd help in any way."

He shook his head. "You go on and get some rest. I'll stay the night. We'll know more by morning." Creases lined his balding head as he peered up at her. "But if he hasn't improved, I dare not wait any longer."

The grave tone of his voice made her shiver. Waiting risked further infection and greater loss of limb. She gave a tentative nod, knowing Doc Pruitt would do what he deemed best regardless of her biddings.

Strong hands clasped her shoulders. "Come, Esther."

She gave into Chad's pull, but not before casting a final glance at Stew, his lifeless form shredding every ounce of joy from her soul. She'd not realized how much he meant to her, how much her heart had knit with his. Throughout the night, she would plead for the Lord's grace and mercy upon Stew. And, Lord willing, when morning dawned, he would be whole.

STEW PRIED HIS EYES OPEN, staring into the dim surroundings. Where was he? He blinked back the blurriness clouding his vision. The log rafters resembled those of his cabin's. How did he get here? His memory seemed as jumbled as his eyesight. Last he recalled, he was racing alongside Esther.

No, wait. The calf. They'd found it, then...

That sound.

A rattlesnake.

He tried to swallow, but his parched tongue and throat made it near impossible. Had he been bitten?

Pain shot through his left leg, leaving no doubt. He attempted to rise, but fell back, his limbs pulling at him like dead weight.

"Lay still, young man," a man's placid voice called out.

Stew lifted his head, straining to see past his chest. "Who's there?"

In the faint glow of lantern light, a shadowy figure leaned over him. "Rest easy, son. I'm a doctor. Doc Pruitt."

Stew wet his lips. "How'd you get here?"

"Chad Avery came for me. Said you'd been bitten by a rattler."

"Chad?" Stew leaned his head back, faded memories forming in his mind. "I found his missing calf. I was picking it up when I heard the rattling. The calf moved, and I jumped. I guess not far enough."

The doctor gave a sad grin. "It appears not."

Stew's thoughts began to clear. "Esther. Esther was with me. Where is she?"

"No need to fret, son. She's well and safe. Chad's taken her home." Doc Pruitt patted him on the arm. "Better count your blessings she was with you. That young lady very well may have saved your life."

Stew released a long breath. What he must have put her through. He vaguely remembered her anguished expression and the pain as she cut into him. She'd removed the poison. How brave she'd been.

Another stab of pain shot through his lower leg. "How bad is it, Doc?"

The doctor's slight hesitance hinted the news wasn't good. "You've very poor circulation below the ankle. While I believe your life's been spared, I'm not so certain about your foot."

Stew broke into a cold sweat, the doctor's words penetrating him like a dreaded disease. Losing his foot would steal his livelihood. He swallowed, his palms growing clammy. "What are my chances?"

A low sigh sounded beside him. "If circulation doesn't improve, I'm afraid it'll have to be taken."

Stew clenched his fists. "Does Esther know?"

Another pause. "She knows. It's at her request I've put it off. She has a mind that massaging might help."

"Will it?"

"It might. That and a bucketful of prayers."

With a nod, Stew snapped his eyes shut. Prayer. It seemed his only option about now. Why the Lord should listen to him, a wayward soul who'd neglected his faith for so long, he couldn't say.

But it never hurt to try.

Chapter Thirteen

ESTHER YAWNED, doing her best to stay astride Willow. Her restless night hadn't done her a bit of good. Hopefully, Stew had enjoyed better sleep. She'd knocked on heaven's door repeatedly throughout the night on his behalf. Soon she'd know if her prayers had been answered.

As Stew's cabin came into view, she saw Doc Pruitt's horse still tethered at its front. Most likely he'd not slept much either. Yet his being there gave her some semblance of comfort. His knowledge of doctoring far outshined her own. But Jesus was the great physician. It would be His hand that brought healing. No one else's.

She clutched her bundle of slightly warm biscuits and sausage tighter. Hopefully Stew would be alert and possess more of an appetite this morning. She hated to shirk her duties helping Charlotte, but she seemed to be managing fine without her when she'd left. Had even encouraged her to come.

Esther's stomach knotted. Before long, she'd not be needed at all. The thought garnered a bitter taste in her mouth. She couldn't leave. Not until she knew Stew would recover.

As she neared the cabin, fear washed over her at sight of Doc

Pruitt sitting hunched in a chair on the porch, hands covering his face. The pose didn't lend to good news. Tapping her heels into Willow's flanks, she goaded her faster. Whether good news or bad, Stew would need someone with him.

The doctor straightened as Esther brought Willow to a halt outside the cabin. His trained expression gave little clue as to Stew's condition. With bated breath, she stared down at him, hands atremble as she fingered the reins. "How's Stew faring this morning?"

A weary looking Doc Pruitt stood and sauntered toward her. He squinted at her, rubbing a hand over his bald head. "'Twas a long night, but he's resting comfortably."

A burning question lodged in Esther's throat. One she wasn't certain she wanted to know the answer to. "Did you…?"

He arched a brow. "Take his foot?" With a shake of his head, his expression softened. "No. Seems you must be in pretty good standing with the Lord. For a while, it wasn't looking good, but the closer to morning it got, the pinker his foot became."

Tears welled in Esther's eyes. "Thank the Lord."

Doc Pruitt stretched his back then reached to untie his horse's reins. "Now, if you're here to relieve me, I've an appointment with my bed."

"Thank you, Doc Pruitt." Dismounting, she looped Willow's reins over the porch rail and hurried up the steps.

The doctor caught her by the arm, his bloodshot eyes earnest. "Keep massaging that foot, change his dressing twice a day, and be certain someone stays with him at all times. If he worsens, send for me. Otherwise, I'll be back in the morning to check on him."

She nodded, his grave words reminding her Stew still had a long way to go before he recovered. Infection could set in or some other unforeseen complication might slow his progress. Healing would take time.

Something she was running short of.

She waited for the doctor to leave then eased inside the cabin.

A pungent smell accosted her. Some sort of medicine or poultice remedy? Whatever it was nearly gagged her. The silence within brought a solemnness to her previously joyous mood. Stew lay motionless on his makeshift bed of blankets in the far corner. Still clutching the bundle of food, she tiptoed toward him, startling when his head veered in her direction.

A weak smile pulled at his lips. "Hello."

Her shoulders relaxed as she stepped closer, his casual demeanor putting her at ease. "How are you feeling?"

"Better *now*." His emphasis on the word now, coupled by the welcoming gleam in his eyes, hinted her presence was the cause of his improvement. The revelation sent a rush of warmth to her cheeks.

She knelt beside him and studied his foot. "Your toes seem to have regained some color."

"From what Doc said, I've you to thank for it."

With a shake of her head, she met his gaze. "I only asked for time. The Lord brought the healing."

"Maybe so, but I'd likely not have a foot for Him to heal if you'd not put in a plea with the doc."

She swallowed down the lump in her throat. "I knew if there was any way, you'd want it saved."

"You know me well." He winced, his voice gravelly.

Moving closer, she pressed a hand to his arm. "You're hurting. Is there anything I can do? Doc Pruitt gave me instructions to…"

He placed his hand atop hers, stilling her words, his pale blue eyes boring into her. "Give me reason to hope you'll be here when I'm well."

Esther dropped her gaze. How could she make such a promise? Her life was all but planned out for her. Very soon, Mother would come, expecting her to accompany her back to Cincinnati with a proposal from Lawrence almost certain to follow. And yet, the words she longed to speak, but shouldn't, tumbled from her lips before she could stop them.

"I promise."

"YOU REALLY DON'T HAVE to stay the night. I'll be fine."

Stew's plea seemed to fall on deaf ears as Chad rolled out his blanket. "Doc wants someone with you around the clock these first couple of days."

He had to admit, he was glad for the company. The cabin seemed twice as empty since Esther had left but a short time ago. He could still feel the tenderness of her touch as she massaged his foot, her hands much warmer and soothing than the doctor's.

"I found the cow and calf right where you said they'd be."

The satisfied tone in Chad's voice brought Stew a sense of comfort. "That's good."

Chad tugged off his boots. "Found a snake skin too."

Stew shot a glance at his friend. "The rattler's?"

"Could've been. But don't worry. I had my rifle."

"Wish I could say the same." Stew lay back, his head propped in his hands. "I should've known better than to go traipsing around the prairie unprotected. I'm just thankful it was me that got bit instead of Esther."

Chad settled onto his blanket on the floor. "You gave her quite a scare. She fretted something awful over you."

Warmth surged through Stew, the thought of Esther's concern for him not altogether unpleasant. The caring way she'd tended to his needs, her shy smile, her gentle touch spoke more than mere kindness. Had her feelings for him deepened?

He chuckled in attempt to mask his true feelings. "Ah, you know women. They worry over a hangnail."

Chad turned to him, a hint of a grin playing on his lips. "Nah. This was different. If I didn't know better, I'd say there was a sight more than friendship between you two."

Stew turned and watched lantern light dance along the

shadowy rafters. Esther had promised to stay until he'd recovered, but had given no indication she'd changed her mind about returning to Cincinnati. For weeks now, he'd prayed she would have a change of heart. If she truly cared for him, she'd stay. That hope was all he had.

Hope…and prayer.

Doc Pruitt peeled back the poultice, exposing the flesh-eaten wound. It hadn't taken long for Esther to realize the stench she'd smelled yesterday belonged to the tobacco leaf paste the doctor had concocted to further draw out the poison in Stew's leg.

As he replaced the cloth, Doc Pruitt stared at her and Stew atop his wire-rimmed spectacles. "Well, it ain't purty, but at least it's no worse."

"How long till I'm on my feet?" Stew's eagerness to be active again told in his voice.

"Depends on how quickly you heal. The poison oughta work out of your system in another couple days. Then, if you're able to stand, we'll see about rigging up a crutch of some sort. But take it slow and easy. It'll be weeks, maybe months, before you regain use of your foot."

Stew winced, the news, no doubt, not what he'd hoped to hear. His gentle nod belied the tension in his jaw. How Esther ached to comfort him. He wasn't the sort to sit idle. But then, compared to loss of life or limb, what was a little time to rest and heal?

Doc Pruitt gathered his instruments into his bag then peered over at Stew. "Don't look so glum, son. When you consider the alternative, I'd say you've made out all right."

Stew shrugged. "I reckon."

Doc Pruitt leaned closer, his voice softening. "With such a pretty nursemaid, I'd not be in too big of hurry to recuperate."

The doctor's wink brought a rush of heat to Esther's cheeks. She seemed to be doing a lot of blushing since she'd met Stew.

He glanced her way, a playful smile replacing his glower. "I see your point."

Esther shook her head, fighting a grin. "Honestly."

The doctor's laughter echoed through the small cabin as he clapped Stew on the shoulder. "I'll be back to check on you in a couple of days."

With a nod, Stew stuck out his palm. "Thanks, Doc."

"Glad to help." The two men shook hands, an obvious rapport between them. At last, Doc Pruitt stood and turned to Esther. "How about seeing me out?"

"Certainly." She knit her brow as she skirted around Stew. The doctor's face wore a jovial expression as they strode to the door, but sobered once outside. Something akin to dread swept through her. "What is it?"

Doc Pruitt paused beside his horse, releasing a long breath. "I fear your friend's in for a rather lengthy recovery."

"But you said…"

"I know what I said, but there looks to be some nerve and tissue damage that may complicate the healing process. Between the lack of circulation and the cutting, I'm afraid his foot may not work properly."

Esther drew in a breath. With trembling voice, she forced out the dreaded words. "You mean I may have crippled him for life?"

Doc Pruitt touched a hand to her arm. "Now don't go blaming yourself. What you did may very well have saved that foot and possibly the young man's life. I don't know as things would have turned out any different had I cut the poison out myself. The important thing is to give him something to work towards. Keep him hopeful, positive."

She nodded and leaned against the porch rail. "What can I do?"

"Keep massaging that foot and tending the wound. Be encouraging. We'll see how he's doing in a few days. Only time will tell how much use he'll have."

Untying his reins, the doctor glanced at the cabin. "That young man has a lot of grit. Lord willing, he'll come through better than most."

Esther swiped a tear from her cheek. Stew mustn't see her upset. She had to be strong, for his sake. *Lord, grant me strength to encourage.*

THE CREAK of the saddle grated at Esther's nerves as she rode toward the Circle J Ranch. Had she been convincing? Had she fooled Stew into thinking recovery was all but certain? For hours she'd put on a pleasant act, doing her utmost to smile and render a positive persona. Alone now, there was no cause for pretense. Silent tears streamed down her cheeks. The possibility that she'd played a part in rendering Stew without use of his foot had shaken her to the core. To know he could be maimed for life was almost more than she could bear.

The chatter of birds flying overhead seemed to chasten her. She watched the pair of robins flit and dart effortlessly through the air before landing in a treetop. Drying her eyes, she scanned the vast prairie, a sense of peace and humility washing over her. The Lord knew every bird and flower of the field. Hadn't He promised to love His people all the more? Stew was alive. His foot had been spared. Couldn't the Lord bring about healing as well? And if He chose not to, didn't He still have a plan for Stew? For her?

She lifted her gaze to the cobalt sky. *Forgive me, Lord, for doubting You.*

Lazy smoke drifted from the chimney of Chad and Charlotte's cabin in the distance. Chad's horse stood saddled and ready, awaiting her return. How grateful she was Chad was willing to stay with Stew when she could not. She'd make no mention of Doc

Pruitt's dismal prediction. Why burden Chad and Charlotte with such? The Lord would do as He saw fit. Only time would tell if Stew would walk unhindered.

As she neared the cabin, muffled voices sounded from within, ones she couldn't quite distinguish. Company? Dismounting, she smoothed her dress and pinched her cheeks. What a time for neighbors to visit, with her teary-eyed and in a sullen mood.

With a steadying pause, she practiced a smile then gave a gentle knock before tugging the latch-string. As the door pushed open, she sucked in a breath, eyes wide.

"Mother!"

Chapter Fourteen

ESTHER STEPPED INSIDE THE CABIN, struggling for words. "You— you're here."

Her mother's forehead creased. "Why so surprised? I told you I'd come."

"Yes, but I wasn't expecting you just now." Nor was she ready for her. Not with Stew still recuperating. She'd made a promise.

Her mother's left eyebrow shot up. "I must say, I was rather stunned to find you were off tending to some ranch hand when I arrived rather than lending your energies to care for Charlotte and my grandchildren."

The nettling tone in her mother's voice rendered Esther speechless and a tad belittled. There was no use trying to explain. Her mother would only find her attachment to Stew odd, disconcerting. He wasn't the sort she'd warm to easily. He was too simple and easy-going, in her mother's perspective, an uneducated man of little substance.

Charlotte stepped to her defense, young Michael cradled in her arms. "Mr. Brant is not a ranch hand. He's a friend. And at the moment, he's in more dire need of Esther's help than I am."

"Well, if I'd known such, I'd have come sooner." Puckering her lips in a bit of a pout, Mother reached for her grandson, and Charlotte slipped the babe into her arms. An animated smile transformed her face as she sought to entertain young Michael. In unfamiliar arms, the infant's coos soon digressed into whimpers. Mother joggled him, shifting him every which way before finally passing him back to Charlotte when his gentle sobs blossomed into full-fledged cries.

Mother smoothed her dress, a hint of added pink in her cheeks. "It seems I'm a bit out of practice where baby boys are concerned. I'm much more adept at raising little girls."

She reached to where Rachel sat playing with her corn-husk doll before the hearth and patted her on the head. In response, the youngster stopped her play and retreated behind Charlotte's skirt.

Mother pressed a hand to her loose chignon, her face losing its merriment. "Well, it appears I have some catching up to do before my grandchildren have anything to do with me."

Esther suppressed a grin. As far as she was concerned, the longer it took the children to warm to their grandmother the better, if it meant a delay in their departure.

"SOME HELP I've turned out to be. Here less than a month and laid up for who knows how long." Stew shifted on his blanket, his muscles craving activity.

"Couldn't be helped." Chad yawned and rubbed the back of his neck, obviously tired from endless hours on the go.

"Just look at you, more tuckered than when I first came. It's bad enough you having to carry the load in my absence, but what's worse is, I'm keeping you from your wife and young'uns of a night."

With a shrug, Chad spread his blanket on the floor near Stew's makeshift cot. "Truth is, tonight I'm glad to have an excuse to be away, what with Charlotte's ma there."

Stew tensed. "She's here?"

"Is she ever. And I get the feeling she's not too keen on Charlotte having stayed behind and marrying a cattleman. Kept going on about her poor grandchildren growing up in such primitive conditions."

With a sigh, Stew locked his fingers together over his chest. It appeared he had his work cut out for him. Not only would he have to convince Esther staying was a good idea, but win her ma over as well. "How long do you 'spect she'll stay?"

"Not sure. A few days. A week. The sooner she leaves the better as I see it. Seems she's gotten accustomed to the fancier side of living and has little tolerance for simpler ways."

Stew offered a half-hearted nod, realizing Chad's gain would be his loss. When his mother-in-law left, so would Esther. Would she hold to her promise to stay until he was on his feet?

Chad reached to snuff out the lantern but paused, his gaze fixed on Stew. "Why do you ask?"

For a moment, Stew was tempted to bare his soul to his friend, then relented. "No reason."

Liar. There was every reason. A few days and Esther would be lost to him.

"Uh huh." Chad's playful tone hinted he knew more than he was letting on. He cleared his throat. "Then maybe it's Esther you're worried about leaving."

Stew jerked his head toward Chad, barely catching his friend's humored expression before he doused the lantern flame. As darkness shrouded the cabin, Stew sank back on his blanket, an unsettled churning in his stomach. There was no need to answer. His silence spoke for him. Though certain Chad meant to encourage rather than gall, his friend's words pricked at Stew like a thorn.

He'd known from the start how futile it would be to surrender his heart to Esther. And yet, he'd done it anyway. Miss Delta Fanning had broken his heart undeservedly. This heartache over Esther was of his own making. Despite every intention not to, he'd come to love her. Now he'd pay the penalty for his mistake. Soon her pleasant features and endearing smile would be but a distant memory.

One he hoped in time he could forget.

A single spark of hope flickered inside him. Growing up, he'd listened to story after story of how the Lord worked miracles in the direst of circumstances—Daniel in the lion's den, Noah and the ark, Jesus rising from the dead. If God could work wonders on such a grand scale, surely He could do something so small as to give Esther the notion to stay.

Couldn't He?

Closing his eyes, he breathed a silent prayer. *Lord, I know I'm not the most perfect of souls. But I'm trying. So I ask you once more. Give Esther a mind to stay.*

THE SNORES EMANATING from the loft were enough to convince Esther she'd done well to abandon her regular sleeping quarters to join Charlotte and the children in the bedroom. With Chad away for the night, Johnny had taken to the barn early. Whereas Mother had at least attempted to bond with the younger children, she'd barely acknowledged Johnny. Whether due to the fact he wasn't her blood relation or her unfamiliarity with boys on the verge of manhood, Esther couldn't determine. But she sensed Johnny's urgency to render himself scarce.

With a final glance toward the barn to assure his lantern was no longer lit, Esther barred the door and drew in the latch-string for the night. She strode toward the bedroom, pulled by the gentle glow of lantern light within. As she eased the bedroom door closed behind her, muffled snores found their way inside. She sighed, having forgotten how horrendous her mother's snoring could be. How thankful she was to have her bedroom at the far end of the hall from where her mother and stepfather slept at their home in Cincinnati.

Turning, she smiled at the sight of young Rachel sprawled across Charlotte's lap while she nursed baby Michael in the rocker. Charlotte's labored expression hinted she could do with a bit of help. Tiptoeing to her side, Esther slid her hands under the sleeping Rachel. The tiny girl fell limp in her arms, her red curls bouncing with each step as Esther carried her to the thin mattress tucked in the corner of the room. She brushed a strand of hair from Rachel's forehead, struck by the fleetingness of the moment. Within these past few weeks, Esther had developed quite a fondness for her young niece and nephew.

One more reason she balked at the thought of leaving.

Charlotte mouthed a "thank you" to Esther as she rose from her chair and laid Michael in his cradle. With a nod, Esther slid into bed. Dousing the lantern, Charlotte slipped in beside her. As her eyes adjusted to the dimness of the room, Esther turned to view the silhouette of her sister's profile, memories of their childhood leaping to the forefront of her mind. Years had passed since they'd slept side-by-side in the small loft, sharing secrets and dreaming dreams. They'd not always gotten along, but there was a kinship between sisters, something they'd lost for a time but now had revived. Except now, it ran much deeper.

Charlotte shifted her face toward her. "I'm so glad you came. I'm going to hate to see you go."

Moisture welled in Esther's eyes at her sister's hushed words. "So will I."

Charlotte released a tired sigh. "Ma certainly has changed. Did you see her face when I kept calling her Ma?"

Esther did her best to stifle a giggle. "I warned you."

"I'm glad to know city life hasn't tainted your sweet nature. Refuse to, won't you?"

"I'll do my utmost. But if Mother has her way and I become

Mrs. Lawrence Del Ray, I'll be expected to be prim, proper, and refined."

Charlotte turned on her side, her tone low but intense. "That will ruin you."

With a soft groan, Esther shifted toward her. "What choice do I have? Mother is set on me marrying a well-to-do husband."

"Not some cattle rancher like Chad, huh?"

Esther hugged her middle, the truth of Charlotte's words ringing in her ears. How could she answer? Many a time her mother had made mention of Charlotte settling for less of a life than she was meant for. And yet, Esther had witnessed the deep-seated love between her sister and Chad. What greater joy could there be than to love and be loved, truly, and from the heart?

She closed her eyes, envisioning Stew's ready smile and pale blue eyes. Neither would Mother approve of him. No home of his own. Uneducated. Lacking in spiritual fervor. Near penniless, with only a horse and the clothes on his back to call his own. And now injured and near helpless. To her mother, he would seem the epitome of someone unworthy of a second glance. But Esther saw something in Stew, something hopeful and pure.

An endearing quality she would never forget.

ESTHER WAS LATE. Would she come at all? From Chad's description of her mother, Stew gathered she was a bit demanding. Would she refuse to let Esther come? Or maybe Esther preferred to spend the time with her family rather than play nurse-mate to him.

Truth be told, he was a bit fearful she would come and give the word she'd be leaving. Even if she did stay, what did he have to offer? Next to nothing. He scrubbed a hand over his face. The more he prayed, the worse things seemed to get. If the Lord cared, if He was truly listening, somehow He'd make a way for them to be together.

The canter of hooves sounded outside the cabin, setting his heart in motion. He pulled himself to a sitting position, cringing when he tried to move his injured leg. Not only was it sore but both legs had gone stiff from lack of use. He strained to see out the window and caught a glimpse of Esther as she dismounted. Brushing a hand through his hair, he willed himself to appear casual.

With a light rap, the door pushed open, and Esther smiled in at him. "Good morning."

"Hello." He nodded to her, unable to hold back a grin. The way her golden hair framed her oval face was prettier than moon-glow on a glassy lake. She strolled over to him, and his stomach rumbled at the sweet scent of cinnamon. His gaze drifted to the bundle in her hand. "If that's my breakfast, it sure smells good."

"Cinnamon buns. Freshly baked this morning." She handed him the cloth bundle. "But I can't take all the credit. It's Charlotte's recipe."

Unfolding the cloth cover, he lifted one to his nose and drew in a breath. "Heavenly."

Her smile deepened. "Your appetite is improving, as you seem to be as well."

"Not fast enough for my liking. I'm eager to be back on my feet. Soon as Doc brings that crutch of his, there'll be no stopping me." He bowed his head in a quick prayer, having been reprimanded by her yesterday morning for not pausing to say grace.

When he opened his eyes, Esther's expression had sobered. Would she tell him about her mother's arrival? He took a bite of the cinnamon bread, its sweetness satisfying his hunger, but not his curiosity. Wiping a crumb from his lips, he waited in expectation for her to speak. When she didn't, he decided to bait her. "So, what's new at the Circle J?"

Her eyelids flickered and fell. "Oh, you know. The usual. Helping Charlotte with the children. Chad and Johnny keeping busy with the herd. They've even made a bit of progress on the well." She stood and wiped her hands on her day dress. "I'll make you some coffee."

He caught her by the arm, and she gave into his gentle tug. "Chad told me you had a visitor."

She met his gaze, her hazel eyes staring down at him like a frightened doe. "I didn't want you to know just yet."

"Why? Did you think it would be easier to have you up and leave without warning?"

"I suppose not." She dropped back down beside him, her expression solemn. "I'm going to do my best to convince her to stay until you're well. At least well enough to move about."

With a shake of his head, he traced a finger down her cheek. "It won't make your going any easier."

Moisture pooled in her eyes. "It's not my wish to leave. Mother expects it of me. She's rather dependent on me."

Heaviness pulled at Stew's chest. Was there any use trying to sway her by telling her he loved her? He took a hard swallow, sandwiching his hands around hers. "I know I haven't much to offer, and it may be months or years before I can prove worthy of you, but I care for you, Esther. Given time, I hope to think you might care for me too."

Her chin quivered. "I do care. More than you know."

"Then do me this one favor. Consider postponing your return to Cincinnati. Stay the summer. Give me time to get back on my feet. Give *us* time. Will you do that for me?"

Her moment of hesitation seemed an eternity. Stew's hands grew clammy as they cupped hers. He held his breath, praying her answer would be yes.

At last, she wet her lips and nodded. "All right, Stew. I'll give it some thought."

A smile crept onto his face, joy and sweet relief welling inside him. He squeezed her hand. "Thank you."

Chapter Fifteen

"Why must you spend your time catering to that cattle herder? I've been here four days and hardly seen you more than an hour of a morning and evening. A young woman of your age alone with a man in his home. Why, it's indecent."

Esther's hand clutched the door-frame, her mother's judgmental words stilling her in her tracks. Pivoting toward her, Esther did her best not to sound disrespectful. "I assumed it was Charlotte and the children you'd come to see. Not me."

"Well, even so, I don't like the thought of you traipsing off to some strange man's cabin. A man I've never so much as met."

Her mother's indignant tone grated at her. If she could only get to know Stew, witness his kindness and infectious spirit, perhaps she'd be more receptive, not only to him, but also to her staying. Each day Stew was making progress. Now that he was strong enough to walk with the help of a crutch, maybe he would enjoy a friendly outing. She shot a glance at her sister. "Charlotte? Would you be opposed to my inviting Stew to join us for supper this evening?"

A wry grin crossed Charlotte's face. "Not at all. Ask away. I'm sure Chad or Johnny would be happy to fetch him in the wagon."

With a pronounced nod and a determined glance at her mother, Esther spoke in a tone that surprised even herself. "Very well then. If he's willing, you'll have your opportunity to meet Mr. Brant."

"YOU LADIES SURE PUT out a fine spread." Stew leaned back in his chair, trying to ignore the throbbing in his foot.

"So glad you're well enough to join us." Charlotte offered him a cup of coffee, which he declined.

"Sure is a treat after being confined so many days." He stretched his leg out from under the table, sensing Esther's mother's scrutinizing glare upon him. Though she'd spoken only a handful of words to him, she seemed to ingest his every move. Esther, too, seemed stifled, stiff. He couldn't decide if she was nervous, annoyed, or just plain bored with the lagging conversation. He had a feeling there was more to the supper invitation than merely getting him out of his cabin.

Not one to delay the obvious, Stew turned his gaze on Esther's mother. Though her fair hair was flecked with gray and her figure not as trim as her daughters, Clara Leifer shared similar attractive features. "Well, Mrs. Leifer, I can certainly tell where your daughters get their fetching looks."

When the comment garnered only a slight grin, he leaned forward and cleared his throat. "I suppose you're wondering just how I came to be a guest in this household."

Seeming taken aback by his directness, the older woman stilled then wiped the corners of her mouth with a handkerchief. "Now that you mention it, I am rather curious of your background, Mr. Brant."

He shrugged. "Not much to tell. Born and raised in Missouri, I'm the eldest of nine children. I left home at seventeen and have worked on cattle drives ever since. That's where I met Chad. I happened by here a few weeks back, and he was kind enough to offer me a position."

"Just about the time Esther arrived, I suppose."

"Yes, ma'am. That was a pleasure I hadn't reckoned on."

He flashed Esther a quick glance, noting her face had blanched. Was it her mother's insinuating tone or his response that had embarrassed her?

Humored grins spilled onto both Chad and Charlotte's faces as though they shared some unknown secret. Dropping his gaze, Stew locked his fingers together on the table. At this rate, he'd not succeed in winning Esther or her mother.

"You seem to be recovering well." Charlotte interjected as she wiped food from Rachel's soiled face.

Grateful for the change of topics, Stew nodded. "Making progress anyway. But I'm eager to get back to work."

Mrs. Leifer harrumphed. "By the discomfort you're in, it appears that may be a while. You certainly can't expect to be paid while you're unable to work."

"Mother!"

Stew placed a hand on Esther's arm to still her and met her mother's gaze. "No ma'am. I don't expect to be. But, I am obliged to the Averys for their generosity and their willingness to see to my needs while I recuperate."

Chad set his jaw, his eyes narrowing as he took in his mother-in-law. "Don't you worry none, Clara. Stew pulls his weight around here. We're fortunate to have him."

Mrs. Leifer moistened her lips, but gave no reply as she stuffed her handkerchief in her lap.

Stew slid his hand from Esther's arm, his stomach knotting. Coming here had been a mistake. He could no more gain this woman's approval than run a three-legged race.

The uncomfortable silence was interrupted by a baby's muffled squall. "Sounds like Michael's ready for his supper. If you'll excuse me." Standing, Charlotte started toward the bedroom, Rachel trotting after her.

Tension hung in the air.

"May I be excused?" Johnny's tentative voice broke the silence.

At Chad's nod, the boy stood then smiled over at Stew. "I've been practicing my roping, Mr. Brant. Gettin' pretty good at it too."

For the first time since he'd arrived, a sense of pleasure enveloped Stew. "That's good, Johnny. You keep at it."

The boy gave an enthusiastic nod before tramping outside.

A glance out the window assured Stew the sun had already set. If the stunted conversation hadn't already convinced him it was time to leave, the darkening sky would have. But first, he needed to talk to Esther. Alone. Not try to sway her in his favor, but encourage her to see things for what they were. He understood now what she was up against. Her mother was an overbearing snob bent on having her way. Esther deserved more than a life chained to such a woman.

Shifting his gaze toward her, he mustered a shallow grin. "Miss Esther, would you care to join me on a short walk?"

Choking down a sip of water, Esther's eyes widened. "A walk? But you can't..."

"I can manage a short one."

His tone must have been convincing for she smiled and nodded. Handing him his crutch, she helped him to his feet.

Without a backward glance, Stew hobbled to the door with Esther. An excited Rubie greeted them on the porch, tail wagging. A rub on the head seemed to satisfy for she returned to her rug.

The darkening sky and soft breeze were a refreshing change from the confines of the cabin. Crickets and katydids trilled in the yard, their gleeful chant accented by an occasional "moo" from the herd as they settled in for the night. Stew took a deep breath, letting go of the unpleasantness of the recent conversation.

Gripping his arm, Esther helped him down the porch steps then gazed up at him. "Are you sure you're up to this?"

He nodded. "I can make it to the yard fence over there."

To his pure delight, she kept her hold on his arm as they plodded along at a turtle's pace. With each step, Stew leaned into the wooden crutch, trying to formulate the words rattling around in his head. Had Esther made up her mind? Would his failure to impress her mother have a bearing on that decision? There seemed no better time than now to ask as they stood beneath the starry sky. No distractions or hindrances to hamper the honesty of their words.

Winded from the walk, Stew steadied himself against the split-rail fence. The moon's glow painted a bluish cast over the prairie, its vastness engulfing them like an endless sea.

"Are you all right?"

Esther's words, spoken so tenderly, sent a tingle through him. Taking her hand, he smiled at her. "Couldn't be better."

He propped his knee up on one of the hewn timbers, his smile evaporating into a playful scowl. "I take that back. I'd be much better if I knew you'd decided to stay."

Moisture glistened in her eyes as she stared up at him. She squeezed his hand. "You asked *me* a favor. Now I'm asking one of *you*. Give me time to think things through, pray, and decide what to do."

"But your mother will—"

Her finger against his lips stilled him. "Please. Just a few more days."

With a sigh, Stew brushed a lock of hair from her forehead. "All right, Esther. I'll say no more until you're ready to give your answer."

Like fresh morning dew, sweet relief seemed to trickle over Esther's face. She leaned into him, and he slid his arms around her. Like a beacon of hope, the silvery moon shone down on them.

And yet, Stew had to wonder if he would ever stroll with her under moonlit skies again.

ESTHER STEPPED into the cabin ahead of Stew, hoping the flush in her cheeks wouldn't be evident in the lantern light. The warmth of his touch still lingered in her senses, as did the affection in his eyes.

Hunching to fit his tall frame through the doorway, he tipped his hat. "Thanks much for the victuals, Miss Charlotte."

"Any time, Stew."

He turned to Mother, his expression stoic, but cordial. "'Twas a pleasure to meet you, ma'am."

In response, Mother offered a curt nod and returned to her stitching.

The obvious slight stung at Esther. Her mother's attempt to become acquainted with Stew had been meager at best. More interrogative than sociable. Esther's stomach lurched. She could as much as guess her mother's response if she requested to delay her return to Cincinnati.

Which, in her heart, she longed to do.

In attempt to soften her mother's rebuff, she caught Stew's eye and flashed a cheerful smile. His expression lightened, and he tossed her a wink before turning to go.

Chad stood and leaned to kiss Charlotte. "With it so late, I believe I'll stay the night with Stew again."

Stew poked his head in the doorway. "This is the last time I'll steal him from you. Promise."

With a chuckle, she waved them on, Rachel asleep in her lap. "Safe travels."

No more were they out the door than Mother set her stitching aside and glared at Esther. "I can see you favor that young man."

If she'd been flushed before, she surely was more so now. With his bad leg, Stew couldn't be more than two steps from the window and certain to overhear. Gritting her teeth, she motioned for Mother to lower her voice.

As if in revolt, her mother's volume increased. "I should have known better than to send you here unchaperoned. You've taken on all sorts of foolish notions."

Rachel stirred in Charlotte's lap, and she rose from her chair. "Ma, please."

Mother's chin dipped, her voice softening as Charlotte carted Rachel to bed. "If I thought for an instant you'd take up with some cow hand, I'd never have sent you."

Esther bristled, taking her time to answer and hoping Stew was out of earshot. "First of all, I've not taken up with anyone. Stew is a friend and much more of a man than you give him credit."

With a sideways jerk of her head, Mother "humphed". "And to think Lawrence has been fretting over you every second you've been away. Why, he's as much as said he wants to marry you. Or have you forgotten?"

A clatter on the porch step made Esther's blood run cold. By the time she found the courage to step to the window for a look, the wagon was pulling away. She leaned into the windowsill and rubbed a hand over her forehead, praying he hadn't overheard.

Oblivious to her distress, her mother snapped, "I'll wager you haven't whispered a peep about Lawrence to that young man."

Esther straightened. "There was no reason to."

"Of course not. Why, Mr. Brant is half the man Lawrence Del Ray is."

Esther clenched her jaw, turning to face her mother. Everything in her wanted to scream that Stew was ten times the man Lawrence was, but she held her tongue. Instead she replied, "You barely know Stew."

Mother drew in a decided breath. "Well, I can say one thing. This evening has convinced me it would be in your best interest to cut our stay here short. The sooner you're back in familiar surroundings, the sooner you'll forget all about this Mr. Brant."

Esther melted into a chair. Arguing would only further aggravate her mother and risk an even shorter stay.

If she did leave, would her fondness for Stew lessen? Would his for her?

Her time to decide was running short. There was but one person to turn to. Someone who understood what it meant to make a difficult choice, a sacrificial one. Tomorrow morning she would make good on her promise and pay a visit to her cousin Becky.

THE BUMPY MILE ride across the prairie did little to relieve the pain in Stew's foot.

Nor the one in his heart.

So, Esther *did* have a beau. A man who thought enough of her he wished to marry her. All this time, and she'd said nothing. The very thought seared his senses. Resigning caution, he'd opened his heart to her, even begun to believe she cared for him.

How wrong he'd been.

Thoughts of Delta churned inside him. Her betrayal. The hurt and emptiness that had followed. She'd promised to be his bride only to turn to the arms of another in his absence. The sting of it still burned in his chest.

Had he been duped yet again?

"What has you tied in knots?"

Chad's words jolted Stew back to reality. "What?"

"Something eatin' at you? You haven't said two words since we left."

Stew slipped back into silence then ran sweaty palms over his trouser legs. "You ever hear Esther mention a fella by the name of Lawrence Del Ray?"

Chad tapped the reins across the horses' rumps. "Not Esther, but Charlotte spoke of her knowing a gentleman by that name back east. Why?"

Stew blew out a breath. "I overheard something I wish I hadn't."

"Such as?"

"Such as this Lawrence feller is considering asking Esther to marry him."

Chad slipped Stew a sideways glance. "Is that a problem?"

"It might be." Try as he may, Stew couldn't rid the tension from his voice.

A crooked smile edged across Chad's lips in the moonlight. "So, you'll finally admit she means something to you."

There was no sense denying it. Chad had him pegged dead to rights. "Lot of good it's gonna do me. What chance does a broken-down cowboy stand against some dandy socialite?"

"Well now, I don't know. Esther seems mighty fond of you. Besides, if she was so smitten with this Lawrence fellow, she'd most likely have voiced it by now, don't you think?"

Stew stared out over the whiteness of the moonstruck prairie, his pulse quickening. "Unless she's been playin' me for a fool."

The humor fled from Chad's voice. "You and I both know Esther better than that. She's straight and honest as they come."

"Then you tell me why she's not been straight with me about this Lawrence character?"

"I don't know. Why don't you ask her?"

Stew pursed his lips against the rising tension. He'd do just that, but not until she'd made her decision to stay or go. Unless he missed his guess, she'd give some feeble excuse why she had to leave.

If so, he intended to have his say.

Chapter Sixteen

"I'm so glad you finally stopped by."

Becky's warm hug trickled through Esther like soothing balm for her troubled spirit. "I'm sorry it's taken me so long, but between helping Charlotte and Stew…Mr. Brant's injury, it's been difficult to find the time."

"Well, you're here now. That's what counts." Becky looped her arm through Esther's and ushered her deeper inside the cabin. "Pa's out back working at his lathe. He'll be so thrilled by your visit."

Esther balked. "Could we wait to disturb Uncle Joseph? I have something I'd like to discuss with you."

Becky's eyes searched hers as though sensing the delicacy of the matter. "Certainly. Have a seat. I'll heat water for tea."

Esther slid onto a chair, a wave of uncertainty washing through her. How could she seek Becky's advice without disclosing the full nature of her dilemma? Would she be able to find the right words, or make a fool of herself trying?

"Aunt Clara looks well." Becky called as she stooped to put a kettle of water over hot coals, the babe in her womb more evident each passing week. "I hardly recognized her when she walked into the church building Sunday."

Esther forced a smile. "Yes. She's changed considerably since you've seen her."

"When did she arrive?"

"Last Thursday." Esther wrung her hands in the moment of silence, a gesture she almost never resorted to. As unnerved as she was, how would she ever convey what was on her heart?

Becky took a seat across from her, the happy expression she'd worn moments ago dissolving. "By chance, does her coming have anything to do with your visit?"

The pointed question peeled back the layers of pretense, allowing Esther the freedom to find her voice. "Mother is of a mind to leave for Cincinnati sooner than I'd hoped. I'm not looking forward to returning."

Becky laid her hand atop Esther's. "I understand well how difficult it is to leave the prairie."

"That's why I've come." Esther leaned in closer, her words flowing easier. "When Mother chose to relocate to Cincinnati after Pa died, I was but a young girl and felt obligated to accompany her. But now, having been home, I find myself longing to stay."

Becky nodded. "Life in the city can be heart-wrenching when your heart is elsewhere."

"And yet, you seemed to have found yourself in St. Louis, were nearly content to stay."

With a shake of her head, Becky's expression softened. "No, Esther. I *lost* myself there. It was the Lord I found."

"What do you mean?"

Becky laced her fingers together on the table, a gentle smile touching her lips. "It was there I learned to fully entrust my life to Him, rather than hold onto my hurts and expectations. When Pa and I left here, I was so bitter at God. I thought He'd abandoned us. It wasn't until I let go of my hurt that I realized He had a plan for my life. The entire time I was away, I wanted nothing more than to return home to the prairie. But when the time came to choose whether to stay or go, I knew what truly mattered was being where the Lord wanted me. Not where I wanted to be."

Esther's mouth twisted. "And yet, you came back. What convinced you this was where God wanted you?"

"The Lord removed my need to stay and gave me every reason to return home."

"Would one of those reasons be a certain young pastor?"

A sly grin spread across Becky's face. "It might."

They shared a chuckle, vanquishing any remnants of unease. At last, Becky leaned back in her chair, arms cradling her rounded belly. "And then there was Pa. Though he left the decision to me, I knew the prairie was where he wished to be. I wanted to honor him as well."

Esther's smile faded as the gravity of her cousin's words seeped into her thoughts. The decision to stay or go involved more than just her. There was Stew to consider and her mother. And most importantly, the Lord. What did He wish for her?

Honor thy father and thy mother.

The familiar command flashed through her mind, drudging up unwanted feelings. It was out of respect for her mother's wishes she'd gone to Cincinnati the first time. Was she to return for the same reason?

She pushed the thought aside only to have it return. Louder. Stronger.

Honor thy father and thy mother.

The tension she'd grappled with earlier burrowed in deeper, wielding a crushing blow. Becky had had to sacrifice her own wants before the Lord gave her the desires of her heart.

Something told Esther, He was calling her to do the same.

STEW SAT ON THE HEARTH, sore leg outstretched and spatula in hand. Boredom and hunger had driven him to attempt a bit of cooking. Thankfully, Esther had supplied him with a few staples to manage with. The scent of hot lard drifted up as he scooped the half-cooked griddlecake out of the skillet and flipped it over. Its sizzling did little to ease the silence of the vacant cabin.

Esther's absence seemed to scream at him from all four walls. Why she hadn't come didn't matter. The morning alone had given him time to think.

Maybe too much time.

Her unwillingness to be honest with him about her beau left a bitter coil lodged in his gullet. If she'd only hinted her affections lay elsewhere, he'd have kept his distance. Not allowed himself to become so fond of her. But then, she'd seemed just as eager for his company. It pained him to think she'd taken advantage of his affections.

Sweet memories of their time together taunted him—their moonlit stroll, her infectious smile, and her attentiveness in caring for him these past couple of weeks. Had it all been an act? A cruel joke played on him for amusement?

Esther didn't seem the type to want to rip a man's heart out. And yet, that's what she'd done. Maybe overhearing her mother's words was God's way of bringing the truth to light. He'd known all along he wasn't good enough for her. Or was it the other way around that, like Delta, she was no good for him? After two misguided relationships, he was beginning to wonder if anyone was good for him, or he for them.

A burnt smell invaded his thoughts. With a quick thrust, he slid the spatula under the overcooked griddlecake and plopped it on an awaiting tin plate. Smoke billowed from remnants of batter left in the skillet. With a disgusted groan, he set the hot skillet on the hearth and tossed the rag he'd held it with on the floor. It was no use. Since last night, his mind had been in a tizzy. Yesterday, he'd had hope. Now his hopes were as singed as his griddlecake.

A familiar tap drew his attention to the door. His traitorous heart reacted with a quickened beat. Before he could gather his senses, the door pushed open, and Esther peered in at him through the smoke-laced cabin air. Her nose crinkled as she set down her bundle and stepped to open the window. Turning toward him, she waved a hand in front of her face, a hint of a smile touching her lips. "I'm glad to see you're making use of your supplies."

Stew coughed, rubbing his hands over his pant legs. He opened his mouth and then snapped it shut, dropping his gaze to the charred bits of batter in the skillet.

Esther joined him on the far side of the hearth. "I'm sorry for not stopping by earlier. I…uh…had some business in town to tend to."

With a shrug, he picked up the fallen rag. "I managed."

"I can see that."

The humor in her voice made him all the more determined. He reached for the half-filled pitcher of batter only to have her slide her hands around it first. "Here. Let me."

"I can do it." He took it from her, sloshing some of the contents on his shirt.

He wiped it with the rag, doing his best to ignore her steady gaze. Pouring some batter into the skillet, he placed it over the fire.

"Are you angry with me?" Her softened tone held an element of hurt.

He slid a glance in her direction. "Do I have reason to be?"

Her brows pinched as if she was doing her best to decipher his thoughts and coming up short. In answer, she stood and gazed out the open window. Her lack of response only confirmed his suspicions. She'd not only made up her mind, but refused to tarnish herself by conveying the whole truth of the matter.

When Esther did voice her decision to leave—which seemed inevitable—he'd seek no explanation. Whatever excuse she gave, she'd get no argument from him.

He'd not give her the satisfaction.

ESTHER PAUSED inside the cabin door, the telling look on her mother's face and the telegram in her hand reminiscent of when they'd received news of Pa's death. She eased closer. "What is it?"

Mother sniffled and handed her the telegram. "William has had a spell with his heart. The doctor says he's recovering, but suggests we return at our earliest convenience."

Esther read over the telegram, the unwelcome news expelling any hope she had left of staying.

Moisture pooled in her mother's eyes. "I've lost one husband. I couldn't bear to lose another."

Esther placed a comforting hand on her mother's arm. Since Pa's passing, Mother's emotions had been fragile, if not unstable. To let her return home unattended now was unthinkable. "I'm certain he'll be fine."

Mother clung to her, dabbing her eyes with her handkerchief. "I've decided we shall leave first thing tomorrow morning."

Like a gavel pronouncing judgment, Mother's declaration sealed Esther's fate. Since her visit with Becky, an ominous cloud had settled over her. Stew had sensed it too. Without so much as a word, he seemed to have guessed the conviction in her heart to abide by her mother's wishes. His agitation had surprised her. She'd expected disappointment, sadness, even genuine regret. But anger?

Heaviness weighted Esther's chest. How would he respond when she actually voiced that she'd be leaving as soon as tomorrow?

There was so little time to set things right. It tore her up inside to think of leaving a man she'd come to care for so deeply. In time, would he forgive her? Would the scars of her leaving heal?

Would her own?

A nervous knot balled in her stomach. She had but one final call on Stew to make, one she dreaded almost as much as leaving.

THE LOOK on Esther's face as she approached said more than words ever could.

She was going.

Whether by her own will or forfeiting to her mother's, she was as good as gone.

Turning, he set another chunk of wood on the stump and heaved the ax over his head. With a quick downward chop, the block of wood splintered in half and flung onto either side of the stump.

Esther's gentle boot steps stopped beside him as he leaned to pick up the hewn logs. "It's good to see you out and about."

Her tender voice washed through him like summer rain. He had to be strong, convince her she was free to go. Straightening, he tossed the firewood into his growing pile. "Beats sitting around feeling sorry for myself."

For a long moment, her hazel eyes remained locked on his, their moistness sparkling in the morning sunlight. With a gentle nod, she wet her lips. "I've come to tell you Mother and I are leaving for Cincinnati tomorrow morning."

Stew tensed, forcing himself to stand firm in his conviction not to show his disappointment. "You don't say?"

She lowered her head, and her face disappeared beneath the rim of her bonnet. "We've received news my stepfather is ill. My mother needs me just now. I'm sorry."

If it weren't for the knowledge of her beau back in Cincinnati, Stew might have been convinced. Instead, he choked down the ache in his heart and mustered a weak grin. "No need to be sorry. I think that's just what you should do."

Esther lifted her face from its hiding place, the shock of his words evident in her eyes. "You mean, you want me to go?"

He jutted his lower lip and nodded. "Probably for the best. The more I consider it, the more I see you're better suited for city life."

He gritted his teeth against the outright lie, hopeful she wouldn't see through his hypocrisy.

Moisture pooled in her eyes, bringing out the hint of green at their center. It was all he could do not to drop his pretense and pull her into his embrace. He stared down at his boots, shifting the ax head back and forth in the dirt. "I'm appreciative of all you've done to help me out. You've been a good...friend to me."

She stepped closer, testing the very core of his being. "I thought you...wanted me to stay."

The tremor in her voice drew his eyes back to hers. His breaths grew shallow as he took in the delicate features of her oval face and golden hair. Any longer and his resistance would be spent. There was no denying it. He loved her.

But she wasn't his to love.

He eased back in attempt to ward off the urge to take her in his arms. Her mother's words scrolled through his thoughts, giving him courage to forge ahead. "I did. But it seems you've more reason to go."

Her chin quivered, and she wiped a tear from her cheek, seeming to sort through his response. At last, she stretched out her arm, a Bible clutched in her hand. "I want you to have this."

He shook his head, knowing she'd make better use of it than he would. "I'm not much of a reader. Keep it."

She pushed it toward him. "Please. Take it."

Reluctantly, he reached for it, his heart pounding in his ears as his fingers brushed hers.

Her eyes crimped, and she threaded her fingers together at her front. "If nothing more, I hope it will remind you of our time together."

"Much obliged." With a nod, he clutched the leather Bible tighter in his palm, the triteness in his tone belying the boulder-sized ache in his heart. Since last night, he'd tried to convince himself her leaving didn't matter.

But it did. Everything about her mattered.

Her moist eyes fastened on his, her voice as unstable as the wind. "Goodbye, Stewart Brant. The Lord keep you." With that, she whirled around and returned the way she'd come. For a long while, he watched her, hoping against hope she'd turn and give him one last glimpse.

But like their love, it wasn't to be.

PART II
MISGIVINGS

Chapter Seventeen

Friday, June 3, 1859

ESTHER CLOSED HER EYES, drinking in her sister's one-armed embrace. Every moment they'd spent together had been pure joy. Now their season of reunion had come to an abrupt end.

As had her friendship with Stew.

The sting of his less-than-sorrowful attitude at her leaving lingered inside her like rancid meat. His sudden change of heart struck her as odd. The evening of their moonlit stroll, he'd seemed so intent on her staying. And yet, yesterday, he'd shown no remorse at her decision, hadn't even seemed to care.

Stepping back from Charlotte's embrace, Esther forced a smile. "I've so enjoyed this time with you and getting to know your family."

Charlotte gave her hand a gentle squeeze, holding Michael in her other arm. "Don't wait for another baby to come. We'd love to have you anytime."

"Thank you."

Michael's clear blue eyes stared up at Esther, his thin, sandy hair and boyish features favoring his father. A bright toothless smile erupted onto his face as Esther bent to kiss his forehead. He gave a soft squeal and joggled in Charlotte's arm, forcing her to secure him with both hands. He'd grown so much over the month Esther had been here. She hated to think how much he would grow before her next visit.

A wave of regret swept through her at the thought of not having the opportunity to really get to know her niece and nephews. In a few months, she'd be all but forgotten. Tears welled in her eyes as she stooped to give Rachel a hug. "Goodbye, sweetie."

The youngster stuck out a pouty lip then slid her arms around Esther's neck. "Don't go."

Esther's throat thickened, threatening to choke off her voice. She turned her head to kiss Rachel's cheek. "I'll come again. Promise."

The youngster clung to her until Charlotte tapped her on the shoulder. "Time to let them go."

Loosening her hold, Rachel stepped back and leaned her head against her mother.

"Come, Esther."

Mother's plea from atop the wagon prodded Esther to stand and retrieve her satchel. Johnny stood at a distance, kicking the toe of his boot against the ground. She'd not had a great deal of time to spend with him, but the one feature she had noticed was how much he idolized Stew. Many an evening Johnny had practiced his rope skills in hopes of impressing him. Perhaps the boy could prove a bright spot in her friend's otherwise solitude life.

Stepping over to him, she reached out her hand. "Goodbye, Johnny."

He clasped her outstretched palm. "Bye, Aunt Esther."

Softening her voice, she leaned closer. "Take care of Stew for me, will you?"

He gave a nod, his face brightening. "Sure thing."

Straightening, Esther panned the prairie to the west in hopes that somehow Stew would be there, riding out to voice his regrets or at least say goodbye. But she knew it was for naught. He'd never be able to mount and ride so far himself.

And even if he were able to, would he have come?

Chin quivering, she turned toward the wagon. Chad kissed Charlotte and the children goodbye and then moved to help Esther into the straw-covered bed, her mother's ample frame not allowing room for the three of them on the bench. Climbing into the driver's seat, he released the brake and peered down at his family. "Be back as soon as I can."

With an understanding nod, Charlotte returned a gentle smile.

He turned his gaze to Johnny. "You look after things and check in on Stew now and then."

The boy gave a brisk nod. "Yes'r."

Tapping the reins across the horses' backs, Chad gave a shrill whistle. As the wagon jerked forward, Esther gripped the sideboard, drinking in the small homestead and her loved ones huddled together. Soon this would all seem like a pleasant dream.

One that had ended all too soon.

EVERY HINT of a sound outside the window pulled Stew's attention to the closed cabin door. Time seemed to crawl as he listened for Esther's gentle rap.

But none came.

He stood and swiped a hand over his face. By now, she'd be well on her way to Cincinnati. Did he really expect her to stop by after the aloof send-off he'd given her yesterday?

His chest clenched. Chances were he'd never see her again. And if he did, more than likely, she'd be married to that high-falutin' city fella. Given time, she'd be as uppity as her mother. The thought turned his stomach. He'd do well to forget he'd ever laid eyes on her.

Limping over to the fireplace, his gaze drifted to the Bible resting on the mantel. Why had he even accepted it? Sight of it would only keep the wounds inside him festering. He picked it up and flipped through its worn pages. A sweet scent wafted up at him. Lavender or roses. He held the Bible close to his face and drew in a breath. The scent returned him to his waking moments after the snake bite and to a dozen other times when he'd been in close proximity to Esther. She'd no doubt spent many hours absorbed in its pages.

He ran his fingertip over the frayed edges of the leather binding then placed it back on the mantel. Praying had done him no good. More than likely, reading the Good Book wouldn't either. Even if he could decipher what it said.

Propping his lame foot on the hearth, Stew scratched at his chin. Could be God hadn't answered his prayers because he'd not made much of an effort to get to know Him. Then again, maybe the Lord had His favorites, those who always said and did the right thing. The privileged and well-to-do sort.

If that were the case, he'd never measure up.

A knock at the door set Stew's heart racing. Before he could answer, a voice called. "Mr. Brant? It's me. Johnny."

Stew's shoulders sagged as he released the breath he'd been holding. "Come on in."

Johnny pulled on the latch-string and pushed the door open.

Still in the routine of leaving the latch-string out for easy access into the cabin, now that Stew was back on his feet and Esther wouldn't be stopping by, he'd need to curb that habit. But then, what did it matter? There was nothing of value to be had anyway.

Johnny sauntered inside, head held high. "Mornin', Mr. Brant."

"How are you, Johnny?"

"Fine." The eleven-year-old puffed out his chest. "I've come to check in on ya."

A humored grin tugged at Stew's lips. "Is that so?"

"Yes'r. If'n there's anything you need, I'd be pleasured to help with it."

"Well now, there's a fine offer." Stew crossed his arms over his chest, glancing over the meager contents of the cabin. He'd had little time or notion to fix up the place, let alone fill it with furnishings. Maybe it was time he put some effort into making this rundown shack a home. "Have you any experience at making furniture?"

The boy's mouth twisted. "Cain't say I have, but I'm willing to learn."

"All right then. Hows about you helping me make a bedframe? It gets a mite monotonous picking myself off the floor every morning."

An eager grin lit Johnny's face, and he stood taller, wiping the smile from his lips. "Yes'r. Just so as I'm home in time to check on the cattle. Chad left me in charge while he's away."

Stew mustered a grin, pressing down the ache of knowing where Chad was headed. "Well now, with such important responsibilities, I'm obliged at you taking time to stop by."

"Oh, I promised Chad and Miss Esther I'd look in on you."

Stew stilled, his grin fading. "Miss Esther asked you to look in on me?"

The boy nodded. "Sure did. She wasn't too keen on leavin', I could tell."

Turning his back to Johnny, Stew fidgeted with the ladle hanging from a peg over the fireplace. No doubt Esther looked upon him like an injured pup, a poor soul in need of benevolence. Had he mistaken her sympathies for affection? If she had any regrets about leaving, it had more to do with her attachment to her family than him.

Ignoring the sudden burning in his chest, he straightened. He didn't need anyone's pity. What he needed was a fresh start.

One that didn't include a person of the feminine persuasion.

Chapter Eighteen

ESTHER HELPED her mother into the Concord stagecoach, then turned and extended a hand to Chad. "Thanks for everything. You've been more than kind to bring us all this way."

"My pleasure. We're grateful for your help with the young'uns."

A heartfelt smile crept onto Esther's face. "That was truly *my* pleasure."

With a tip of his hat, Chad clasped her arm and helped her into the coach.

The stagecoach door clicked shut behind her, rendering a sense of finality to her visit. It seemed only yesterday she'd made the journey here. Now, too soon, it was over.

An unsettled feeling churned inside her at the thought of her final conversation with Stew. Something didn't set right. Stew hadn't been himself. Had he hidden his true feelings, hoping to make her departure easier? Or had he simply been put-out at her for going? The uncertainty of it hounded her relentlessly. More than likely, she'd never learn the truth.

"Don't make yourself a stranger," Chad called to Esther as he handed the Whip their baggage.

She forced an uncertain grin. "I won't."

An air of foreboding seemed to shroud the cramped compartment as the stagecoach lurched forward. Esther waved to Chad, then settled back in her seat, her gaze drifting to the young mother and child seated across from her. Sorrowful frowns lined both of their faces, their black garb suggesting they'd recently lost a close loved one. A husband and father perhaps? Esther's heart grieved the thought.

As the coach picked up speed, dust filtered through the openings in the doors and windows. Mother coughed and fanned a handkerchief in front of her face. "Oh, this dreadful business of traveling. You'll not find me making this journey again any time soon. If Chad and Charlotte wish a visit, next time let them come to us."

Esther wrapped her arms around her waist, realizing how difficult and costly such a trip would be for her sister's family. Traveling such a distance by stagecoach wasn't cheap. With their growing family and meager income, it would be near impossible for them to make the trip.

Glancing out the open window, Esther caught a glimpse of the sturdy, white columns of the Old Vandalia State House, its pristine white walls bright against the morning light. "It's a grand building, don't you think?"

"Not compared to those of Cincinnati. I'll be relieved when we get home." With that, Mother turned and pulled down her shade, as if to shut out any semblance of what her life had once been. Was she really so desperate to escape the past that she had no tolerance for anything not tied to Cincinnati?

The cluster of buildings began to fade away as the stagecoach meandered out of town into the countryside and further along the Cumberland Road. The only true passage connecting east and west, many a wagon and stagecoach daily traveled its wide, worn trail. Esther dreaded the long trip home much more than when she had come. How her heart ached to speak again with Stew, to ensure there were no hard feelings between them.

Not one to let situations go unresolved, this time, it seemed, she had no choice. She could only hope one day she and Stew would cross paths again. Until then, it would be her constant prayer that he would seek the Lord and render a heart of forgiveness toward her.

"You're certain you won't go with us?"

With a decisive nod, Stew leaned against the porch rail and tapped at his knee. Though he appreciated the Averys' invitation to ride into church service, he just wasn't in the frame of mind to go. His external wounds might be healing, but the wound in his heart was still raw and tender.

"Not sure my leg's up to it just yet. Thanks anyway."

Charlotte's gaze seemed to bore right through him. He was making excuses, and she knew it.

Chad thumbed his hat higher on his forehead and took up the reins. "Maybe next time."

"Maybe so." Stew managed a slight grin, holding in the questions burning his tongue. Now that Chad was back, the smidgen of hope Stew had held onto that Esther might change her mind had vanished. Had she voiced any regrets or given any indication she cared for him? With the family present, now wasn't the time or the place to ask. Instead, he waved them on their way.

As the wagon rambled out of view, Stew rubbed a hand over his stubbled jaw. He could use a shave. Between his injury and Esther's leaving, somehow he'd lost all sense of motivation.

Making his way inside the cabin, his gaze again drifted to the Bible atop the mantel. Irritated that it seemed impossible to enter the room without glancing its way, he pulled it from the shelf intent on laying it aside. Instead, he crumpled onto the fireplace hearth, holding the Bible in both hands. Was it the connection to Esther that drew him to it or something more powerful?

His throat thickened as he flipped it open and thumbed through the pages of the Old Testament. When he was a boy, his ma had often shared stories of the shepherd boy, David, who bested the giant, powerful prophets who called down fire from heaven, and Moses and the plagues on Egypt. But now, as he leafed through its pages, the difficult words and funny-sounding names seemed foreign to him. It would take hours to decipher a single paragraph, and still he would gain little from it.

With a defeated sigh, Stew snapped the Bible shut. It wasn't worth the effort. Lacking any better place to put it, he slid the Bible back on the mantel and reached for his blade. Shaving seemed a better use of his energies. Despite his prayers, the Lord had let the one meaningful part of his life slip away. The best thing to do was to keep busy and resign himself to the fact he was destined to live out the rest of his days alone.

THE CHURCH BELL beckoned the people on the street into the framed church building. It seemed the entire town was turning out for services. Esther strolled alongside her mother, feeling out of place amid the unfamiliar setting and faces. The stagecoach town of Casey boasted many a traveler en route along the Cumberland Road. With only one leg of their journey complete, it would be several days before they would reach their destination. Given the delay to attend church service, they'd likely gain only a few miles by nightfall on the afternoon stage.

Esther hiked her skirt as she climbed the church steps. It was difficult to decipher the locals from the travelers. Other than an occasional nod or smile, everyone seemed intent on making their way inside the mid-sized church building to secure a seat. Stepping inside, Esther spotted an empty bench to the far right and pointed it out to her mother. "Over there."

They skirted their way toward it and slid onto the bench just as the song leader made his way to the front. Esther smiled at the woman next to her, garnering only a faint acknowledgment in return. How her heart ached to be back at Miller Creek seated alongside Stew, Chad, Charlotte, and dozens of other friendly faces. Or even in Cincinnati where she'd grown accustomed to regular attenders. Loneliness nipped at her like a chilling breeze. How was it possible to be in the midst of a crowd and yet so alone?

"Have you forgotten your Bible?"

Her mother's hushed question startled Esther from her thoughts. Glancing down, she laced her fingers together in her lap in attempt to ward off the heightened sense of emptiness plaguing them. Mother would never approve of her having left the Bible with Stew. She leaned close to her mother's ear, determined not to divulge the entire truth. "I believe I left it behind."

Mother's scowl came just as the song leader roused them to their feet for the opening hymn. As the congregation broke into singing "Rock of Ages", Esther couldn't help but wonder if Stew had made it into service. Was he, at this very moment, clutching the Bible her own hands were missing? Was she wrong in hoping he would think of her each time he took it in hand?

She smothered a yawn, having gotten little sleep amid her mother's snores and the uncomfortable inn bed. Mother's less than subtle nudge set Esther to singing with renewed vigor. Yet inwardly, weightiness filled her chest. Despite her sense of obligation to her mother and stepfather, everything in Esther wished to undo her decision to leave. The short stay had revitalized what four years in the city had stolen away. Her heart belonged to the prairie, to her father's memory, and to the people she knew and loved.

Her voice hitched. And—if the longing inside her were any indication—to Stew.

As the song ended, Esther blinked back tears. She would return to Cincinnati out of obedience to the Lord, praying He would one day see fit to grant her the desires of her heart.

Chapter Nineteen

S<small>TEW</small> <small>TAPPED</small> the final canvas strap into place and pulled at the corner of the bed frame to test its strength. "That oughta do it. Now, let's get that straw mattress in here."

With a nod, Johnny started after him.

A stiff breeze caught the door as Stew pulled it open. He squinted into the afternoon sky, the gathering clouds hinting of rain. He clapped Johnny on the back. "We'd best get at it so you can be on your way."

Lifting the lumpy mattress from the porch, they tipped it upright to fit through the doorway. Stew lowered his end to match Johnny's as they carried it to the far corner of the cabin. Together they plopped it down on the wooden bed frame. Stew pushed at it to ensure the canvas straps beneath would hold, then eased down onto it.

Johnny slipped his hands in his pockets. "How is it?"

"Beats a blanket on the floor. You be sure to thank Chad and Charlotte for the mattress and supplies for me."

"Yes'r. Anything else I can help you with?"

The boy's eagerness brought a faint smile to Stew's less-than-cheerful demeanor. "Well now, I don't want to be accused of keeping you from your duties. How's the well coming along?"

The boy bowed his head, scuffing the toe of his boot against the floorboards. "It ain't. We need someone to draw the buckets of dirt up, and I haven't the strength."

Stew sat up and swung his legs over the side of the bed. How selfish he'd been to take time off to lick his wounds while Chad and the boy struggled to keep up. Surely his leg was well enough to manage hauling off buckets of dirt. If he could mount Scout, there'd be no reason why he couldn't do his part.

Keeping busy might help mend his wounded heart as well.

Stew placed a hand on the boy's shoulder. "You tell Chad to expect me first thing tomorrow morning."

A bright smile spread over Johnny's face. "Yes'r."

"Now, scoot on out of here before you get yourself drenched."

With a wave, the boy trekked toward the door. "See you, Mr. Brant."

Stew returned his wave, his grin fading the moment Johnny stepped outside. He'd pitied himself long enough. Chad and Charlotte had been more than patient. Whether he felt like it or not, it was time to start pulling his weight.

And, as much as he hated to, make a fresh start.

THE SUN'S warmth soaked through Stew's shirt as he reined Scout closer to the Circle J. He breathed in the fresh morning air, grateful to have taken the initiative to venture out. Despite his troubles, it was good to be back in the saddle. The mile ride was what he'd needed to clear his head and rejuvenate his unsettled spirit.

A twinge of pain shot through his ankle, and he slid his injured foot from the stirrup, letting it dangle. Holding it in the same position so long was taking its toll. Would he ever regain his agility, or had his freedom to ride and walk unhindered been lost to him?

Up ahead, Chad's Hereford cattle stood grazing, their red and white coats dotting the prairie landscape. At his approach, several cows lifted their heads then resumed eating, paying him little mind. A quick count tallied three additional calves since he'd last counted. The sign of a vibrant, growing herd.

Chad's border collie let out a high-pitched bark as Stew neared. Chad paused and stared in his direction, a wide grin spilling onto his face. "Well now, you're a welcome sight."

Stew pulled Scout to a stop, nodding at his lame foot. "Not sure how much help I'll be."

Tipping his hat higher on his forehead, Chad propped his foot on the yard fence. "More than if you hadn't shown up, I reckon."

Unable to argue the point, Stew leaned on his saddle horn. "Tell me what needs done, and I'll get at it."

Chad sank his hands in his pockets, squinting up at him. "Charlotte's getting awful eager for her well water."

Stew stuck out a palm. "Say no more. If you'll tackle the digging, Johnny and I'll do our best to haul away the dirt."

"Fair enough. I'll let Charlotte know there'll be an extra mouth for dinner." With a grin, Chad pivoted toward the cabin.

"Tell her not to go to any bother!" Stew called after him. Since he'd been laid up, he'd had little appetite. Esther's leaving had only made matters worse. His lean physique had deteriorated to the point his suspenders were all that kept his pants from slipping to his ankles.

Dismounting, he eased down onto his bad foot then quickly shifted his weight to his other leg. By the time he'd limped his way to the windlass, Chad had returned. "Charlotte's happier than a robin in spring. I've sent Johnny to gather more rocks to line the well. Let's get started."

Stew nodded, wishing he shared his friend's enthusiasm. He had to admit, it felt good to do something other than stare at his cabin walls.

Or so he thought.

Hours later, his energy was spent. His lame foot throbbed from the unaccustomed use, and his arm muscles ached from the constant strain of turning the windlass handle and heaving buckets. Being laid up so long had sapped his youthful vigor.

Not to mention his adventuresome spirit.

He shouldn't complain. At least he had a roof over his head and a steady position. Still, somehow he felt half a man with his maimed foot and injured pride. He'd not minded the well digging at first. But now, the monotonous task of drawing and lowering the buckets left him wishing he was back on a cattle drive.

Or was it his outlook that had changed?

Esther's leaving had affected him more than he cared to admit. Being jilted twice did something to a man. Delta Fanning had merely robbed him of his pride.

Esther had stolen his heart.

The turn of a wheelbarrow over the grass alerted him to Johnny's approach, and he turned. The boy struggled to maneuver the heavy load of rocks, and Stew moved to help him wheel it into the yard and over to the well hole. Each bucket of dirt Stew carted away was replaced by a load of flat rocks and sent down for Chad to use to line the walls. It was grueling work for all of them, the end of which couldn't come too soon.

The cresting sun, along with his rumbling belly, gave Stew hope of a reprieve. He needed a break, though he would never admit it. He'd hold out until Chad gave the word to stop. Surely his friend would be due for a break soon as well.

A tug on the rope told him Chad had filled yet another bucket. Again, Stew twisted the handle on the windlass and drew up the heavy bucket. The rich, dark topsoil had gradually changed to heavy, damp clay and then loose, dull, yellowish well soil, the color of prairie grass in the fall. This load had a darker cast to it and a hint of moisture. He could only hope the change meant they'd soon tap into a stream.

Stew locked the rope in place and swapped the full bucket for an empty one. Leaving Johnny to fill it with rocks, Stew strode over to the growing pile of dirt and dumped the contents of his bucket. A creaking sound from behind drew his attention to the windlass. His heart leapt to his throat when he saw Johnny struggling to still the churning windlass handle. Somehow the rope had slipped, sending the bucket of rocks plummeting downward, Chad trapped beneath.

Johnny peered over at Stew, his eyes round as saucers. "I can't hold it!"

Stew lunged toward him, ignoring the pain that shot through his ankle with each grueling step. Reaching over Johnny, Stew clasped hold of the handle and gradually brought it to a stop.

Johnny peered down the hole, his face ashen. "You all right?"

Stew tensed, unwilling to relinquish his hold on the handle. Had he stopped it in time? His pulse raced as he cocked his ear to listen. Long seconds ticked by in silence. *Please, Lord, spare him.*

A faint sputtering sounded from deep within the hole, followed by Chad's muffled voice.

Stew released the breath he'd been holding, his shoulders sagging in relief.

Johnny straightened. "He says to pull him up."

With a nod, Stew strained to press the handle forward, the load easing slightly with Johnny's help. The muscles in Stew's arms shook mercilessly, not only from the added weight, but also the realization that his friend and his family had almost suffered a terrible tragedy. One Stew wouldn't have been able to forgive himself for. Whether the fault was his or not he'd have carried the guilt the rest of his days.

The windlass rope grew taut. Moments later, Chad emerged, legs wrapped around the oversized bucket. He squinted against the brightness of the sun, his expression marred by confusion. Smudges lined his shirt and brow, and his chestnut hair was powdered white with dirt. Unwilling to trust the rope to stay in place, Stew kept a tight hold on the handle while Johnny helped Chad to his feet.

Stew cast a weary glance toward the cabin, thankful Charlotte hadn't witnessed the incident. He and the Lord might not be on the best of terms, but He'd been gracious in sparing them all needless heartache, and for that Stew was grateful. He scratched at his chin, looking Chad up and down. "You sure you're all right?"

"I reckon. What happened?"

"The rope gave."

Chad brushed off his soiled clothes. "A couple feet more, and I'd have had one powerful headache."

"It was my fault." Johnny stared at his feet, a tear streaming down his cheek.

Stew shook his head, refusing to let the boy take the blame for what likely was his own doing. "If it was anyone's fault, it was mine. Must not've had it locked in place well enough."

Chad raised a hand to stop them. "It happened. No one's to blame. Thank the good Lord it didn't come to any harm." Slipping off his work gloves, he placed a finger under Johnny's downcast chin. "Now, what say we break for dinner?"

The boy's eyes lifted. "Yes'r."

Lowering his voice, Chad leaned over and gripped the boy's shoulder. "We'd best keep the incident under our hats though. No need to worry Charlotte, right?"

Johnny hesitated then nodded, his expression brightening.

Chad peered at Stew as though waiting for him to comply.

Stew's lips twisted in a grin. "Right, but if you expect to keep it a secret, you'd best not go in like that."

Chad glanced down at his soiled clothing. With a chuckle, he rubbed at a stain on his shirt. "You two go on. I'll stop off at the water trough and be right in."

The aroma of beef stew and fresh-baked bread wafted out at Stew as he and Johnny entered the cabin. Warmth and vitality flowed freely from within, so unlike his own abode. Charlotte greeted them with a welcoming smile, juggling her attention between stirring the steamy kettle and young Rachel tugging at her skirt. "Have a seat. Dinner's about ready."

Stew nodded and limped his way to the table, tired in mind and body. More than nourishment, he needed revival. When he'd come here, he'd been full of zest for life. Now, a mere few weeks later, he was a shell of the man he'd once been.

Charlotte divvied out bowls, glancing expectantly at the door. "Where's Chad?"

"Cleaning up. He'll, uh, be along directly." Stew avoided looking her or Johnny in the eyes, fearful his telling expression would relay too much.

Johnny pulled a chair up beside him. "How'd the new bed sleep, Mr. Brant?"

"Real good. Thanks for your help."

At Stew's wink, Johnny's grin widened. "I've gotten real good at lassoing."

"I bet you have." Though Stew did his best to sound enthused, he couldn't quite wipe the downcast tone from his voice. Nothing held his interest anymore.

And he knew why.

"Would you have time to watch me later?" Big blue eyes stared up at him expectantly.

Stew scrubbed a hand over his face. Normally the request would have pleased him, but, truth be told, he was in no mood for socializing. Esther's absence seemed to taunt him from every corner of the room, from the empty rocker where he'd stolen his first glimpses of her to the missing place-setting at the table. The four days she'd been gone seemed like weeks. He cleared his throat. "Well, uh, maybe another time."

Stew caught Charlotte's scrutinizing gaze. The woman had the intuition of a fox scouting prey. Nothing got past her. She gave Johnny's shoulder a gentle squeeze. "Why don't we give Mr. Brant a few days to gain his strength back before we put too many demands on him?"

The boy's shoulders sagged, his expression sobering. "Yes'm."

The door creaked open, and in walked Chad, his shirt blotched with water-stains. Stew cringed when his friend removed his hat and a cloud of dirt settled to the floor. He'd neglected to brush off the part of him he couldn't see.

Charlotte's hands flew to her hips. "What on earth happened to you?"

He peered down at the powdery residue at his feet then scooted back onto the porch, reappearing a moment later hat and hair a bit less dusty. An apologetic grin crossed his face as he tossed his hat on the bench. "Being at the bottom of a well's dirty work, right fellas?"

Stew gave a slight cough. "Sure is."

Charlotte knit her brows, keeping her gaze fixed on her husband. "You look as though half the dirt fell in on you."

Chad's face flushed as he loosened the buttons on his shirt and reached for a clean one on a peg. For a brief moment, Stew feared Charlotte would learn the truth, but an infant's cry from the cradle in the corner, diverted her attention. Her shoulders drooped, and Stew wondered if she was missing Esther as much as he was.

Chad finished buttoning his shirt then rubbed a hand along Charlotte's upper arm. "I'll get him."

"Thank you." She gave a soft grin, her gratitude genuine.

Chad strode over and picked up baby Michael, cradling him in the nook of his arm. Pride radiated from his face as he took a seat at the table. With practiced ease, Charlotte scooped Rachel up into her chair then set a large bowl of beef stew at the center of the table. Sitting opposite Chad, she flashed a contented grin.

As Stew bowed his head for Chad to say grace, he warred within. He should be the one down the hole taking risks. If something happened to Chad, Charlotte would be devastated, cheated out of years of happiness, his young family robbed of the father they needed and adored.

Stew had no one.

It was hard not to be envious while in the midst of such a loving home. But life hadn't always been so pleasant for Chad. For whatever reason, when Stew had first met him he'd been down and out.

Now, those days seemed a lifetime ago.

As the prayer ended, Stew lifted his head, casting a glance around the contented family. Was there hope for him as well? Not likely. His hopes for a loving wife and family had vanished right along with Esther.

Chapter Twenty

THE STAGECOACH JOGGLED UNMERCIFULLY as the driver urged the team of horses faster along the route from Richmond, Indiana to Cincinnati, Ohio.

Mother groaned, wiping her sweat-dampened forehead with a handkerchief. "After this, I never wish to ride in one of these dreadful stagecoaches again."

Half in agreement, Esther clung to the coach seat, each jolt threatening to bounce her onto the floorboards. Having switched to a smaller stagecoach for the final leg of the journey, they'd veered away from the Cumberland Road and onto a less travelled route. They'd parted ways with the gentle, grieving woman and child, along with a handful of other riders who'd made it to their destination or continued eastward. In their stead sat a young couple so intent on each other they seemed not to mind the jostles.

Stealing a glance in their direction, Esther squirmed under their starry-eyed gaze and clasped hands. Would she ever be so enamored with someone? Given time, could she and Stew have grown so fond of each other?

She shifted her attention outside, to the distant foliage and the hilly landscape, her thoughts turning to Lawrence. The man was certainly fine looking, bright, successful. But could she love him? It seemed she had little choice in the matter. Mother had come to expect it of her. In returning to Cincinnati, she had more or less sealed her fate.

Esther settled back on her seat, trying to ignore her mother's continual groans and outbursts of complaints. Why was she plagued with being the dutiful daughter, born with a keen sense of conformity? Why couldn't she be more like Charlotte? Confident. Headstrong. Unafraid of challenge. Esther stifled a grin at the memory of her sister shouting "Goodbye, Ma!" to her mother's chagrin.

With each turn of the wheels, the joy she'd embraced with Stew and Charlotte's family seemed to fade into nothingness. Soon it would seem as if she'd never left the crowded city or the routine that had all but squeezed every ounce of adventure from her soul.

Until she succumbed to Lawrence's persistent attempts to woo her, she would cling to the hope that the Lord would allow her to marry for love. Even Mother had known that blessing with Pa. Her grief at his passing had born witness to her deep affection for him. Though obviously, she'd grown quite fond of William Leifer, her marriage to him was more one of necessity and convenience than love.

When they'd first arrived in Cincinnati, they'd been forced to rely on the kindness of relatives until they could secure an apartment of their own. At fifteen, Esther had taken a job tutoring fellow students to help meet expenses.

Then came William, with his affluent shipping operation and his ultimate proposal of marriage to her mother. Without a moment's hesitation, Mother had agreed, ensuring they would never want for anything.

Nor had they.

Though William had been kind to Esther, he was certainly no

father to her. Mother had fit the shoes of a wealthy socialite's wife instantly. Esther, on the other hand, had longed for the life she'd once had—a life filled with love, family, and community. All the wealth in Ohio couldn't replace the simple pleasures she'd known in her youth on the prairie.

Heaviness pulled at her chest. Unless she missed her guess, upon their return, Lawrence would take up right where he'd left off, seeking to impress her with his many self-proclaimed attributes. Why he'd chosen her to pursue, she couldn't say. Nearly ten years her senior, he'd had ample time to secure a marriage. And yet, he seemed intent on making her his bride.

As the wife of Lawrence Del Ray, her every need would be met. She'd rub elbows with the cultural elite and be expected to entertain his business associates and their wives. Could she embrace such an affluent lifestyle if and when it was offered? Already she sensed the flame of hope of marrying for love extinguishing within her.

Life with Stew would have been much less refined and grand. And yet, she couldn't help but think it might have been much more genuine, more suited for her true nature. But in the end, he'd more or less encouraged her to leave, as if she'd been a pesky relative he was eager to be done with. The change had taken her off guard. She'd never known him to be moody or irritable. What had evoked such an alteration?

Perhaps she should write and ask him to explain.

No. What would it accomplish? They'd parted ways. She'd best leave it at that.

A bend in the road allowed Esther a view of the hills nestled around Cincinnati. As the coach crested an incline, she caught a glimpse of the winding Ohio River to its south.

Mother patted her arm, a smile replacing her recent frown. "We're home."

Esther drew in a breath, not sharing her elation. With a population of over one hundred fifty thousand, the grand city boasted every advantage imaginable—colleges, medical facilities, a vast array of stores and businesses, opera houses and theatres. And yet, it lacked the one thing she longed for most.

A sense of belonging.

Chapter Twenty-One

One Week Later

THE AFTERNOON SUN beat down on Stew, soaking into his shirt. He leaned over the well hole, coolness wafting up at him. The scrape of the shovel assured him Chad was still hard at work. Despite Stew's attempts to persuade his friend to let him take on the riskier job, Chad had refused, citing Stew had no business bearing weight on his bad leg so long or maneuvering in and out of the now four-teen-foot hole. Stew didn't argue the point, though hauling away buckets of dirt in the blistering heat was no easy task for him either.

The past week and a half had been among the loneliest he could recall. Though work helped to fill his days, it did nothing to relieve the void Esther's absence left in his heart. By now she'd settled back into her life in Cincinnati. Had she even given him a second thought?

More than likely she'd forgotten him the moment she'd stepped into the stagecoach. The thought soured in his stomach. He'd provided her a bit of amusement while she was here, but his sort couldn't compete with the well-to-dos Esther was accustomed to.

A tug on the rope stirred Stew from his reverie. Clasping the handle on the windlass, he cranked it around, drawing the bucket up for what seemed the millionth time. The windlass handle turned harder than usual, like there was a kink or more weight pulling at the rope. As the bucket neared the surface, he understood why. Mud, rather than dirt overflowed the sides of the bucket. Just yesterday they'd hit a trace of water. Now, the moist earth had turned to glops of mud. Tapping into a stream couldn't be far off.

With more enthusiasm than he'd felt in weeks, Stew lifted the bucket from the rope and made his way to the growing pile of dirt. He poured out the contents of the overturned bucket, scraping out what remained with his glove. With a low sigh, Stew wiped sweat from his brow, for the first time seeing an end in sight to the tiring project.

"That looks promising."

He started at the female voice behind him, its pitch so similar to Esther's. Turning, he mustered a weak grin when he saw Charlotte poised behind him, a tin cup in her hand. "Yes, ma'am, it does. Another day or two should do it."

She held the cup of water out to him. "I'm certain it's a job you'll be glad to put behind you."

With a nod, he took it from her. "It will at that, though it's been sorta nice having something to occupy my time."

"Well, Chad and I are most grateful for your help. He's made much better progress with you back."

"Glad to know I'm good for something," Stew said under his breath. He gulped the creek water down in one long swig and handed her the empty cup. "Much obliged."

She cradled it in both hands, squinting up at him beneath her bonnet. "I've been meaning to tell you, I received a telegram from Ma and Esther a few days ago saying they'd made it to Cincinnati."

He nodded, mention of Esther stirring unwanted angst in his chest. His face flushed hot against Charlotte's stare until he felt compelled to answer. "I reckon that's good news."

Turning his back to her, he limped over to the windlass and fastened the rope onto the bucket. Soft footsteps trailed after him, stopping just to his left. As he lowered the bucket down the hole, he kept his gaze fixed on the cattle grazing in the distance.

"Good news for Ma. I'm not so certain about Esther."

He cocked his head to the side. "Why do you say that?"

Charlotte tapped her finger against the bottom of the empty cup. "I don't think Esther was too eager to return there."

Stew stared at his dusty boots, tension edging into his voice. "She had her chance to stay."

"Oh?" The heightened pitch in Charlotte's tone hinted he'd said too much.

He pushed his hat back on his head and leaned against the windlass. "I mean, it looks like if she wanted to stay she would have."

"Sometimes obligations get in the way of what a person really wants."

"How so?"

Charlotte released a long breath. "When Ma chose to relocate to Cincinnati after my pa died, Esther was too young and amiable to balk against Ma's wishes. She's come to depend heavily on Esther, so much so, she felt duty-bound to go with her."

"And marry some fine-mannered city fella, no doubt." Stew interjected.

Charlotte's mouth twisted. "Ma never warmed to the idea of me staying behind to marry a cattleman. She's become a bit of a snob, I fear, hoping Esther will do better for herself than I did."

Stew scuffed the heel of his boot in the dirt. "Did you do so bad?"

"Not at all. I can't imagine a better life than what Chad and I have together. That's Ma's thinking. Certainly not mine. Nor Esther's."

He met her gaze, weighing the truth of her words. Convinced she was in earnest, he still couldn't bring himself to believe the same of Esther. Bitter thoughts—long pent up inside—threatened to spill out. Maybe baring his soul would help ease the hurt balled up within him. His breaths shallowed as he opened his mouth to speak. "Your ma's way of thinking must have rubbed off on Esther. I asked her to stay, and she chose to go back and take up with some Lawrence feller."

Charlotte's green eyes flared wide, then she brandished a wry grin. "So that's why you've been moping about like a thrashed puppy these past couple of weeks." She shook her head. "Esther has no love for Lawrence Del Ray. She returned to Cincinnati out of a sense of duty, nothing more. When Ma received word her husband was ailing, Esther didn't have the heart to say no."

Stew swallowed the walnut-sized lump in his throat, not hearing much after the part about having no love for Lawrence. "You sure?"

"She told me so herself." Placing a hand on his arm, Charlotte's smile widened. "I do know she's quite fond of you though."

The sun's heat paled in comparison to the fire Charlotte's words ignited in his chest. All this time he'd thought Esther had merely toyed with his affections when she'd been nothing but truthful.

But what did it matter? Hundreds of miles lay between them. Even if what Charlotte said were so, Esther had chosen duty over love. There were no guarantees she loved him at all, least not enough to leave her life in the city. She'd said no once. More than likely if asked, she would again.

THE CLOCK on the mantel chimed seven. Esther pushed her

embroidery needle through the sampler, trying to tune out the drone of conversation between her stepfather and Lawrence. Back in Cincinnati less than a week and already she'd tired of talk of finance and shipping.

Mother paused from her needlework and peered over at the two men. "Enough talk of business, William. Remember, the doctor said you're not to overdo."

William glanced her way, his pipe smoke making the already stuffy room more confining. "Yes, dearest."

Esther's mouth twisted as she stabbed the needle into the material. Perhaps giving up his pipe might be of benefit too. Other than being a bit fatigued, her stepfather had shown little sign of weakness, making Esther wonder if her mother had made more of the issue than necessary. Had her trip here been for nothing?

She sensed Lawrence eyeing her from across the room.

"Yes, William. I fear I'm neglecting Esther." His chair creaked as he stood and walked her way.

Pretending not to notice, she kept her eyes trained on her stitching. No doubt he would shower her with compliments and seek to persuade her to accompany him on some outing as he did each time he called on her. Thus far she'd made the excuse she was travel worn. But how much longer could she put him off?

A warm hand brushed her shoulder, and she tensed as Lawrence's shadow darkened her needlework. "My, but you are talented, Esther. Wouldn't you agree, Mrs. Leifer?"

Mother lowered her own sampler and offered a matronly smile. "I quite agree. One of her many fine abilities."

"Thank you." Esther tipped her head to the side enough to glimpse Lawrence's cleft chin poised inches from her face.

Returning her gaze to her embroidery, she rubbed her fingertips over the half-finished tree and lambs framed by a colorful border. An empty spot at the center would soon display the words: *The Lord is my Shepherd, I Shall Not Want* from the twenty-third Psalm.

Lawrence pulled a footstool up beside her chair and gently pried the sampler from her hands. "However, too much time spent on one's individual talents can detract from more amiable pursuits." He flashed a winsome smile, one handsome enough to make a girl swoon. He truly was dashing with his coal-black hair, dark eyes, and thin mustache.

And yet, something in his nature caused her heart to revolt.

"I find my needlework most rewarding." In truth, she found it tedious, but wasn't about to admit it. How much more invigorating was the thought of racing across the prairie with Stew on horseback.

She reached for the sampler only to have Lawrence clasp her hand. "You've been back nearly a week, and we've not so much as attended a play together."

Her gaze fell away. "The trip home was exhausting. I've needed time to rest."

Placing a finger under her chin, he lifted her face, scrutinizing her with narrowed eyes. "I fear your venture to the wilds of Illinois must have taken something out of you."

Esther eased back, holding in a frustrated groan. If anything had stripped away her vitality it was returning to the city. Her trip to the prairie had fostered freedom and a renewed spirit. She mustered a grin. "I'm fine. Really."

"Good. Then you'll do me the honor of accompanying me to a play tomorrow evening?"

His words were more statement than question.

"Why, of course she will," Mother interjected from across the room, her concentrated gaze pinning Esther to her chair.

Knowing she could put them off no longer, Esther gave a consenting nod.

Lawrence's smile broadened. "Wonderful. I look forward to it."

Something akin to feelings of betrayal sparked within Esther. How could she enjoy Lawrence's company so long as her heart was knit with Stew's? But then, what good would it do to pine away for someone she might never see again? Stew had been lost to her the moment she'd chosen to return. There was no choice now but to forget him.

The sooner the better.

STEW RAPPED his fingers on the stone fireplace, unable to rid his mind of Charlotte's words. Was she right? Had Esther been in earnest about her affections for him? The thought both thrilled and haunted him.

Esther's Bible seemed to call to him yet again, this time like a forgotten friend. The only remembrance he had left of her, save his memories, he slid the book of Scriptures from the mantel. Opening it at its center, he came upon the Psalms. Though he'd never read any himself, he recalled his ma being partial to the eighty-fourth Psalm. Flipping to it, he ran his finger down the page, struggling to sound out the words. Ever so slowly, he made his way down it, pausing on the final verses to read them through a second time.

> *"I would rather be a doorkeeper in the house of my*
> *God than dwell in the tents of wickedness.*
> *For the Lord God is a sun and shield; the Lord will*
> *give grace and glory. No good thing will He*
> *withhold from them that walk uprightly.*
> *Oh Lord of hosts, blessed is the man that trusteth in*
> *Thee."*

Closing the Bible, Stew leaned against the rough stones of the fireplace.

No good thing will He withhold from them that walk uprightly. Blessed is the man that trusteth in Thee.

Was that all there was to it? Do the right thing and God would bless you? It couldn't be that simple. Though he'd not done anything too horrific in his past, he couldn't say he'd "walked uprightly" either. For some time now, he'd known his relationship with the Lord was sorely in need of improvement. Yet, his efforts had been meager at best, mainly prayers pleading for Esther to stay and attending church more out of desire for Esther's company than the Lord's.

No wonder the Lord had turned a deaf ear to him.

He clutched the Bible to his chest. Barring some miracle, it was probably too late for him and Esther. And yet, the verse said the Lord withheld nothing from them that walked uprightly. It said right in Psalm eighty-four the Lord blessed those who were faithful to Him. Maybe that's what Esther had wanted him to learn. More than once she'd inquired about his relationship with the Lord. Was that what had been lacking between them? Had she left her Bible with him in hopes he'd grow in his faith?

Hope stirred in his chest as he returned the Bible to the mantel. From now on, he'd make every effort to be the man of faith Esther had longed for him to be. If he gave it his all, maybe the Lord would make a way for him and Esther.

He swiped a hand through his hair. If he had the chance to do it over, he'd handle things differently. It hadn't been fair to either of them to send her off the way he had. He'd let his anger get in the way of good sense. If Charlotte was right about Esther, she deserved to have her say.

His heart drummed in his chest at the sudden notion churning over in his mind. He must be crazy. Esther had only been gone a couple of weeks. Besides, he and his leg weren't up to anything rigorous. And yet, he longed to know the truth, and the only way to know for certain how Esther felt about him was to ask.

In person.

Chapter Twenty-Two

ESTHER CLASPED LAWRENCE'S outstretched hand and allowed him to help her from the carriage on the corner of Fourth and Vine Street. Before her loomed the newly constructed Pike's Opera House. Though it had opened weeks before she'd left for Illinois, she'd only viewed it from a distance. Seeing it up close for the first time was as impressive as visiting one of the wonders of the ancient world.

She tilted her face upward, at a loss for words. With widened eyes, she took in the impressive five-story sandstone building, its array of windows crested by four stone figures representing the fine arts. At the building's apex rested a majestic eagle, wings outstretched, perched atop a globe.

With a chuckle, Lawrence leaned in close, his voice muffled against the noise of the crowd. "If you think this is something, wait until you see inside."

Reluctantly, she surrendered to his pull. They moved toward the arched entrances, meandering their way through the throng of people. A poster for the much anticipated romantic comedy opera, *Martha,* decorated the wall at each of the three entrances.

The rows of patrons inched forward, each lady and gentleman decked in their finest, chattering excitedly between themselves. Lawrence's lips moved, but his words went unheard as Esther's mind traveled back to the prairie. What would Stew think of such an extravagant structure? More than likely he'd never set foot in Cincinnati, let alone a fancy opera house. Her chest squeezed. As striking as the place was, she'd forego the visit if only she could take in his ready smile and stroll with him under moonlit skies once more.

"Esther? Is anything wrong?"

Lawrence's concerned tone, along with a tug on her arm, pulled her to her senses. A huge gap rested between them and the couple in front of them. "It's all a bit overwhelming."

"You're in for quite a treat, my dear." He grinned, urging her forward.

Mustering a weak smile, she matched his quick stride, thankful her response seemed to satisfy. If he'd known the true reason for her preoccupation, she'd not have been so easily forgiven.

Having purchased their tickets in advance, Lawrence handed them to the attendant and escorted Esther inside. Black and white marble tile paved their way into the vast three-tiered auditorium lit by a string of gas lights dotting the outer walls. Her breath caught at sight of the domed ceiling lined with colorful fresco paintings.

Lawrence smiled as he ushered her to a seat. "Didn't I tell you it was grand?"

A stir of excitement welled within Esther. She'd not wished to come, but now that she was here, was glad she had. The sheer thrill of being in such a pristine place made the outing worthwhile. "It truly is marvelous. There must be more than a thousand people here."

"I hear tell it can house eighteen hundred." He leaned closer until his warm breath brushed her ear. "And yet, I feel as if you and I are the only ones in the room."

Esther's mouth went dry as he slid his hand atop hers, the familiarity in his tone and touch rendering her speechless and more than a little uncomfortable. Heat climbed up her neck, spilling into her cheeks. Unlike her companion, she was suddenly relieved to be in the midst of a crowd. How could she endure the advances of a man who incited such a reaction in her?

She wet her lips, doing her best to ignore the drumming of her heart in her ears. Averting her gaze to the curtained stage, she listened to the orchestra tuning their instruments in the pit below it. "I-It appears they're getting ready to start."

"So it does." She attempted to slide her hand from under his, only to feel his hold tighten. "Glad you came?"

Until a moment ago, she could have honestly said she was. But now, she wasn't so certain. As she opened her mouth to speak, the orchestra struck up a vibrant chord and the lights dimmed. The curtains opened, revealing a woman dressed in a striking burgundy dress poised at the center of the stage. Thunderous applause broke out around the packed auditorium. Esther used the moment as a welcome excuse to pull her hand from Lawrence's. She breathed a soft sigh, wondering how she could ever entertain the thought of accepting the man's almost certain future offer of marriage when she could barely abide his touch.

"GOOD TO SEE YOU HERE, Stew. You've been missed."

Stew reached for Pastor Brody's outstretched palm. "Thanks, Preacher." He hadn't the heart to tell him that this, his first week back, would most likely be his last. At least for a while. Yesterday he'd helped Chad put the finishing touches on the well. Then and there, Stew had determined the time had come to find out the truth about him and Esther. All he need do was find the right moment to break the news to Chad.

Guilt pricked at Stew's middle. Since he'd agreed to work for Chad, he'd been off work more than he'd been on. Other than the well, he'd not been much of a help. Would Chad be annoyed with him for leaving? Stew couldn't blame him if he gave him the boot for good.

Regardless, it was something he had to do. Not knowing the full truth behind Esther's leaving was driving him mad. He'd be little use to Chad or the Circle J until his relationship with Esther was resolved one way or another. Otherwise, the matter would continue to eat away at him.

He shook Mrs. Brody's hand then donned his hat as he stepped outside. Limping his way down the steps, he squinted against the brightness of the sun. Scout stood in the shade of a tree on the far side of the street, seeming more eager than Stew to begin the long ride back to the cabin. He patted the horse's neck. How Stew hated the thought of leaving him holed up in a livery for days, maybe even weeks, while he was away.

But what else could he do? The trip into Miller Creek and back was taxing enough on his ankle. There was no chance he could make it to Cincinnati. Besides, if he was successful in persuading Esther to return with him, he couldn't expect her to ride double the whole way. Though he didn't have a lot of money, he could cover the cost of the stagecoach.

The question was, how could he ever provide for Esther? *If* she would have him.

"Hey Stew, wait up!" Chad's familiar voice hailed from across the church lot. Stew turned as the Avery family downed the steps and headed his way.

Stew slid Esther's Bible into his saddlebag then sauntered toward them. Now seemed as good a time as any to share his plans —especially since he hoped to leave first thing in the morning.

Stepping up beside him, Chad wielded a broad smile. "Come join us for dinner to celebrate the new well."

Stew twisted his mouth to one side. One last home-cooked

meal was more than tempting. He'd grown accustomed to the family's hospitality, which made leaving all the more difficult. "Much obliged, but I have some things I need to tend to this afternoon."

Charlotte shifted young Michael in her arms. The boy seemed to grow bigger every time Stew laid eyes on him. "You sure? We'll have plenty of victuals."

With a nod, Stew mustered a weak smile. "Yes, ma'am. Not that I don't appreciate the offer. It's just, I have some gettin' ready to do."

"Going someplace?" Chad's brows pinched.

Stew cleared his throat. "I, uh, thought I'd head out to Cincinnati a spell."

He couldn't miss the flash of Charlotte's emerald eyes nor the notable upturn of her lips. "I, for one, think that's a splendid idea."

Heat rose in Stew's cheeks as Chad's curious stare shifted from him to Charlotte and back again. At last, his expression mellowed. "How long you figure on being gone?"

Stew dropped his gaze to his boots. "All depends on how things go. Not long, I hope." He swiped a hand over his jaw. "I hate to inconvenience you like this after missing so much work already, but..."

"Don't give it another thought." Charlotte interjected, edging closer to her husband. "You and Johnny can manage a while without him, can't you, Chad?"

He met her gaze, a hint of humor in his eyes. "I reckon so. Now that the well's dug, there's nothing pressing till we brand cattle. How soon till you leave?"

Stew straightened, hope stirring in his chest. "First thing tomorrow morning."

"Then I'll not take no for an answer. You'll join us for dinner today, and I'll send you with a bundle of leftovers for your journey."

At Stew's hesitation, Chad arched a brow. "May as well say yes. She'll have her way regardless."

"Then, I'll not waste time refusing." With a chuckle, Stew backed toward Scout, experiencing the first sense of joy he'd felt in a long while. The Averys had been more than accommodating.

Now, if only Esther would be so obliging.

Chapter Twenty-Three

THE KNOCK on the door wasn't unexpected. Lawrence was as predictable as he was persistent. Hardly a day had passed since Esther's return that he hadn't stopped by. But tonight, he bore an added air of confidence.

A curious smile played on his lips as he removed his tall hat and entered the sitting room. With a bow, he reached for Mother's hand and then her own, his eyes dancing as he leaned over her. "You're looking extraordinarily becoming tonight, my dear."

"Thank you." Esther drew her hand away, shifting under his steady gaze.

His smile widened, as if he were harboring some unknown secret. Though his eyes never left her face, he addressed her stepfather. "I wonder if I might have a moment alone with you, William."

"Certainly." The older man lowered his pipe and stood, pulling his brown suitcoat over his rounded belly. A good six inches shorter than their visitor, with his stocky frame, William looked a bit like a duck waddling up next to a swan. He reached a hand up to clasp Lawrence's shoulder. "Well, my boy, shall we go into the study?"

"As you say." Lawrence gave a slight bow then turned to Esther, a roguish gleam in his eye. "I won't be long, my dear."

Esther's gaze darted from one smiling face to another, all seeming to possess an element of unspoken delight. Her heart pulsed in her ears. Surely Lawrence didn't intend to ask for her hand so soon after her return.

The two men disappeared down the hall. A moment later, the door to the study clicked shut. Perhaps she was wrong. They were business partners after all. And yet, Lawrence had never sought privacy in discussing matters before. Nor had he worn such a buoyant expression. Almost as if he already knew the meeting's outcome.

"How splendid!" Mother's giddy, but hushed voice quipped from across the room. "Didn't I tell you once you returned a marriage proposal would soon follow?"

A sickened feeling washed through Esther as she ventured a glance at her Mother. "You can't be certain…"

"What else could it be? It's plain the young man is entranced by you."

In her heart, she knew her mother was right. With each outing, Lawrence's attentions had become more intense. More than once, he'd hinted of clearing his schedule in coming weeks for a more pressing matter. Though he'd refused to disclose what that matter was.

Setting her needlepoint aside, Esther stood and strode over to the window. Her stepfather's mansion sat atop a hill overlooking the city. The few trees dotting the landscape seemed swallowed up by the vast array of houses below. How different from the wide open golden plains of the prairie. The two locations were as diverse as Lawrence and Stew—one bursting with security and ambition, the other full of hopes and promise.

She'd come to this place on her mother's behalf and, more or less, returned for the same reason. Would she settle for whom her mother deemed advantageous for a husband as well? The churning in her stomach made her fearful. She'd wished to marry for love, not wealth or station. And yet, to refuse Lawrence would shame him and bring reproach from her mother and stepfather who held him in highest regard.

What other option did she have but to accept if he offered? She couldn't very well throw away a proper marriage proposal on account of Stew when he'd done nothing more than ask her to lengthen her stay. He even seemed to have changed his mind about that in the end.

Closing her eyes, she bowed her head. *Lord, give me the courage to do what's right. Above all, I wish to honor You. If Lawrence is whom you intend for me to marry, may I submit to the decision with grace and dignity. But if not, may You place a barrier in our path and take me in the direction You desire.*

Men's laughter echoed in the hall as the door to the study opened, bringing Esther's prayer to an abrupt end. The two men emerged, seeming quite pleased with themselves. Without a moment's hesitation, Lawrence crossed the room and brushed a hand along her upper arm. "Fetch your bonnet, my dear. We're headed out for the evening."

Esther moved to retrieve her green felt bonnet. "Where are we going?"

"Given the occasion, I think a carriage ride and evening stroll seem in order."

Lawrence flashed a smug grin, his response seeming as much for William and Mother's benefit as for hers.

Esther opened her mouth to speak, but instead took the arm Lawrence offered, all but certain she knew the reason for his sudden urge to escort her.

Lawrence's rig awaited them at the front of the house, the driver seated still as a statue at the reins. Taking her hand, Lawrence helped her onto the cushioned seat then hopped in beside her. He rapped on the outside of the carriage and poked his head out the opening. "To the riverfront, Charles."

"Yes, sir," came the muffled reply.

As the carriage lunged forward, Lawrence settled in closer, his leg and shoulder pressed against hers. Esther eased away, uncomfortable with the closeness. Not that her companion had ever been anything but a gentleman, but since her return, with each outing, he seemed to gain boldness where she was concerned.

The sky flared crimson as the setting sun dipped low on the western horizon, casting long shadows over the city. The view from the hill, though spectacular, lacked the raw beauty of the prairie. Nothing manmade could ever outshine the Lord's handiwork.

"An evening stroll followed by a savory meal seems a perfect way to celebrate, don't you think?" Lawrence's tenor voice cut into her thoughts.

Her mouth went dry at the one question burning to escape. She cleared her throat, struggling to keep her voice steady. "And what is it we're celebrating?"

He arched a brow and took her hand in his. "All in good time, my dear." Keeping his dark eyes fixed on her, he raised her gloved hand to his lips.

Mustering a weak grin, she turned her attention to their surroundings. Silence fell between them as the driver diverted the carriage around the core of the city to its outskirts. Below them, to the south, lay the Ohio River, much of it obscured by buildings and riverboats lined along its bank. How wonderful it would have been to view the rolling terrain before it was touched by human hands, when only hills and trees had dotted the landscape instead of smokestacks and tall buildings.

The carriage rolled to a stop atop the rise overlooking the river very near her stepfather's shipping business. Though the Leifer Shipping Company bore William's name, Lawrence now owned a healthy share and more or less managed its affairs. Having no male heirs of his own to pass the business onto, her stepfather had made his intentions clear that one day the company would be turned over to Lawrence. Given his affluent lifestyle, business seemed to be more than adequate. Had he brought her here to gloat?

"Ah, here we are." Lawrence exited the carriage then reached to help Esther down. In uncharacteristic fashion, rather than clasp her fingers, his hands moved to her waist.

Taken off guard, Esther drew in a hasty breath. When Stew had lifted her from Willow, it had seemed a polite, gentlemanly gesture. Not so with Lawrence. His firm grasp and determined stare sparked of possessiveness. She tensed under his hold, grateful when her boots touched the ground. He offered her his arm. "Shall we?"

With a hesitant nod, she looped her arm through his. They meandered down the slope to the water's edge just as one of the Leifer cargo boats pulled into dock. She arched a brow, Lawrence's boldness bolstering her own. "Have we come for the view or to see how business is faring?"

"Why, the view, of course. I wouldn't think of boring you with matters of business, least of all, tonight." Lawrence nodded to the man at the helm, tipping his head closer to her ear. "Though I do like to keep tabs on how things are going. Not all our workers are, shall we say, the most upstanding of fellows."

Esther's gaze flicked to the scraggly dressed workers atop the steamboat. One of the men's eyes fastened on her, his stare trailing slowly down her and up again. She turned away, a shiver running through her. "I see what you mean."

Keeping in step with her companion's unhurried pace, Esther accompanied him to an open area away from the cluster of steamboats lining the bank. She stared out over the scenic river. A soft breeze drifted across the water, tousling loose strands of her hair. She breathed in the smell of the river, listening to the sloshing of the waves against the shoreline. Boat traffic slowed but never stopped along the Ohio.

"You like it here."

Esther gave a nod in answer to Lawrence's astute observation. Despite her misgivings, she sensed herself relax. There was something tranquil in standing at the water's edge. "I believe this is my favorite part of Cincinnati. When Mother and I first moved here, I came to the river often. Now, living on the far side of the city, such pleasures come less frequent."

"We shall have to remedy that." Loosening his hold on her arm, Lawrence draped his arm around her shoulders. "A beautiful scene to be sure, though it pales in comparison to your beauty, my dear."

Esther tensed under his touch, uncertain how to respond. Such blatant flattery. She couldn't recall Lawrence ever complimenting her on her sweet nature or thoughtfulness toward others. Always her beauty. Was her appearance all that mattered to the man?

She let her gaze drift to the far shore, determined to find out. "Outer beauty is fleeting. It's what comes from within a person that makes one beautiful."

A chuckle erupted from her companion. "I didn't know you were such a philosopher. I shall have to seek your advice often in the future."

"The wisdom isn't mine to claim, but comes from God's Word."

"Ah. Well versed as well as beautiful. What a splendid asset you'll make me, my dear."

Pulling away from his hold, she gazed up at him. "What do you mean?"

He brushed the back of his fingers over her cheek. "I've asked William for your hand, and he's agreed to it." His matter-of-fact tone made the declaration sound like a company merger.

Esther pulled her gaze to the wide river. "My hand isn't William's to give."

"Of course." He turned her toward him, taking her hands in his. "That's why I've brought you here, to ask you personally."

The blood drained from Esther's face, any doubts about his intentions fleeing away.

He gazed down at her, his smile tender, expectant. "Will you do me the honor of becoming my wife?"

She took a step back, doing her best to conceal her growing angst. Such a proposal would be the envy of many a lady. What young woman wouldn't relish marrying an attractive, wealthy, upstanding businessman such as Lawrence? There was no finer calling for a woman than to wed, bear children, and be well provided for. And yet, the thought of such a union with him left her emotionless. Hollow.

"Esther?" Lawrence's heightened tone pulled her back to the question at hand.

"I..." For a brief moment, she thought she could say "yes", but her mouth refused to form the word. She drew a long breath, praying he would not be put off by her hesitancy. "I'm honored by your kind offer, Lawrence, but I must beg for time to consider it."

"Time?" His tone held an air of disbelief, if not astonishment.

"Y-Yes. I've been home such a short while. Your proposal comes quite sudden."

Letting loose her hands, he smoothed his thin mustache, a gesture she'd witnessed him display on more than one occasion when deep in thought or agitated. "But surely you must have known, even before you left, how I felt about you."

"I suppose I did, but please understand, I need to think things through. There's much to consider."

"Such as?" His eyes narrowed slightly as though scrutinizing the reason hidden beneath her words. Had he assumed she would jump at the chance to secure a future with him? Was he so certain of his charms that he thought she couldn't refuse?

She laced her fingers together, struggling for words. "Well, for one thing, I-I'm not certain we know each other that well."

He tugged at the cuffs of his sleeves, the tension in his face easing. "That's easy enough to remedy. We shall spend the next few days becoming better acquainted. Come, my dear. We'll dine out and you can ask me anything you wish. I've nothing to hide."

Taking the arm he offered her, Esther pasted on a smile, doing her best to seem enthused. She'd bought herself a few days at best. Given Lawrence's reaction, more than likely, a second refusal would not bode well.

Chapter Twenty-Four

S TEW PATTED S COUT'S NECK, feeding him some well-deserved grain. They'd put in a day. Traveled more miles than either of them had cared to. Now he was paying the price—a stiff, sore ankle and worn out body. The thought of a warm bath and soft bed awaiting him at the inn were almost more temptation than he could stand. But the small amount of cash left in his pocket after purchasing his stagecoach ticket quickly made up his mind for him.

He'd bed down in Scout's stall for the night and save what money he had for later. No telling how expensive things were in a city as large as Cincinnati. He must be crazy to spend all his earnings on what might prove a hopeless pursuit.

Crazy, or in love. Maybe a bit of both.

The room dimmed as twilight settled in. Stew leveled the straw at the far end of the stall with his boot and spread his blanket over it. Scout arched his neck and gave a soft whinny. Stew hated to leave him holed up here so long, but what choice did he have?

The stable boy had assured him he'd give Scout the best of care. Still, Stew felt like he was abandoning his faithful companion. What was worse, he didn't know how long Scout would have to stay here. If all went well, most likely he and Esther would be back inside of a week. If not, his stay might be longer.

Or shorter, depending on how his unexpected visit was received.

His stomach rumbled, reminding him he'd not eaten. He rinsed off his hands with water from his canteen and dried them on his pant legs. Reaching in his saddlebag, he pulled out the bundle Charlotte had sent with him. The scent of smoked ham overpowered the earthy smell of the livery as he pulled away the cloth. Mouth watering, he took out a small portion along with one of the biscuits. The Lord bless Mrs. Avery for her thoughtful gesture. She'd saved him many a hunger pang. Splitting the biscuit apart, he slid the slab of meat between the two halves.

"Sure you wanna bed down here, mister?"

Stew paused mid-bite at the stable boy's query. "I've slept worse places."

The young man's lips lifted in a sideways grin. "Can I get you anything?"

"An extra lantern would be nice, if you can spare one."

"Can I trust ya not to burn the place down?"

"I wouldn't think of destroying the place that's boarding my best horse."

The young man chuckled and handed him the lantern from two stalls down. With a nod of thanks, Stew hung the lantern on a peg on the far wall. As the stable boy moved on, Stew returned to his meal. As the savory taste of hickory-smoked ham filled his taste buds, he paused his chewing, recalling he'd not said grace. Removing his hat, he bowed his head and offered up a silent word of thanks for the grub, adding a plea for a successful journey.

With a few quick bites, he finished off the ham and biscuit. He brushed the crumbs from his hands and reached in his saddlebag for Esther's Bible. True to his promise, these past few days he'd taken up the habit of reading a few verses at bedtime. Though it remained a struggle to decipher some of the words and meanings, he'd come to enjoy the nightly routine. Having abandoned the Old Testament for the New, he'd skipped over the first couple chapters in Matthew—with its difficult names—and delved into chapter three.

The parts about Jesus interested him. Over the past few days, he'd worked his way to the sixth chapter where Jesus was speaking to the huge crowd of followers. Finding his place, he held the Bible closer to the lantern.

> *"Lay not up for yourselves treasures upon earth,*
>   *where moth and rust doth corrupt, and where*
>   *thieves break through and steal:*
> *But lay up for yourselves treasures in heaven, where*
>   *neither moth nor rust doth corrupt, and where*
>   *thieves do not break through nor steal:*
> *For where your treasure is, there will your heart be*
>   *also."*

Stew paused. He shouldn't have much to worry about there. Outside of Scout, he didn't own anything that could be considered treasure. The part about not taking stock in earthly possessions made sense, but how did one go about laying up treasure in heaven?

It was plain he had a lot to learn where faith was concerned.

His eyes grew heavy, and he closed the Bible and turned down the lantern. Looping his hands together behind his head, he breathed a long sigh, letting his eyes adjust to the dark. Esther wanted a man of faith. He could never come close to having the qualities Jesus demonstrated.

All he could do was try. And pray it was enough.

"WHAT A DELIGHTFUL MEAL." Lawrence dabbed the corners of his mouth with his napkin and pushed aside the remains of his catfish dinner. "Now, what would you like to know about me?"

Esther sat back in her chair, caught off guard by his straight-forward approach. It was hard to know where to begin. All she really knew of him was that he had a mind for business and a knack for running her stepfather's shipping company without so much as doing a bit of the manual labor, so far as she knew.

Drawing a breath, she folded her hands in her lap. "Well, I know you have a vested interest in Leifer Shipping, but what exactly do you do?"

With a slight chuckle, he arched a brow. "Why, my dear, I oversee every aspect of the company. Every crate and barrel shipped is subject to my approval. William entrusts every detail, from finances to hiring workers, to my discretion. Of course, I often delegate the more trivial matters, but more or less, the Leifer Shipping Company doesn't make a move without my consent."

Esther managed a slow nod. "William must have great confi-dence in your abilities."

Her words produced a wide smile from her companion, seeming to stroke his already swollen ego. "I would say he trusts me implicitly as I hope you do as well."

She pasted on a smile, but gave no reply. Though Lawrence had never given her reason not to trust him, something in his over-confident demeanor didn't set well.

He leaned over the table, circling his finger around the rim of his half-filled water glass. "Now, what other curiosities are bouncing around in your pretty head?"

One more question burned on her tongue. She lifted her chin. "I've not heard you speak of your relationship with the Lord. Are you a devout Christian?"

The corners of his mouth curved upward in a taunting sort of way. "I attend services with you most every Sunday. What more proof do you require?"

Dropping her gaze, she toyed with a crumb on the tablecloth. "I only wish to learn how deep your faith runs. Such an attribute is very important to me in my husband."

"How quaint." Reaching across the table, he clasped her hand in his. "I assure you, what matters to you, matters to me."

Esther bristled inwardly. His words lacked earnestness. True, he attended services, though she wondered if it was for her benefit rather than the Lord's. More often than not during sermons, she'd caught Lawrence jotting notes in his company ledger, or peering at her or out the window. Stew, at least, had listened intently to the message.

Lawrence gave a soft chuckle and pressed her hand to his lips. "Don't look so glum, my dear. Given opportunity, I promise I shall be the devoutest of husbands."

She nodded, though his pledge left her wanting. Lawrence had many alluring qualities, but lacked the ones most dear to her heart. All the charm, wit, and attractiveness in the world couldn't replace a love that was true and God-centered. Could she overlook his less than ideal attributes in favor of his dashing good looks and daring personality?

In a matter of days he'd expect a final answer to his proposal. No doubt he cared for her deeply and would provide well for her needs. The question was—could she compromise her convictions for what she knew in her heart wasn't best?

"You...what?"

Esther cringed at her mother's harsh tone. Certain the news wouldn't be well received, she'd waited until her mother had forced the issue before disclosing her delay in response to Lawrence's proposal. "I needed time to think."

"Whatever for?" Mother's silk skirt rustled as she stood and paced back and forth across the sitting room. "Why, any woman would be a fool to pass up an opportunity to become the wife of Lawrence Del Ray."

Pursing her lips, Esther drew a calming breath. "I haven't refused his offer, merely asked for time to consider it."

Her mother froze in place then pivoted toward her, mouth drawn. "It's an insult. By putting him off, you've jeopardized your entire future. You'll be fortunate if he doesn't shift his attentions elsewhere from here on."

The thought left Esther cold and unsettled. "If Lawrence is so easily put off, I dare say he isn't as fond of me as he professes."

Mother's chin tipped upward. "Men don't like to be put to the test. Why toy with his affections? What cause do you have to detain your answer?"

Esther's mouth twisted. In truth, she could think of several reasons, the most important being her lack of affection for him. His suave disposition and handsome features might cause many a lady to swoon, but something about him seemed fraudulent—conniving even—as if he were too good to be true.

Maybe it was Stew's easy-going nature that had spoiled her. She'd felt at home in his presence. Comfortable. Herself. Not so with Lawrence. There always seemed an element of practiced falsehood, as if she feared her true self wouldn't measure up to his expectations. Could she stomach a life of pretense?

She sat forward in her chair, attempting to still the quiver in her voice. "I don't love him."

Her mother chuckled. "Love isn't everything, child. You must think of your future."

"But you loved Pa. Didn't his love bring you more happiness than all of this?" She lifted her hands, gesturing to the fine furnishings.

Moisture pooled in her mother's eyes, their blueness reflecting a hint of her old self. She crossed the room and took Esther by the hand. "I'll always treasure the years with your pa. He was my first love, the man I'd hoped to spend the rest of my days with. But,

William has been good to me, and I've grown to care for him deeply. He's provided us with an affluent lifestyle and a secure future that we could otherwise never have known. You may not have strong feelings for Lawrence as yet, but, in due time, your fondness for him will grow. Don't throw away this opportunity. Mr. Del Ray is a respected man of substance. One you'd do well to latch onto."

Her mother's words penetrated deep inside Esther, wrestling with her deep-seated convictions. Was her mother right? If she married Lawrence, given time, could she come to love him the way she'd hoped to love a husband? Or would she feel forever trapped in a loveless relationship, wishing she'd waited for true love to find her?

Thoughts of Stew hounded her. How she wished they'd had more time together. But what would it have accomplished? If they'd allowed the seeds of love to grow between them, it would only have brought more misery. Her sense of obligation to her mother would remain, and Stew could never stomach living in the crowded city. Nor could she ask him to. He would surely shrivel and die inside.

If only she held for Lawrence even a smidgen of the attachment she felt for Stew. Then, she could agree to the proposal without reservation. But as things were, the proposition seemed just another obligation she'd been asked to fulfill. Should she rid her mind of Stew completely? Abandon any hopes of a God-centered marriage based on mutual love and affection?

She mustered a weak grin. "Thank you, Mother. I'll bear that in mind."

Her mother let loose of her hand and touched her fingers to Esther's cheek. "I know you will, dear. You've always been the daughter I could count on not to disappoint."

Esther tensed, the words seeping into her like bitter water. The would-be compliment seemed more a sentence of lifelong servitude. Charlotte had been the one to know her mind and go her own way. When they'd been younger, her sister's obstinacy had annoyed Esther. But now, she'd come to envy her sister's independent nature.

And wished, for once, she'd have the grit to stand up for her own way of thinking.

PART III
ENTRAPMENTS

Chapter Twenty-Five

Wednesday, June 22, 1859

STEW LOWERED the stagecoach blind and held it against the frame with his knee, doing his best to keep the spray of rain at bay. Water continued to trickle in, soaking his pant leg. As if the constant jostling and cramped quarters weren't bad enough, now his whole left side was soaked to boot. The annoyance made him all the more impatient to reach Cincinnati.

Three days of travel should have landed them just shy of the Ohio border. Instead the pouring rain had turned the Cumberland Road to mud, slowing progress. At this rate, it would be a week before they reached their destination. The thought rendered his spirits as damp as his clothing.

His elbow bumped the rather large man seated next to him, who, by his tailored suit and lap full of books, looked to be a teacher or professor. The fellow peered over his book at him through wire rims, forehead furrowed. Stew drew his arm back and leaned into the carriage wall as the man returned to his reading.

With nothing to do but stare at the frowning gentlemen passengers across from him, Stew chose instead to close his eyes and pull his hat over his face. The crowded compartment reeked of body odor, causing him to further regret his decision to take the coach instead of ride horseback. Being drenched and in discomfort atop Scout seemed favorable compared to the cramped, disagreeable confines of the stagecoach.

He could only hope the outcome of the journey would make the trip worthwhile. Charlotte's words had given him hope, but the fact remained, Esther had chosen to leave. There were no guarantees he could convince her to return with him. Winning her mother over seemed the key. But how could he accomplish such a feat when she appeared to loath everything about him?

To her, he was a lowly cattleman with no place to call his own and no means to provide for her daughter. The woman's mind was so set against him there was little hope of changing it. The very thought of trying to win her approval sapped his energies. He realized he had little to offer. He didn't need a hifalutin' city woman to convince him.

But shouldn't the willingness to commit and love her daughter count for something?

He crossed his arms over his chest and scrunched farther down on the seat. He had half a mind to head home and forget the whole thing. But something wouldn't let him. One question, one hope, spurred him on—the need to know if Esther loved him.

The stagecoach jolted to a stop. Stew straightened, sliding his hat from his face. A man's muffled voice shouted in the distance, followed by their Whip's irritated reply. "All right, but we're behind schedule as it is."

Lifting the blind high enough to see out, Stew glimpsed an oncoming Conestoga wagon bogged in the mud, its six-horse team looking winded and drenched to the bone.

His studious companion lowered his book. "What goes on?"

"The road ahead's blocked by a freight wagon."

Grumbling under his breath, the man hid his face behind his book once more.

The Whip clambered from his seat atop the stagecoach and stepped to Stew's side of the compartment. Pulling aside the blind, the driver peered in, the run-off from his hat further soaking Stew's pant leg. "Any you fellers willin' to lend a hand unloading freight, come on out. They need some weight off the wagon before they can pull free."

Without hesitation, Stew donned his hat and unlatched the door. If it would get them moving again, he was all for it. While Stew and the two men opposite him vacated the coach, the professor returned to reading. Mud coated Stew's boots as he sloshed his way toward the Conestoga wagon. He kept his hat low, shielding his face from the pouring rain. Any attempt to keep dry had gone by the wayside.

Along with any hopes of reaching Esther anytime soon.

"THERE IT IS. MY HUMBLE HOME."

The carriage rolled to a stop, and Esther followed Lawrence's gaze to the two-story brick house situated atop the hill to her right. Anything but humble, the sizable home rivaled her stepfather's fine mansion. "It's beautiful."

Taking her hand, Lawrence helped her from the carriage. "Ah, but how much more beautiful and full of life it will be with you gracing its halls."

Esther met his gaze with a raised brow. He truly was a master at flattery. "We agreed I had until the end of the week to make my decision."

His lips thinned in a wry grin. "So we did. Forgive me. I'm a bit too eager, I fear. You have my word as a gentleman, no more coercion until two nights hence." He pressed her hand to his heart, his smile broadening. "But until then, I shall do my utmost to dazzle you with my charms."

Esther sensed herself weakening. Would marrying Lawrence be

so bad? He obviously loved her and would cater to her every whim. Maybe her mother was right. In time, perhaps she would grow to love him as well. Though she'd not been keen on her mother's marriage to William, it had proven beneficial and timely for their needs. Could she settle for such a marriage arrangement for herself?

Lawrence squeezed her hand, his expression childlike. "Come. I'll give you a tour."

Before she could respond, he'd taken her arm and whisked her forward. An array of flowering rose bushes fringed the walkway leading to the front door. Lawrence snapped off one of the crimson heads and handed it to Esther. Her lips tugged in a gentle smile as she took it from him. Touched by the kind gesture, she lifted it to her nose and breathed in its sweetness. Her companion may not be the man she'd envisioned for herself, but he certainly had a flare for making her feel special.

The door slipped open as they neared the front step, and a well-dressed servant bowed and ushered them inside. Esther paused, wondering how he'd known the exact moment to open the door. Had he been watching them? Did the affluent life Lawrence offered allow for no semblance of privacy?

A young maid stood just within. She curtsied as Lawrence handed her his hat. "Good evening, sir. May I take your hat, miss?"

With a nod, Esther untied her bonnet, venturing a glimpse around. A grand staircase decorated the room's center, leading to the upstairs balcony. A huge chandelier with countless tiny gaslights glittered overhead.

She handed the maid her bonnet, wondering what it would be like to be mistress of such a fine mansion, to have maids and servants waiting on her hand and foot. As the wife of Lawrence Del Ray, she'd be expected to entertain his elite friends and business associates. Could she stomach all the expectations placed upon her?

How different life would be for her here than what she'd envisioned. As a girl, all she'd dreamed of was marrying a farmer or laborer like her pa and owning enough land to start a homestead. The very thought of managing a grand household such as this left her a bit light-headed. A log cabin on the prairie was about as far from this place as one could fathom.

"Shall I alert the cooks you'll be dining in with a guest tonight, sir?"

Lawrence nodded to the maid, keeping his gaze fixed on Esther. "Yes. Tell them Miss Stanton deserves nothing but the finest."

Esther pasted on a smile, her palms growing clammy. Was this God's plan for her? Were the two of them to wed and perhaps use their wealth to aid the poor and downtrodden? She could justify such a union if it would somehow benefit the Lord. But would Lawrence agree to part with a fair portion of his income to help others?

There was still so much she didn't know about him, how he spent his time when they were apart. More than once she'd witnessed him conversing with a shady-looking fellow on the street below before making his way to her stepfather's door. Each time she asked him about his business duties, he shrugged it off as nothing of concern to her. And yet, he and William would settle in a corner of the room for hours at a time discussing matters of finance and shipping.

Once wed, would Lawrence tire of romantic notions and become further engrossed in his business dealings? If he refused to discuss such matters with her, would they lose all sense of intimacy? She would become bored and complacent sitting idle with nothing to do but pass her time ordering servants about and planning social events.

She'd hoped to run her own household and take a vested interest in her husband the way Charlotte did. Was she instead simply to decorate her husband's arm and wait for him to return home each evening? Would she ever again know the satisfaction of hard work or experience the pleasure of toiling alongside her husband to make their house a home?

She'd promised Stew not to allow herself to become too stuffy and steeped in city ways. Could she hold true to that promise if she married Lawrence?

The question was one she had little time left to find answer to.

STEW PEELED off his soiled boots and trousers. What a sight he was. Soaked clear down to his skin. Freeing the Conestoga wagon from the road's muddy grip had proven more difficult and time-consuming than any of them had dared to guess. The delay had cost yet another afternoon of travel. A day later, here he was in Richmond, Indiana with only the final stretch of road to Cincinnati left to go.

The rain had finally let up just outside of Richmond. Darkness had settled in before they'd arrived. Too late to catch the stage-coach heading south. At least he'd have the chance to clean up a bit, change clothes, and rest his weary muscles. He'd splurged and put himself up in a hotel for the very purpose of making himself presentable before he made it to Esther's doorstep.

A nervous tingle rippled through him as he pulled his shirt up over his head. What would she think of him coming all this way? Would she be put out at him for following her or overjoyed to see him? He had an inkling it would be one or the other. But he didn't care to venture a guess which it would be.

He set his wet, muddied clothes aside to wash up later, then sank down in the claw-foot tub of warm water the attendant had drawn for his bath. Too long-legged to stretch out fully, he bent his legs at the knees, his muscles tense from all the hauling of supplies from the wagon. It seemed to be taking far more time to regain his strength from being laid up than it had to lose it.

Soap in hand, he rubbed it between his palms, his thoughts

again turning to Esther. All the scrubbing in the world couldn't make him as refined and handsome as her city fella was sure to be. A glance down at his distorted ankle reaffirmed his doubts. His limp, though improving, continued to plague him like a nagging cough in the dead of winter.

Would Esther even give him a second look?

His mouth went dry at the thought of coming all this way for nothing. Regardless of what happened, he'd done what he had to do. Knowing Esther didn't want him was better than wondering the rest of his days if he'd missed out. He leaned down and doused his head under the water, his wet hair clinging to his face when he sat up.

A hair cut wouldn't be a bad idea either if he could swing one.

He scrubbed a hand through his wet hair. Soon he'd know the truth. He'd either be a happy man, or return to Illinois empty-handed. Lord willing, she'd at least give it some thought.

As he finished washing, his gaze skimmed the quilted mattress. Good thing he'd enjoyed a bath because he had a suspicion he'd wasted money on a bed. The way his mind was churning, more than likely he'd not get two winks of sleep.

Chapter Twenty-Six

ESTHER'S FACE blanched as the servant announced Lawrence had arrived early. Not that it mattered. She'd made her decision. Voicing it a few hours sooner than expected wouldn't change anything. And yet, a shadow of dread spilled over her. She met her mother's knowing smile with a stiff grin, an invisible hand choking off her air.

"Show him in, James," Mother chortled.

Esther's heart raced. All night she'd weighed her options, warring back and forth within. She'd prayed for guidance and received no clear answer. Yet, the time for wavering had come to an end. What could she do but surrender to what seemed her best option?

Mother's soft chuckle startled her from her thoughts. "Don't look so alarmed, child. He's asking you to marry him, not putting you in shackles."

She gave a brisk nod and drew a steadying breath. Odd her mother would make such a comparison. For in marrying Lawrence wouldn't she, in a sense, be chaining herself to a man she didn't love for a lifetime? No matter what her answer, she stood to disappoint someone—herself or others.

The click of Lawrence's heels in the hall jarred her from her thoughts. Though over recent weeks, the sound had become a familiar one, now each click drummed in Esther's ears like the ticking of a clock on the mantel, stealing away precious moments.

At last, he appeared in the sitting room doorway, face awash in emotion. At once, his dark eyes engulfed her as though probing her every thought. Did he guess her uncertainty? With a bow, he turned to her mother. "Good afternoon, Mrs. Leifer. I hope I'm not intruding, but I wonder if I could speak privately with Esther."

"Why, of course." Mother bolted from her chair as if she'd sat on her embroidery needle. "I was just about to check what Cook had planned for the evening meal. Would you care to join us?"

His eyes found Esther's once again, their intensity all but undoing her. "I should be happy to, should the evening turn out favorably."

Heat crawled up her neck and flamed in her cheeks. Could she do this?

She must. Despite her unsettled heart.

The moment her mother stepped from the room, Lawrence was at her side, her hand sandwiched between his. "Forgive my eagerness, but I simply must have an answer. Will you do me the honor of becoming my wife?"

For a brief moment, time seemed to stand still. Memories of Stew clogged Esther's senses, his gentle laugh, his ready smile, the wave of his hair, the blueness of his eyes. She'd known him such a short time, and yet he'd wedged a place in her heart that none other had. Was she being fair to herself? To Lawrence?

To Stew?

Lawrence pulled her closer, his hold on her hand tightening. "Esther, please. Don't make me wait any longer. Will you marry me?"

Flames of resistance engulfed her, and she pushed them aside, holding to her resolve. She wet trembling lips, trying to find her voice. "I…yes, Lawrence. I'll marry you."

He breathed an audible sigh, the tension on his face easing. A smug grin replaced his look of uncertainty as he raised her hand for a kiss. "You'll not regret the decision, my dear, I assure you."

Esther took in his handsome features, trying her best to convince herself he was right. They would have a good life together.

They would.

But to do so, she'd have to push thoughts of Stew and the life she'd hoped for to the far recesses of her heart and mind.

Something she would find a challenge to do

THE FIRST THING Stew noticed as the stagecoach neared Cincinnati were the hills. Sight of them made him homesick for Missouri. Except, nestled within these mounds lay a mass of buildings the likes of which he'd never seen. The winding banks of the Ohio River hedged it in to the south, the flowing water bustling with a steady stream of traffic. Never had he seen such an assortment of vessels—steamboats, fishing boats, rowboats—all of various shapes and sizes.

As the stage rounded a bend in the road, he lost sight of the river and much of the city. He wiped sweaty palms on his pant legs, watching the sun sink lower in the sky. A break in the back axle just outside of Richmond had put them hours further behind schedule. Now it was well toward evening. Would it be too late to track Esther down?

Though the final stretch of the journey had proven less troublesome, it had seemed the longest. Every mile an eternity. Now, with his destination within reach, to go another day without seeing Esther would be agonizing. He'd envisioned their reunion dozens of times. In his mind's eye, her response to his unexpected visit was always pleasant. In reality, he had no idea how she would react. The uncertainty of it gnawed at him.

He'd parted ways with the professor and the other passengers when he'd vacated the stage continuing along the Cumberland Road to board one bound for Cincinnati. A family of four now shared his compartment—a well-dressed couple, their prim daughter, and a rather rambunctious son. Stew felt a tug on his pant leg and peered down to see the young boy grinning up at him, his hands covered with dirt from the stagecoach floor. The boy's mother scooped him up, her expression apologetic as he let out a squeal. "I'm so sorry."

"Not a problem." Stew dismissed the incident with a grin. He had more tolerance for pent up youngsters than most. With eight younger siblings, he'd had to endure more than his fair share of being pestered. A sudden ache balled in his chest. Nearly a year had passed since he'd been home to see his family. Maybe instead of this foolhardy trip to Cincinnati he should have headed to Taylor Springs like he'd originally planned.

Forget he'd ever met Esther Stanton.

He stared out the window at the cluster of tall buildings flicking by, their long shadows periodically shading the coach interior. He swallowed, his heart pumping faster. Too late to back out now. They'd arrived.

As the stagecoach rolled to a stop outside the station, Stew reached for the latch. Eager to be on his feet, he stepped from the coach and glanced around the bustling street. Though he'd been on the outskirts of Chicago numerous times with cattle drives, not once had he ventured into the heart of the city. Now, hemmed in on all sides by buildings and people, he felt akin to a fish plucked from a clear-flowing stream and dropped in a crowded bucket.

Retrieving the duffel bag Chad had loaned him from the rear compartment, he slid a glance in both directions, wondering where to start. All the noise and hubbub was dizzying. He needed to move someplace less confining and figure out how to go about finding Esther. Her stepfather was in shipping. If he ventured toward the river, maybe he'd come across someone who could head him in the right direction.

Why hadn't he thought to ask Charlotte for a street name?

His stomach rumbled, reminding him he'd eaten little since breakfast. Ignoring his body's plea for food, he headed south, mindful of the deepening shadows settling over the street. He paused occasionally to ask if someone knew of Esther or the Leifers. With the shake of their heads, they hurried on. At last, he happened upon someone who'd heard of Leifer Shipping and pointed him to the western edge of the riverfront.

Quickening his pace, he dodged the onslaught of people in his path. He touched a hand to his pants pocket, the slight bulge assuring him the money for his and Esther's fare home was still safely tucked away. There it would stay until he had her answer.

Even if it meant going hungry.

The crowd and buildings began to thin as he neared the river. An amber glow in the western sky ensured nightfall would soon be upon him. Once the streets were darkened, it would be impossible to locate Esther. Would he do well to find somewhere to stay the night and start afresh in the morning? His pronounced limp further dampened his hopes.

A hotel in this place would likely rob him of every cent he had. Besides, he'd have to backtrack to the heart of the city to locate one. If he stayed on the outskirts, maybe he could find a cranny where he could bed down under the stars.

The sound of flesh meeting flesh pulled his focus to a darkened corner of the street up ahead. A loud moan, followed by angry, hushed voices, drew him closer. He squinted into the shadows, trying to decipher what was happening. At last, he made out the figures of two large men standing over a smaller fellow. One of the larger men drew his arm back and sank his fist in the smaller man's belly. Doubling over, the man let out another agonizing moan.

Passersby gave the three men a wide berth, crossing over to the opposite side of the street. Stew clenched his jaw. Whether it was wise to get involved or not, he couldn't stand idly by and see a man beaten. No matter the men's differences, the injured man was outnumbered. "Hey!" he called, venturing toward them.

At his shout, the larger men straightened and turned. Stew strode closer, heart pounding. With any luck, he'd scare the brutes off. But, instead of running, they stood their ground. With a sigh, he pressed forward, still unable to make out the men's shadowed faces. "You fellers have had your fun. Let the man be."

"By whose order?" one of the men jeered.

"Mine, I reckon."

The man who'd spoken crossed his arms over his chest. "And who might you be?"

His burly silhouette stood out against the twilight, giving Stew pause. If the men turned on him, he'd likely meet with the same fate as the other fella. Had he come all this way to be beaten to a pulp?

Set in his resolve, he jutted his chin, refusing to back down. Most ruffians were cowards at heart. "Someone who's willing to even the odds."

The man took a step forward only to have his companion pull him back. "Come on, Snoot. The boss don't want no trouble."

A long moment passed and then, ever so slowly, both men backed away, giving the injured man a final shove as they stole away into the night. The beaten man fell to his knees, steadying himself with his hand on the ground.

With a jagged breath, Stew hurried over and bent down next to him. The man's dark skin shed light on the reason for the ruckus. Stew would have expected such treatment in regards to a colored man back in his home state of Missouri where slavery was the rule. But here in Ohio, blacks were free.

Apparently, such freedom wasn't honored by all.

"You all right?"

The man gave a faint nod, blood trickling from a gash to the side of his face. Blood stained his shirt in more than one place. He glanced up at Stew, his left eye nearly swollen shut, his voice raspy. "Thanks, mis'er. The Good Lord was a smilin' on me when you happened by."

Stew couldn't deny that, but with the shape this fellow was in, it was amazing he could find something to rejoice about. "Just sorry I didn't get here sooner."

He helped the man to his feet, his short, stocky frame barely reaching Stew's shoulder. The injured man cringed and pitched forward, holding a hand to his side. Judging by his labored breathing and stooped posture, he likely had a broken rib or two. "We need to get you to a doctor."

Through shallow breaths, the man shook his head. "Just see me home. My Abigail will know what t' do."

Stew hesitated. Already the delay had cost him valuable time. If he helped the man further, he'd lose what little daylight he had left to get a lead on Esther. Yet, the man was in no condition to go it alone. With a soft sigh, he clasped the man's arm. "Which way?"

Chapter Twenty-Seven

"Such wonderful news. William and I couldn't be happier."

Mother's words fell flat on Esther's ears. She should feel the same, and yet her heart refused to rejoice. A marriage should be anchored in mutual faith and trust, neither of which described her relationship with Lawrence. Her bond with him was shallow at best. Even after a week of attempting to fill in the missing gaps of their relationship, she hardly seemed to know the real Lawrence. Thus far, they'd shared little of substance. His true self remained locked deep within.

And yet, in the Bible, Rebekah had left her home and family willingly to marry Isaac, whom she'd never met. Esther traced her finger along the decorative swirl in the ivory tablecloth. Perhaps she simply needed time to allow herself to love Lawrence.

And forget Stew.

She sensed eyes upon her and drew her hands from the table. Glancing to her left, she noted Lawrence's expectant stare, as if he'd made a comment and received no reply. Had he spoken? She straightened. "I'm sorry. Did you say something?"

His expression brightened. "Only that we are equally overjoyed."

Smoothing her napkin in her lap, she pasted on a smile, though she couldn't quite force herself to nod in agreement. William, too, seemed more bent on eating than celebrating.

Mother clapped her hands together, stealing his attention away from his food. "I have just the thing. William and I shall host a dance tomorrow night to announce your engagement."

Esther sat forward in her chair. "So soon?"

"Why not? The night is young. We can ready the invitations this evening and have them delivered early tomorrow."

Lawrence reached to clasp Esther's hand, the warmth of his touch only increasing her angst. "A splendid idea. And a timely one, since I'd like our wedding to take place within a fortnight."

Mother framed her face with her hands. "Oh, dear. That doesn't leave much time to prepare."

William wiped his lips and grinned. "Less time for all the fluff."

Tightness closed off Esther's words as she tried to wrap her mind around the thought. It was all happening so fast. She'd hoped for more time to console herself to the idea of marrying Lawrence. A couple of months as least. Everything in her ached to slow the pace, allow herself time to think and breath.

She cleared her throat, attempting to find her voice. "That *is* quite soon. I wonder, could we hold off a few weeks? To rush so would take the enjoyment out of it."

"I suppose a slight delay wouldn't matter." Lawrence drew in a breath then tapped his knuckles decidedly on the table. "We shall set the wedding four weeks from tomorrow. The last Saturday of July."

Heat flamed in Esther's cheeks as she ventured one more straight-forward request. "I was thinking more toward September to allow for my sister Charlotte to make arrangements to attend if possible." Though fairly certain Charlotte would have no means to come, the suggestion made for a logical motive.

Lawrence slid his hand away, his dark eyes probing hers, as

though attempting to pry into her deepest thoughts. "Is that the only reason you wish to further postpone our wedding?"

Lowering her gaze, she took a sip of water, fearful she'd pressed too hard. "That a-and the weather is much more tolerable in early autumn."

"That is true," chimed Mother. "The ceremony will be much more enjoyable when the weather is less stifling."

Hope stirred within Esther at her mother's words. Unnerved by Lawrence's silence, she ventured a glance in his direction. Though his expression still held an element of uncertainty, his piercing gaze eased considerably. At last, a weak smile settled onto his lips. "All right, my dear. If it pleases you, we'll make it the first Saturday in September."

Relief washed over Esther. "Thank you."

His eyebrow shot up as he leaned closer, his voice laced with caveat. "But no later."

She nodded, taken aback by the sternness in his tone. For a brief instant, she felt she didn't know him at all, his insistent manner causing even her mother's jaw to drop a bit. Esther had won her way, but clearly, Lawrence would not be put off again.

Come September, Lord help her, she'd become Mrs. Lawrence Del Ray.

"THAT'S OUR PLACE. OVER THERE."

Stew's gaze flicked to the small shanty up ahead and to the right, situated in the midst of dozens more like it. The rickety structures seemed out of place amid the grandeur of the surrounding city. As they started toward it, his injured companion's steps swaggered, and Stew tightened his hold on his arm. "Stay with me. You'll soon be home."

Dim light flickered from within the small plank house. As they neared, a woman's gentle hum filtered through the open window, her voice clear and sweet. A pained grin edged out the tension on the man's face. "That's my Abigail."

Stew gave an affirming nod and helped him onto the dilapidated porch. It seemed almost a shame to interrupt the woman's moment of contentment with the disturbing news of her husband's attack.

With a sigh, Stew lifted his fist and rapped on the door.

The humming stopped, and in its stead, a youngster called, "Who is it, Mama?"

Her hushed reply and delay in opening hinted of uncertainty.

The man strained to speak. "Open up, Abigail. It's me, Isaac."

A scurrying sounded within, followed by the latch lifting. The door swung open, and a dainty black woman in her mid to late twenties smiled out at them. Her grin faded as her eyes settled on Stew. She shifted her puzzled gaze to her husband and drew in a sharp breath. "Oh, Isaac. What happened?"

"Two fellas jumped me."

Widening the door, she pulled her curious child out of the way. The curly-haired boy hid behind his mother's skirt, peeking at Stew with widened eyes. The scent of ham and corn bread wafted from within. No doubt wife and son had been awaiting Isaac's return and most likely fretting over his delay.

Stew ducked through the short doorway and helped his injured companion to the cot at the far corner of the room. Isaac cringed as he eased down onto the thin pillow. Casting Stew a leery glance, Abigail brought a bowl of water and a dampened rag and sat on the edge of the mattress. Stew stepped back to give her room to work, wondering whether he should stay or go.

Tears welled in the woman's eyes as she dabbed at the wound near her husband's eye. "Who did this?"

He gazed up at her, his lips parched and dry. "I think ya knows who."

Her slight nod and turbulent eyes confirmed she did. Pursing her lips, she dipped the bloodied rag in the water and wrung it out.

Obviously, they intended to keep the knowledge to themselves. And why wouldn't they? Stew was a white man and a stranger, neither of which qualified him to earn their trust.

It shamed him to say that back in Missouri he'd have been chastised for associating with coloreds in such a manner, though he'd never cottoned to the idea of labeling one race as superior. As far as he was concerned, the Lord never intended one man to own another.

Abigail finished washing her husband's face and then set the rag and bowl aside. With careful hands, she unbuttoned his blood-stained shirt and gave his ribs a few gentle pokes. His face pinched, confirming Stew's suspicions. Leaning forward, she brushed dampened hair from Isaac's forehead. "You've two broken ribs. I'll git some cloth t' wrap ya."

She stood, her expression hardening as she gestured toward Stew. "Who's he?"

Isaac's cracked lips parted in a weak grin. "An angel sent from heaven whose name I don't yet know. But, I'd not have made it home without him."

In other circumstances, Stew might have scoffed at being referred to as an angel. But the gravity of his new friend's predicament kept him from it. Removing his hat, he cleared his throat and met the woman's probing gaze. "Name's Brant. Stewart Brant."

She offered a polite nod, her expression softening. "Isaac and Abigail Simmons. That there's our boy, Benjamin."

When Stew glanced his way, the youngster dashed behind the bed out of sight.

"Benji's a bit shy of...strangers." Mrs. Simmons shook her head, turning her attention back to her husband. "I declare, love, you've done got yourself in a fix."

Stew cleared his throat, eager to be on his way and yet not wishing to desert them in their time of need. "Is there anything I can do?"

Mrs. Simmons stared up at him, her eyes flickering between

confusion and gratitude. She pointed to the far side of the cabin. "There's an old sheet in the corner. Would ya mind fetchin' it an' tearin' it into wide strips? We'll use it for wrappings."

Stew crossed the room, returning with the stained linen. Taking it in both hands, he ripped off a section lengthwise and handed it to Mrs. Simmons. The young boy stood at the foot of the bed, his coffee-brown eyes following Stew's every move. He shot him a friendly smile, and something akin to fear flashed in the boy's rounded eyes as he hid behind the bed a second time.

A pang of remorse washed through Stew. Plainly these people had little regard for his kind. And for good reason, given the recent encounter. Had there been other incidents?

Stew helped ease Isaac back into a sitting position and then finished ripping the sheet into strips while Abigail wrapped the makeshift bandage snuggly around her husband's middle.

She eyed him as he handed her another strip. "You ain't from around here is ya, mis'er?"

"No, ma'am. I've just arrived from Illinois." He didn't dare mention he was from Missouri, a slave state, and undo any sense of trust he'd gained.

Isaac groaned under his wife's gentle tug on the sheet. "You travel light, Mis'er Brant. Er you here on business?"

Stew glanced at his lumpy duffel bag on the floor, wondering how he should answer. "More on a personal matter."

His response met with silence. Feeling suddenly awkward, he reached for his bag. "Well, uh, if there's nothin' more I can do, I'd best be on my way."

Isaac shook his head. "Not till you've been properly thanked for your trouble. My Abigail's a fine cook. The least we can do is feed ya."

In all the excitement, Stew had forgotten his hunger. The mention of food—coupled by the savory scent of pork—was enough to set his mouth to watering. "I should probably go."

Mrs. Simmons finished pinning the bandage in place then

looked Stew over. "You needs a good home-cooked meal. By the looks of ya, you've not had one for nigh on a week."

She had him pegged right. How could he refuse? "All right, then. Much obliged."

Abigail stood, hands on hips. "I's indebted to ya for lookin' after my Isaac, Mis'er Brant, so if'n you'll help him to the table, I'll set another plate."

With a nod, Stew tossed his duffel bag aside and helped Isaac to his feet, a twang of regret rippling through him. By the time they finished eating, it would be pitch dark out. Too late to find a decent place to lay his head or locate any sort of lead on Esther. Much as he'd liked to have avoided the delay, he couldn't help but feel a sense of satisfaction in having brought Isaac safely home to his family.

The Lord had placed him in the right place at just the right time. Was this what Jesus had meant in laying up treasure in heaven? The thought gave him hope that he'd not made the trip for nothing.

Chapter Twenty-Eight

STEW AWAKENED to the smell of bacon frying. He breathed in the welcome scent, and his stomach growled. Daylight filtered through his eyelids as he tried to collect his senses. It wasn't like him to sleep past sun up.

Something soft and warm skimmed the top of his hand. He opened his eyes, surprised to see young Benji kneeling over him, hand outstretched. The boy seemed more than a little intrigued with his light skin. Likely he'd not seen a white man up so close. It only stood to reason he'd be inquisitive.

Not wanting to frighten him, Stew lay still, smiling up at him.

"Let Mis'er Brant be, young'un."

At his mother's soft rebuke, the boy jerked his hand back and scrambled to his feet, but didn't run away. A step in the right direction.

"He's no bother." Stew stretched and sat up. For the first time in many days, he'd gone to sleep on a full stomach. Once Isaac and Abigail found out he had no place to lay his head, they'd insisted he stay the night. Reluctantly, he'd agreed and had been rewarded with the best night's rest he'd had in some time. A blanket on the floor beat bedding down in some dark cranny in a strange city.

"Forgive Benji. He's not acquainted with many white folks," Isaac called from his seat on the edge of the bed.

Stew's lips lifted in a grin. "He wouldn't be a boy if he wasn't curious."

Abigail forked the strips of bacon onto a plate and drained off the grease. Setting the skillet over hot coals, she scooped a spoonful of pancake batter into its center. "I knows you is in a hurry t' git goin', but you'll stay t' breakfast won't ya, Mis'er Brant?"

"Yes, ma'am." Stew gathered his bedroll and stood. Two home-cooked meals in a row was too tempting to pass up. "And call me Stew."

Flipping over the griddlecake, she returned a satisfied nod.

Stew slid a glance in Benji's direction, eager to gain his confidence. "What say we give your pa a hand over to the table?"

Benji gave a slow nod and inched toward the cot. Together, they helped Isaac to his feet and walked him over to a chair. He eased down onto it, still in obvious pain. Drainage seeped through the cloth bandage Abigail had fastened over his swollen eye. It would take weeks for his ribs to heal. Would he have the means to provide for his family?

Stew pulled a chair up to the table catty-cornered from Isaac's. "How'd you sleep?"

"I've had better nights," Isaac answered, rubbing a hand over his ribcage.

Stew cleared his throat, lacing his fingers together on the table. "It's none of my business, but will your injuries throw you out of work long?"

Isaac's chin tipped upward. "I'll lay low a few days, but no ruffians are gonna keep me from earning my wages. And come Sunday, you'll find me at the African Union Baptist Church. Same as always."

The man seemed determined not to let the incident get the better of him. Likely his solid frame was one of the reasons he was faring so well. A man of lesser strength would be laid up indefinitely. Perhaps his faith had a bearing on his recovery as well.

Scooping the last of the pancakes onto a chipped platter, Abigail carried the stack to the small, oak table. "Don't you worry none about my Isaac, Mis'er Stew. Lord willin' he'll snap back quicker than then a man half his age."

Benji slid onto the chair opposite Stew, his gaze still riveted on him. Clasping hands, the family bowed their heads to pray. Stew followed suit, warmed by the accepting way the couple had welcomed him into their home. The Simmons weren't wealthy as most would define it, but they were rich in what truly mattered.

Once the "amen" was said, Stew forked a couple of the golden griddlecakes onto his plate. "Have you folks lived in Cincinnati long?"

With effort, Isaac leaned forward in his chair and stabbed at a slab of bacon. "All our lives."

Stew gave a quick nod as he dabbed butter onto his cakes. It was hard to imagine experiencing only the city. He'd been here less than a day and already yearned to be free of the smoke-filled air and oppressive atmosphere. What he wouldn't give for the open prairie and clear blue sky. And yet, the couple's familiarity with Cincinnati may be helpful in locating Esther. They'd made no attempt to impose upon the reason for his visit. Perhaps opening up would do no harm. "Would you by chance know of Mr. or Mrs. William Leifer? I believe they own a shipping company here."

Isaac and Abigail shared a flustered look, an air of tension seeming to wedge its way into the conversation. "You acquainted with the Leifers?" Suspicion edged out the friendliness in his new friend's voice.

Stew shook his head then downed a bite of food with a swig of water. "Not really, but the person I've come to see lives with them."

Isaac arched a brow. "Does he now? Your friend is among the well-to-dos then, I take it."

Stew hesitated. He'd gone this far. Might as well spill everything. With a sigh, he plunged ahead. "William Leifer is her stepfather. Her mother married him after the loss of her first husband."

A slight grin replaced Isaac's disgruntled features. "So, it's a lady friend you've come all this way t' see."

Abigail passed him the pitcher of sorghum. "You set your sights mighty high, Mis'er Stew. The Leifers are among the wealthiest in the city."

Heat crept up Stew's neck and spilled into his cheeks. He cleared his throat, feeling as awkward as a school boy at his first dance. "She's not the sort to let wealth go to her head. Would you know where to find them?"

"I hear tell the Leifers make their home among the hills on the far side of town. Somewheres we here in the basin rarely see, 'cept from a distance."

Cynicism saturated Isaac's words. That a huge gap existed between men of color and the wealthy white class was undeniable. Stew could understand the couple's resentment. Even here, where blacks were free, they seemed to be looked upon as lesser beings. He only hoped his association with the Leifers hadn't damaged his newfound friends' opinion of him.

Abigail wiped her lips, her expression earnest. "I'd not figured you the upper-class sort, Mis'er Stew. You seem so down t' earth."

He snickered. "Believe me. I'm as out of place here as a river bass in an ocean. I just need to know if Esther feels the same."

"I surely hope she's of the same mindset. But if'n things don't work out, you is welcome here anytime." Sincerity lined Isaac's words.

Stew nodded. "Much obliged. I'll remember that."

Seemingly bored with all the talk, Benji cradled his chin in his palms. Stew dug his hand in his pocket and pulled out an Indian head cent piece. With his thumb and forefinger, he propelled the coin into a rapid spin. A smile lit Benji's face. He bent down until his eyes were level with the table, watching the coin zig-zag and twirl. When it came to a stop, Stew rolled it toward him. "Make it spin, and it's yours to keep."

The boy clasped the coin between his fingers, tongue lopping out the side of his mouth as he concentrated. After several failed attempts, he propelled it into a wobbly spin. His eyes were hopeful when he glanced at Stew.

Reaching across the table, he gave Benji's hair a tousle. "That's good enough for me."

The boy beamed up at him. "Thanks, Mis'er Brant."

"You bet."

"Looks like our boy's taken a shine to ya."

Warmth surged through Stew at Abigail's words. He tossed Benji a wink. "I'm right glad he has." With that, he pushed his plate aside and stood, turning to first Isaac, then Abigail. "Well, I should be going. I can't thank you both enough for your hospitality."

"It's us should do the thankin'. Without you, I'd likely not made it home at all." Isaac struggled to stand. "I'll see ya to the door."

Stew motioned for him to stay seated as he gathered his things. "No need for that."

Despite his protest, Isaac eased himself to his feet and moved to open the door. Taking a couple of coins from his pocket, Stew thrust out his hand. "It's not much, but it's a little somethin' in return for your kindness."

With a shake of his head, Isaac shoved his hand back. "Keep your money. The Lord's blessed us ten times over by bringin' ya to us. Besides, I've a full week's wages in my pocket."

Stew knit his brow. "Those men didn't take your money?"

"Weren't money they was after."

"What then?"

Isaac took a quick glance back at his family then ushered Stew outside, closing the door behind them. A shadow fell across his face as he spoke. "Not many white folks are as accepting as you.

Even here, where we is free, there's those who'd profit by takin' away our freedom. We've heard tell of people like us disappearin' without a trace." He nodded toward the river. "Across there, we ain't free no more. I 'spect they had that in mind for me and my family."

Stew swallowed, the magnitude of what his friend had been spared sinking in. "Don't you have some means of proving you're free?"

Isaac shook his head. "Yes, but that don't make no never mind. Once someone's taken, ain't nobody fool enough to go after 'em to prove they is free. The ones that done it would sooner tear up free papers as honor 'em."

Queasiness sliced through Stew. Had he not come along, no telling what might have happened. He'd seen how slaves were treated. Whether Esther obliged him by returning home or not, he was glad for the Simmons' sake he'd made the journey.

Isaac reached to clasp Stew's shoulder. "Now maybe you kin understand why we's so grateful. So keep your money, Mis'er Stew, and go find that lady friend of yours."

Stew hesitated then slipped the coins back in his pocket. "Thanks. I'll do that."

With a good-natured wink, Isaac pointed up the street. "Head north toward the hills and you'll find where you're headed."

Nodding, Stew tossed his knapsack over his shoulder and started off.

"Godspeed, my friend!" Isaac called after him, his voice still a bit labored.

Stew waved, pressing down his welling emotions. Doubtless Isaac would have endured anything to protect his loved ones. Stepping up his pace, Stew laced his way through the spattering of people, more eager than ever to find Esther.

And hopefully return her where she belonged.

Chapter Twenty-Nine

THE CITY HAD NO END. Nestled within the surrounding hills, the mass of tall buildings lay sprawled in all directions. Caged in on every side, Stew lost all sense of direction. Even the sun lay hidden behind a blanket of clouds. After nearly an hour meandering through the streets, he finally gave in and flagged down a buggy. "Could you take me to the William Leifer home?"

Upon mention of the name, the driver nodded, seeming to know exactly where he was headed. Stew sat back on the cushioned seat, his ankle stiff from the excess walking. He should have done this earlier. He only hoped the rate was reasonable.

No sooner had the driver propelled the buggy into motion than it slowed to a near standstill. With the street teeming with horse-drawn carriages and people, walking seemed almost faster. But at least he could rest his leg and stop aimlessly wandering the streets. His gaze drifted to the passersby with their fancy clothing and refined mannerisms. No two ways about it. He didn't belong here. A glance at his dusty boots, worn trousers, and wrinkled shirt convinced him he'd have done well to invest in a new set of clothes before greeting Esther.

If only he weren't so strapped for money.

Deep in the heart of the city, the air was stifling, smoke from the factories mingling with manure and humidity. Not until the buggy touched the foot of the hills could Stew draw a full breath. How did people live like this? If he could pry Esther from under her mother's thumb, it shouldn't be too hard to convince her to leave.

That is, if she cared for him the way Charlotte let on.

The click of the horses' hooves on the cobblestone slowed as the buggy rolled to a stop at the top of a rise. "The Leifer residence, sir."

At the coachman's announcement, Stew peered at the house to his left and whistled under his breath. He'd not expected anything so lavish. No wonder Isaac and Abigail had looked at him strangely. The place was nothing short of a mansion. Convincing Esther to leave such a luxurious place might take some doing after all.

He rubbed a hand over his chin, envisioning his broken-down cabin back home—a cabin he couldn't even call his own. Could he really ask her to give up all this finery and return with him to little more than nothing?

Lord help him, he had to try.

As he stepped from the carriage, voices sounded at the front of the house. He strained to see past the cluster of trees dotting the yard. His heart sank at sight of Esther strolling arm in arm with a dark-haired man. So that was Lawrence Del Ray. Evidently, they were still seeing each other. And by the looks of him, Stew didn't stand a chance.

Retreating into the coach, he watched from behind the curtained window, thankful the driver had stopped some distance from where they were walking.

Esther glanced his direction, and he drew deeper into the coach. He needed to face her alone, not when she was in the company of the man he hoped to woo her away from.

"Sir?" The coachman called from atop the driver seat.

Fearful of being seen or heard, Stew made no reply. He'd pay the man for his time, if he would only be patient.

When he ventured a look again, Lawrence was helping Esther into the carriage several yards in front of him. She glanced back, and he ducked away. Had she recognized him? He couldn't risk it.

Drawing the shade, he moved to the far side of the rig and motioned the coachman to drive on. He slumped back on the seat, certain he'd completely confused the driver. The fare hadn't been a total waste. At least now he knew where Esther lived. He'd lay low and try again later.

Hopefully this evening, he'd find her alone.

ESTHER EASED down onto the carriage seat a bit dazed. Was her mind playing tricks on her? She'd barely caught a glimpse of the man in the carriage parked along the street, and yet what she had seen reminded her of Stew. It took all her resolve not to crane her neck for another look. But she didn't dare. Not with Lawrence eyeing her every move as though guessing her interest.

He cast a dubious glance behind then climbed inside the carriage. "Who's that?"

"I'm certain I don't know. Perhaps it's one of William's associates."

Lawrence's brow creased. "I know all of his associates. He's not one of them."

Esther ventured a look back, as eager as Lawrence to learn the rig's occupant. She had half a mind to volunteer to investigate, but thought better of it. If the unknown man was one of her stepfather's business associates, she would appear foolish. And as there was little to no chance it could be Stew, she was better off staying put.

He smoothed his mustache. "Why would someone hire a rig here and refuse to leave it?"

Esther wavered under his scrutinizing gaze, uncertain if it held an air of protectiveness or suspicion. "If it concerns you, why not go and see who it is?" The moment she'd spoken the words, she regretted it. If by some miracle Stew was in the carriage, how would he explain himself?

Lawrence tapped his foot on the floorboard then reached for the door latch. "I believe I will."

Before he could leave, the carriage behind swept by them, shade drawn. Esther stared after it, her curiosity piqued. She had to admit, the incident seemed peculiar. Though her stepfather's estate was grand to look at, rarely did passersby pause to gawk. And why the closed shade, as if the passenger didn't wish to be seen?

Edging back onto the seat, Lawrence seemed to shrug off the incident as if he'd just shooed away an annoying fly. "Well, perhaps now we can commence with our shopping for tonight's celebration." He rapped twice on the carriage door, his signal to the coachman they were set to leave.

As the carriage lurched forward, Esther cast a wary glance at her companion. How he'd convinced Mother to remain at home and let him accompany her on the outing was nothing short of masterful. By appealing to her mother's need to oversee the preparations at home, he'd easily stepped in to take her place alongside Esther.

It wasn't the first time Lawrence had swayed Mother or William. He seemed to have a knack for manipulating situations in his favor. She had yet to understand how he could discuss business all hours of the night with William and yet miss work at his slightest whim any given day of the week. Would he keep such odd hours once they married, or attempt to align his schedule to suit hers?

Truth be told, she didn't know how he spent his days. He made little mention of his work duties. Or his hobbies for that matter. She'd never known anyone so skilled at concealing his true self. It frightened her to know so little about the man she'd agreed to marry. Was there a reason he refused to share on a more personal level?

Stew had been so transparent, so easy to know. In a few short weeks, she'd come to understand him better than she had Lawrence in more than a year. Her heart ached to experience that same closeness with her future husband. But he seemed too preoccupied with frivolous things to concentrate on deepening their relationship.

What bothered her most was his shallow view of faith, as if attending church was all that mattered. Each time she broached the topic, he dismissed her concerns with a flippant remark. More than once she'd requested they pray together only to have him give some ready excuse why she should pray and he listen. The one time he had complied, his conversation with the Lord had been awkward and aloof. Could she truly become one with a man who didn't share her deep convictions?

Though sadly neglected, even Stew had shown some semblance of true faith.

As they turned onto Elm Street, Esther found herself inadvertently searching for the mysterious buggy, part of her wishing Stew had come to whisk her home. Who was she kidding? More than likely, it had been a newcomer to town out to see the sights or an acquaintance of her stepfather's who'd decided he was too pressed for time to stop in.

Her hopes plummeted as she scanned the busy street. The carriage had been swallowed up by the city. Much like the life she'd given up.

STEW TUGGED AT HIS SLEEVES, feeling awkward as he walked the streets of Cincinnati in his new store-bought clothing. It had taken much of the day to decide how better to spend his money. New clothes or a night in a hotel. He hadn't funds for both. The clothes had finally won out, in hopes of gaining a more positive impression.

Maneuvering his way along the bustling street, he glanced at the street sign to ensure he'd not wandered off course. He'd made a point not to travel too far from the Leifer mansion so as not to lose his way. The buggy ride had cost more than he'd anticipated. Walking seemed the better option this evening.

What he wouldn't give to have Scout here. He'd taken for granted the luxury of a horse to cart him around whenever he needed a free ride. He missed his faithful friend. The only thing that would make the separation worthwhile would be if Esther could be persuaded to make the trip back. He had a feeling she'd be willing, if only she could find the gumption to stand up to her mother.

As the sun dipped lower in the west, lamplighters lit the string of lamps dotting the street, spreading light through the darkening city. Buildings grew sparser as he neared the hilly, residential section of town. With each difficult, upward step, the stress on his leg deepened. Would it be worth it?

As he topped the rise, the impressive mansion came into view, and his heartbeat quickened. He'd intentionally waited until after mealtime in hopes of catching Esther at leisure to meet with him. As he rounded the bend that led to the house, he slowed his pace, taken aback by the slew of buggies parked around it. So much for meeting with Esther alone. It looked as if half the city had decided to drop in.

He eased to a stop, debating on whether to continue or leave. With a frustrated sigh, he plunged his hands in his pockets. He was tired of putting it off. By the looks of things, it was some sort of party or gathering. If so, maybe he could blend in unnoticed and steal Esther away long enough to speak his mind.

With a steadying breath, he continued on, doing his best to mask his limp. The closer he came to the lit-up mansion, the more he had to fight turning back. With weighted steps, he made his way to the door, the scent of roses filling the night air. He wiped sweaty palms on his trousers then lifted his fist to the door.

A lanky servant answered his knock, his puzzled gaze taking in Stew from head to toe. "May I help you, sir?"

Lively music poured from within. Definitely a celebration of some sort. Straightening, Stew clasped his hands together behind his back. "Would Esther Stanton be in?"

The man looked at Stew as if he'd said the mansion was on fire. "Why, yes, of course."

"May I see her?"

The servant's chin tipped upward. "Have you an invitation?"

"Can't say I do."

The doorman's brow creased. "Your name, sir?"

"Stewart Brant." He ventured a glance deeper inside the extravagant home. Not even in his dreams had he envisioned something half so grand.

"One moment, please." Turning, the distinguished looking servant stepped away from the door, his eyes scanning the dozens of people milling about.

Moments ticked by, with Stew garnering stares from those within. He wasn't fooling anyone. Even in his new clothes, he was still pegged an outsider. At last, the servant returned, along with a wide-eyed Mrs. Leifer. She stepped into the doorway, casting a leery glance over her shoulder. "Whatever are you doing here, Mr. Brant?"

Stew's stomach dropped at the less than courteous greeting. "I've come to see Esther."

Mrs. Leifer's upper lip stiffened. "Then I'm afraid you've come all this way for nothing, Esther is not available. Nor will she be. Good evening, Mr. Brant."

Stew caught the door as she attempted to close it. "I aim to see her."

Lowering her voice, Mrs. Leifer's eyes narrowed. "Go back to where you came from, Mr. Brant, and forget about Esther. She's not for you." With that she slammed the door shut.

Stew ground his teeth. That went well. If Esther's mother had been against him before, now she was downright hostile. It seemed he had two choices—bust his way in and create a scene or find another way inside. Obviously, breaking down the door would get him nowhere. There must be some other way to get to Esther.

More guests arrived, and he moved to let them pass. Attempting to sneak in would never work. Now that he'd made himself known, he'd be recognized in a heartbeat. Maybe there was a back way in where he could hide in some dark corner until he caught Esther's eye.

With a glance around to ensure he wasn't being watched, Stew inched his way to the darkest side of the mansion. The music grew louder as he came to a room with thin, long windows. Keeping to the shadows, he ventured a peek inside. The room was filled with ladies in colorful, hooped dresses and men in tailored suit jackets and pants. Couples swirled to the three-tone beat of a lively waltz, their expressions brimming with merriment.

Stew perused the ballroom for Esther, coming up short. Had she tired of dancing and gone somewhere else? The music died away, and the winded dancers retreated to chairs along the sidelines. All but one couple who made their way to the room's center. Stew's eyes bulged when he recognized Esther, looking more beautiful than he'd ever seen her. Her golden hair draped in ringlets around her oval face. Her jade, off-shoulder, hooped dress accented the green in her hazel eyes. How his heart ached to take her in his arms. With her the center of attention, would he even have the chance to speak with her?

Her companion raised a silencing hand to the group of onlookers. Stew pulled his eyes from Esther for a closer look at the man he'd seen with her earlier that day, Mr. Lawrence Del Ray. He was everything Stew was not—suave, sophisticated, handsome.

Bracing himself against the side of the house, Stew listened through the open window.

"We're so pleased you were all able to come on such short notice to share in this joyous occasion." With a smug grin, he raised Esther's hand to his lips then surveyed her at arm's length like a trainer showing off his prized horse. "I'm thrilled to announce this lovely lady has agreed to become my wife."

Stew's stomach clenched as the room erupted into unbridled applause. In one brief moment, his purpose in coming had been snatched away, taking his heart with it. His gaze fled to Esther's face. Her smile seemed stiff, guarded. Was she less enthused by the announcement than her fiancé? If he thought for a moment she was unhappy, he'd not hesitate to interfere.

All at once, she glanced his way and lost her smile completely, her face blanching white. He dodged out of sight, heart pounding. Had she seen him? Should he make himself known or would it be best to leave well enough alone?

He hesitated, indecision eating at him. At last, he scuffed his boot on the ground and pushed away from the house. She'd obviously made her choice. To interfere would only stir up trouble. Starting with her mother. The last thing he wanted was to cause Esther grief. She'd come to resent him for it.

Sinking his hands in his pockets, he started down the hill to the street below. He'd come too late. His only choice now was to let her go.

This time for good.

Chapter Thirty

THE ROOM SWAYED, and a steadying hand clasped Esther's arm.

"What is it, my dear? You look positively squeamish," Lawrence's voice sounded in her ear.

"I…" She must be going mad. Visions of Stew twice in one day? Was she plagued with reservations about marrying Lawrence or was the Lord trying to tell her something? It couldn't truly be Stew. He would never travel all this way with his leg in such condition.

Would he?

All eyes were upon her. She had to find some sort of excuse. To voice the truth behind her odd reaction was unthinkable. Lawrence must never know.

An inspiration pierced her befuddled mind, one that would not only offer explanation, but provide a ready excuse to look around. She fanned her face with her hand. "I fear the heat has gotten to me. Perhaps a few moments of fresh air would do me good."

Nodding, Lawrence tugged on her arm. "I'll go with you."

"No!" She pulled from his grasp, attempting to calm the nervousness in her voice. "There's no need for both of us to abandon our guests. Really, I'm fine."

He arched a brow. "You're certain?"

"Quite." With that, she strolled toward the door.

The night air caressed her cheeks, beckoning her out into the yard. She smiled and nodded to a young couple in her path whose names she didn't know—like so many of Lawrence's acquaintances. Passing them by, she hiked her skirt and rounded the corner of the mansion. Her pulse quickened as she neared the windows of the ballroom.

The deepening shades of twilight mingled with light from the windows, creating shadowy crevices along the outer wall. Esther inched closer, straining to see, not knowing what to hope for. If she found nothing, her heart was certain to be disappointed. But if by some miracle Stew had come, it would only complicate her already trying circumstances.

She'd said no to him once. She wasn't certain she'd have the strength to do so again.

The rustle of grass from behind stilled her movements.

"Esther? What are you doing out here? Lawrence said you'd had a spell of some sort."

Esther tensed at her mother's words. She pivoted, her heart pulsing in her ears. With a final glance around, she stepped toward her mother. "It's nothing. I simply got overheated and needed some air."

"So you go traipsing off alone in the dark? What is it you're looking for?"

Esther bit her lip, wishing for the freedom to confide in her mother. But telling the full truth would only upset her. "I thought I saw someone."

"Oh?" Her mother craned her neck for a look, the tone in her voice sated with unease. "Well, if there is someone, you have no business out here alone. You've had your reprieve. It's time you return to your guests and fiancé." Taking hold of Esther's arm, she tugged her toward the front of the house.

Esther allowed herself to be dragged along, wishing she'd had more time to look around. She cast a long glance down toward the street speckled with the glow of gaslight. Traffic had slowed to a trickle. Only a few pedestrians peppered the street. None of them resembling Stew.

Fragments of color lined the western sky where the sun had kissed the horizon. The sight made her homesick for the prairie. If Stew was out there somewhere, he'd sacrificed greatly to come. Why would he hide? Had he been frightened by all the people or, worse yet, witnessed Lawrence announcing their engagement?

She followed Mother to the door, pausing before going inside. It might all be wishful thinking, but if Stew had found her once, she could only hope and pray he'd find her again.

STEW LOOPED his hands together behind his head, staring up at the starry sky. After walking from one end of the city to another, he was bushed. He'd needed the time to mull things over. Here less than two days and already he had his answer. He'd go home empty-handed. Without so much as a spoken word passing between them, he'd found out the lady who'd stolen his heart would soon belong to another. He must've been daft to think she'd prefer a lame, penniless cowboy like him to the likes of Lawrence Del Ray.

He blew out a long breath. So much for all his prayers and church going. Maybe God really did favor those who did and said all the right things. People of substance, like Esther and her well-to-do fiancé. Trying to fake his way into the Lord's good graces had only brought him misery.

He stretched his legs out on the crate he'd chosen for a bed and listened to the sound of waves splashing against the moored cargo ships. Well, as of tonight, he was done trying. He'd head home just as soon as he could purchase a ticket on the stage. He'd wasted enough time and money on a foolish notion. The sooner he was back to work at the Circle J, the sooner he could move on with his life.

The only drawback was, every time he saw Charlotte, he'd be reminded of Esther. Maybe he'd do well to rethink working for Chad altogether. Go home to Missouri and back to working the cattle drive for Pete Callaway. What he'd hoped would be a step in the right direction had instead added to his already wounded heart.

Men's muffled voices sounded from atop the ship closest to him. He edged farther into the shadows, fearful of being ousted from his sleeping spot. The men's boot steps drew closer, finally coming to a stop at the steamboat's bow. The sound of a match striking wood, followed by a flash of light, alerted him to where they stood. Though he could only see them from the waist down, they carried the look and sound of deckhands. They kept their voices low as if not wanting to be heard.

Stew closed his eyes, attempting to drown out their words. Another night, he might have taken interest in the private conversation, but tonight sleep was all he wanted. But the more he tried to ignore the hushed tones, the more their words seeped into his head like unwanted criticism.

"How soon can we ship out?" one of the men whispered.

A terse, deeper voice responded. "Not till we've enough to please the boss."

"Surely he's not so greedy that lacking one or two matters. Why can't we shove off with the lot we have? I'm tired of the stench and all their whinin'."

Stew knit his brow. What sort of cargo were they talking about?

"You know the boss. He won't let us leave till his quota is met," the deeper voiced man replied.

"'Twasn't our fault that feller came along and spoiled things."

Stew tensed, doing his best to get a better look at the fellows without being seen. This was starting to sound disturbingly familiar. Had he unwittingly stumbled across the men who'd beaten Isaac? He cocked his ear to better listen.

"Just the same, the boss wants another to make up for the one we lost."

"Then let's go."

"Not yet. We wait till there's less movement about this time."

As the conversation ended, Stew sank back on the crate, listening to the clip of boots trail along the deck. Isaac and Abigail's troubled faces played over in his mind. They'd alluded to the fact that there were those who'd stop at nothing to take their freedom from them. Was that what this was all about? Were these men transporting free blacks downriver and selling them as slaves? The Ohio River stood as a natural barrier between the slave states of Kentucky and Virginia and the free sod of Ohio.

Who was behind all this? Who was the boss they referred to? He smothered a yawn, fighting fatigue.

Tired as he was, he knew he needed to stay awake to find out.

Chapter Thirty-One

STEW AWOKE TO THE "BONG" of church bells. Instead of stars, daylight streamed overhead. He sat up, eyes wide. When had he fallen asleep? He cut a glance to the riverbank where the boat had been moored, and his heart sank.

Gone.

Tucking his duffel bag in a crevice, he clutched his hat and swung his legs off the crate which now seemed much too hard. Here, he'd stayed awake half the night waiting to catch the deckhands sneaking off and wound up falling asleep before they'd shown themselves. Now he'd never know what they'd been up to. If there were blacks being stolen away and toted downriver, any proof was long gone.

What time was it anyway? Judging by the position of the sun, it must be nigh onto nine o'clock. He must have truly been exhausted. Thoughts of Isaac and Abigail drummed in his head. Those men had tried once to overpower Isaac. Was there a chance they would seek him out again?

As much as Stew wanted to leave this place and all thoughts of Esther behind, he couldn't rest until he was sure his friends were safe. Yet, he'd never find them in this maze of buildings. All he remembered was that they lived somewhere on the southwest side, in what Isaac had referred to as the Fourth Ward. The makeshift plank houses had all looked the same. There was no sense wandering the streets trying to find them.

More church bells chimed from throughout the city. He'd forgotten it was Sunday. Taking time to attend services wasn't part of his plan either, especially since the Lord had refused him the one request he'd made. But hadn't Isaac mentioned he could be found at a certain church on any given Sunday? But which church? And would he be up to attending, given his injuries?

Stew raked a hand through his hair, trying his best to remember. It was a Baptist church. United? Unified? Union. That was it. Union Baptist Church. Hopping to his feet, he snatched his duffel bag and headed up the embankment. Without an address, it might be difficult to locate. But these hired buggy drivers seemed to know their way around. If he could flag one down, more than likely, the fellow would have him there in no time.

Topping the rise, he cast a quick glance around. He would never grow accustomed to the drab, closed-in feel of the city, with its tall buildings towering over both sides of the street. Traffic had thinned compared to last night. Only a spattering of people strolled along the street. Most of the crowd—dressed in their finest—were making their way toward the church building on the north end. Stew smoothed his new shirt sleeves, now more than a little wrinkled after having been slept in.

They'd have to do.

The absence of carriages led him to the notion he was in for another long walk. With a sigh, he sauntered on, keeping an eye out for someone to point him in the right direction. As the church bells died away, a hush fell over the street. By the time he'd made it halfway to the church, which by now he could distinguish was Presbyterian, only a few stragglers remained.

He hurried to catch up with a man in front of him. "Excuse me, sir. Could you give me directions?"

The elderly gentleman paused and turned, an air of pride telling in his upturned chin. "I certainly hope so. I've lived here my entire life. Where is it you wish to go?"

Stew took a moment to catch his breath. "The Union Baptist Church."

The man's face puckered as if he'd bitten a sour apple. "The African Union Baptist Church?"

It hadn't dawned on Stew that the church might be merely for colored folk. Even in a free state, there appeared to be a wall of separation between the races. "Yes, sir. Could you tell me where I could find it?"

A scowl replaced the man's stunned expression. For a long moment, he stared at Stew then pointed westward. "Three blocks down and to your right. Corner of Western Row and Second. Though I've no idea why a church of that nature would interest you."

Ignoring the comment, Stew tipped his hat. "Much obliged."

With renewed vigor, he headed west until he hit Western Row, then veered left. Before long, he spied the mid-sized stone structure, one much less extravagant than the lush church building he'd left behind. No clanging bell or clock tower decorated this church, nor a tall steeple or stained-glass window. Only a crude sign at its front identifying it as Union Baptist Church and joyous voices pouring from within.

He made his way to the door, hoping his late arrival wouldn't draw much attention. Right now, all he cared about was making sure those no-good deckhands hadn't finished what they'd started. Lifting the latch, he eased the door open. The blend of lively voices rang louder as he stepped inside the packed building. More than a hundred strong, the congregation swayed on their feet to the soulful melody, many with hands uplifted.

Any hopes Stew had had of slipping in unnoticed dissolved as those standing in the back stopped singing and parted around him like the Red Sea, eyes wide as silver dollars. Removing his hat, he smiled and nodded, hoping to put them at ease. Instead they clung to each other, their expressions fluctuating between fear and disdain.

As the hymn came to a close, the congregation took their seats, several whispering to each other and pointing in his direction. Stew slipped down onto the edge of a log bench in the back that had been abandoned. He should have guessed his presence would cause a ruckus, especially given the knowledge he now had about the threat these people lived in daily. No wonder they were leery.

He panned the crowd for Isaac and Abigail, but in the sea of dark-skinned people, most of which had their backs to him, he came up short. Though none were dressed in what Stew would deem fancy attire, he noted a few wore the garb of slaves, like those back in Missouri. These especially watched him with frightened eyes, attempting to make themselves invisible amid the crowd.

Stew made a point not to stare, wondering if this congregation had its own secret abolitionist work going on. After all, it would be relatively simple to cross the river to freedom and find refuge in this black community. Albeit more difficult not to have them eventually found out. If only he could assure them he was no threat.

The song leader strode to his spot on the front bench and a distinguished looking man in his forties took his place at the crude pulpit, Bible in hand. Though the ripple of whispers and backward glances in Stew's direction continued to expand, the speaker seemed unaware of his presence. He opened his Bible, smoothing its pages with his palms. "Our Lord Jesus in His sermon on the mount tells us we are to love our enemies and pray for those who persecute us. In light of what is taking place in our nation, this is a difficult thing to ask. But if Jesus, who was hung on a cross in our stead, could forgive those who spilt His precious blood, so must we forgive those who seek to batter us and steal our very freedom. It's with a heavy heart I come to you today with news that others in our midst have been carried off, spirited away like pieces of chaff blown by the wind."

Soft moans erupted throughout the room, drawing even more eyes toward Stew. He shifted in his seat, hoping they hadn't mistaken him for an enemy. Someone from a center pew stood and approached the pastor. The building quieted as he whispered in his ear. The pastor's gaze slipped in Stew's direction, and the man who'd alerted him took his seat. As he did, Stew caught a glimpse of the man seated next to him. From the back, the man resembled Isaac, but with face downcast, shoulders drooped.

The man turned his head slightly to the left, revitalizing Stew. It was Isaac. The bandage over his eye confirmed it.

The pastor cleared his throat, clasping his hands on the front of his suit jacket as he directed his words at Stew. "May we help you with something, sir?"

Every head veered in his direction. Stew stood, hat in hand. "I, uh, I'm sorry to intrude. The name's Stewart Brant. Isaac and Abigail Simmons paid me a kindness. I merely wished to check on them before I left town."

Isaac rose to his feet and turned to face him, eyes wide. "Is that you, Mis'er Stew? The Lord be praised." A whimper expelled from his throat as he scooted past the others on his bench, fighting his way to the aisle. Oblivious to the stunned stares of those around him, Isaac held an arm to his ribcage and stumbled his way to Stew, a tortured expression lining his brow. Clasping Stew by the arm, he peered up at him, tears streaming down his dark cheeks. "You've gotta help me, Mis'er Stew. Please!"

"What is it? What's wrong?"

Isaac's fingertips pressed into Stew's forearm as he gave full vent to his sobs. Through jagged breaths, he poured out the misery of his soul. "They took...my...Abigail...and my Benji!"

"WHAT HAPPENED?" Stew took a seat across the table from Isaac. The poor fellow had been too distraught on the walk home for Stew to venture the question. Even now, the small house seemed to cry out in empty silence.

Isaac stared at him through bloodshot eyes. "They came in the night, those same two ruffians who busted me up. Must've followed us home the night you brought me, but held off 'cause you was here." His shoulders sagged. "When they saw I was injured, they shoved me aside and took off with Abigail and Benji."

The words chiseled their way to Stew's very core, leaving him hollow, angry. He'd feared for Isaac, never once anticipating Abigail and Benji would go missing. Young Benji must be so frightened. Any trust Stew had earned by now had surely melted into fear in the youngster's heart.

Tears fell afresh as Isaac rubbed a hand over his ribcage. "I tried t' stop 'em, but they knocked me on the head. When I came to, it was daybreak. I didn't know what t' do, so I came here." A spark of hope flickered in his eyes. "Then the Lord brought ya to me. You'll help get 'em back, won't ya, Mis'er Stew?"

A thousand thoughts pummeled Stew. How he longed to flee this place, flee the memory of Esther on another man's arm. By now he'd hoped to be on his way back to collect Scout and leave this unpleasant venture behind.

But he couldn't. The broken man before him needed his help. In this instance, a white man could accomplish what a colored man couldn't. If Isaac attempted to go after his family, more than likely he'd not get far without losing his own freedom—especially given the shape he was in. But how could anyone go about finding them? The boat had sailed. There were dozens of ports along the Ohio where they could have been dropped. The odds of finding them seemed staggering.

He blew out a long breath. "I'll do all I can."

The heaviness in Isaac's expression lifted. "Thank you, Mis'er

Stew. The Lord was surely shinin' on us when He brought you along."

"Save your thanks. I haven't found 'em yet." The truth was, he didn't know where to even start. He raked a hand through his hair. "You mentioned there were papers proving your freedom. Do you have them?"

"Yes'r. I'll fetch 'em."

Stew locked his fingers together on the table with a sigh. How did one go about retrieving colored people who'd been uprooted from their home and taken across river? It wasn't like he could go about asking their whereabouts. He'd be laughed at. Or even scorned. He'd have to be a bit devious about seeking information. Pretend he was someone he wasn't.

Isaac returned with a small wooden box. He set it on the table and lifted its lid. Taking out two folded sheets of paper, he handed them to Stew, his expression somber. "These here is all the means we have t' claim freedom. If'n they's lost, our hope of freedom is too."

Stew took the papers from him, conscious that Isaac was entrusting him with his family's very livelihood. The thought proved a bit daunting. "I'll do my utmost to keep them safe."

Isaac retrieved a small leather pouch from inside the box. He pursed his lips as he handed it to Stew. "You'll be needin' money t' buy 'em back. It won't be enough, but this is all we has."

With a sober nod, Stew took the pouch from him and stuffed it in his shirt pocket.

Isaac slumped back in his chair, rubbing a hand over his anguished face. "There's one more thing you need to know." In the long pause, his eyes locked onto Stew's. "Those men work for Leifer Shipping."

Stew's gut clenched. "You sure?"

His friend leaned forward, his gaze intense. "I'm sure."

The jolting news shed new light on the situation. As owner, did Esther's stepfather have knowledge of the sinister operation? Was he who the men referred to as the Boss? The appalling thought rendered him nauseous. Knowing Stew's association with the Leifer family, it was a wonder Isaac trusted him at all.

Stew wet his lips, sinking the papers deep in his pocket. "All right, then. First thing tomorrow morning, I'll see about getting better acquainted with the crew of Leifer Shipping."

Another thought pierced Stew's heart. Something else needed done as well.

Something he'd just as soon forget.

Chapter Thirty-Two

ESTHER DRUMMED her fingers on the chair arm, as restless as a kitten. Two days had passed since she'd seen Stew. Or thought she had. Surely if he were here, he'd have made himself known by now. Either he'd witnessed her engagement to Lawrence and decided to bow out or she'd imagined him.

She stood and crossed to the sitting room window. What good would seeing him again do anyway? She was stuck here, destined to marry a man she didn't love and only half respected.

"What is it, dear? What's troubling you? The past couple of days you've been in a world of your own." Concern edged out the displeasure in her mother's voice.

Esther peered over her shoulder then returned her gaze to the lawn. "I don't know. My nerves have gotten the better of me, I suppose."

Her mother chuckled. "Well then, perhaps you shouldn't have persuaded Lawrence to postpone the wedding. You'd have less time to fret over it."

Esther pursed her lips. It wasn't the wedding that had her on edge, but the marriage. No matter how long or short the engagement, the end result would be the same. Stew had spoiled her for anyone else. But to voice so to Mother would only agitate the already volatile circumstances.

A knock on the front door pulled her attention from the window. She'd grown accustomed to Lawrence making unannounced visits at any hour of the day. Drawing a long breath, she turned to greet him, but instead of his spry boot steps, James' casual footfall sounded in the hall. He paused just inside the room and turned toward her. "Pardon me, Miss, but a telegram just arrived for you."

She skittered toward him, her first thought a joyous one. Surely it must bring news of Charlotte and her dear ones. But why a telegram rather than a letter? And why was it directed to her alone? Her feet slowed, memories of the telegram that brought news of her Pa's untimely death clouding her joy. Had something happened? She reached for it, clasping it between her fingertips like it had been pulled from hot embers.

"Who's it from?"

Esther flipped it over side to side, Mother's words echoing in her ears. "I'm not sure." She broke the seal with her fingernail and unfolded the thin piece of paper. Blood drained from her face as she read the short, stunning message.

MEET ME BEHIND YOUR HOUSE TONIGHT AT
MIDNIGHT
STEW

She sucked in a breath, her hands atremble. Then she'd been right. Stew was here.

Mother huffed an impatient breath. "Well, what does it say?"

Esther stuffed the telegram in her pocket, struggling to regain her composure. "I-It's merely an invitation from a friend."

Morning mist hung in the air as Stew strolled along the Ohio riverbank. Having traded his new set of clothes for his older ones, he walked with his knapsack draped over his shoulder, eyeing the cluster of men gathered beside the steamboat owned by Leifer Shipping. One of the men, older than the rest, barked orders to the others. Confident the man was in charge, Stew moved closer, waiting until the others had scattered before he approached. "Mornin'."

The bearded man glanced his way, but gave no reply as he finished securing the boat to the dock.

Stew widened his stance, doing his best to look the part of a rough and ready deckhand. "Would ya be in need of another worker?"

The man paused, looking him over from head to toe. "I might. If he be the right sort." He squinted up at him against the bright sunlight. "Ever worked a cargo ship before?"

"I've seen my share of water." It wasn't a lie. Stew had seen many a boat travel along the Missouri and Mississippi Rivers. He'd just never been on one. He hated to mislead, but he needed to get on board and find out what was going on. Being welcomed aboard would arouse less suspicion than sneaking aboard, and perhaps gain him some inside knowledge.

The man rubbed a hand over his scraggly beard. "I've not seen you around before. You new to town?"

"Yes'r. I hale from Taylor Springs, Missouri. Just came in on the stage a couple days ago." If this man was in cahoots with the others, Stew's slave state background would be a plus.

The older man gave a slow nod. "What's your name, son?"

"Stewart Brant." He stretched out his palm. "Stew to my friends."

With a nod, the man reached to clasp his hand, the distrust in his eyes easing. "Charlie Dunn." Releasing his hold, he crossed his arms over his chest. "My boss usually does the hiring, but you look able enough, so I 'spect it'll be all right. When can you start?"

"Any time you say." Stew worked to keep his expression unchanged. How he longed to ask who his boss was, but too many questions might arouse suspicions.

"Good." He pointed to a short balding fellow atop the bow. "Mick there can show ya where t' stow your gear and get ya set up for payroll. Then you can come help load freight."

Stew gave a curt nod. "I'll get right to it."

As he started up the ramp, he couldn't help but revel at how easy it had been to weasel his way onto the boat. Earning some pay in the process wouldn't hurt either. If only it would bode so well with him to find out what he needed to locate Abigail and Benji.

By day's end, he'd accomplished little more than gaining some tired muscles and meeting some of the crew. The few questions he'd ventured had gotten him nowhere. It was hard to keep his emotions in check. Every hour that ticked by was precious time wasted. He could only pray if he did find them, it wouldn't be too late.

Not willing to risk being found out, he'd decided it best not to return to Isaac's for the night. Instead he'd grab a bite to eat and try to get a couple hours of shuteye before making the dreaded trek across town. His stomach tightened. More than likely, after facing Esther, he'd not sleep another wink.

ESTHER AMBLED her way along the back of the house, eyes searching the darkness. By now, it was well past midnight. Had Stew forgotten? She rubbed her arms against the cool night breeze. Her gaze fled to the line of dim gaslights peppering the street below, their flames dancing like fireflies. Perhaps she was simply too eager. Stew would show.

He would.

She smothered a yawn, listening to a cricket chirp a steady beat in a nearby shrub, loud against the stillness. A rustling sound snapped her awake, pulling her attention to the tree up ahead. She edged forward, her heart pounding. "Stew?"

Stillness overshadowed her soft plea, followed by a hushed, "Over here."

On trembling feet, she ventured closer, finally able to make out his shadowy figure emerging from behind the tree. She swallowed, trying to make out his features. His very presence stirred warmth in her cheeks. She worked to steady her voice, keeping it soft and low. "How are you?"

"I'm managing." He stepped from the shadows into the moon-light, tall and lean.

Longing stirred within Esther as she took in his wavy hair and strong jaw, and her pulse quickened. She pressed down the urge to close the gap between them, reminding herself she was pledged to another. "I-I was rather stunned to learn you were here." She locked her fingers together behind her back, a shy smile touching her lips. "More than once I thought I saw you, but decided I must be imagining things."

"You weren't imagining."

His steady gaze beckoned her. She moistened her lips, venturing a step toward him. "Why didn't you show yourself? Why have you waited so long to let me know you're here?"

"I did try to see you and was sent away."

Esther's chest squeezed. "Who sent you away?"

He shook his head, lowering his gaze. "It doesn't matter."

She knit her brow, trying to process who would gain from keeping them apart. Lawrence? It couldn't be. He knew nothing of Stew—although his jealous nature had been aroused by the buggy outside her house. Warmth shrouded her cheeks. If Stew had been found out, how would she have explained him?

No wonder he'd left.

To her knowledge, the only other time Stew had made an appearance was the night of the engagement party. But if Lawrence had seen him, she'd have heard about it.

The only other person who would have cause to send Stew away would be …

"Mother. *She* sent you away."

Stew's eyes lifted, the truth of her words revealing itself in his expression.

"I'm so sorry." She stepped closer, placing a hand on his arm. "Why *did* you come, Stew? Tell me."

Heavy silence enveloped them. At last, Stew gave a soft sigh. "The reason no longer exists. What matters is why I'm here now."

Moisture pooled in her eyes, her mind flooding with questions. "And why is that?"

His expression hardened. "I need a favor."

"What sort of favor?"

He seemed hesitant to respond. "I need you to look through your stepfather's business transactions for suspicious entries."

She pulled her hand away, the unexpected reply catching her off guard. "Whatever for?"

"To see if he's involved in kidnapping blacks and smuggling them downriver to sell as slaves."

"What? Why would you think—"

He raised a hand to quiet her. "Some Leifer Shipping workers are involved. I overheard them plotting to snatch another person to fill their boss' quota."

Her hands flew to her hips. "William would never take part in something so ungodly and underhanded."

"Then he needs to be made aware of it." He clasped her shoulders, his eyes softening. "I don't wish to put you in harm's way, but if you could look for anything unusual, I'd appreciate it."

The warmth of his touch vibrated through her, calming her and mellowing her resolve. How she longed to forget all this nonsense and melt into his embrace. Instead, she shook her head. "I can't intrude upon William's private business. Surely you're mistaken."

"My friend Isaac's wife and son were the ones they took."

She drew in a sharp breath, tears stinging her eyes. "I'm sorry."

He leaned closer, his expression earnest. "Please. Find out what you can. I'll check back with you this time tomorrow night."

She hesitated and then gave a gentle nod.

His lips lifted in a slight grin. "Thank you."

Before she could stop him, he brushed the back of his hand down her cheek and stole away into the night, leaving her with a full head and an empty heart.

Chapter Thirty-Three

STEW SET the heavy crate of supplies beside the others on the lower deck of the *Ohio Belle* and brushed dirt from his hands. The cargo and passenger steamboat was due to set out later that day. To his relief, Charlie had informed Stew he was needed here and not on board when it made its run. Until he found out where Benji and Abigail had been taken, he was better off snooping around the dock than on a boat somewhere.

Despite his gentle inquiries about the goings on at Leifer Shipping, for all he could tell, Charlie, Mick, and the other workers seemed on the up and up. He took every opportunity to poke his way around the ship, but so far had garnered nothing unusual. Had he been wrong or was it only the boat that had left in the night that was used for smuggling?

Welcoming shouts from the men on the upper deck brought him rushing out of the cargo hold. He followed the stares of the other workers to the approaching steamboat. Though almost identical to the *Ohio Belle,* the *Dynasty* was a tad larger and more seasoned.

He sensed someone approach and turning, saw Charlie coming up beside him. "Go grab the line, will ya?"

"Yes'r." Stew downed the plank and stood ashore, waiting for the boat to dock. One of the men on deck resembled Snoot's smaller companion. His chest clenched. Could this be the ship that had transported his friends to some unknown port? The man turned his way, and Stew ducked his head. Would he recognize him? If so, his chances of finding his friends were lost.

"You down there! Heads up."

Stew ventured a glance up just as the man tossed a heavy rope his direction. Reaching for it, he sensed the man eyeing him. He did his best to act casual, breathing easier when the man finally turned and went about his business. If they crossed paths again, he'd do well to keep his distance from both him and Snoot. Tangling with them once was enough. A second round might land him in the same condition as Isaac.

And leave Abigail and Benji without hope of being found.

He tied the rope to the piling, his mind on his friends. Two days had passed since their abduction, and so far he had no real leads. By now, they could well be in the hands of a slave owner and transported who knows where. With each passing hour, his chances of finding them grew slimmer. He needed a lead, and quick.

Mick sauntered by, and Stew caught him by the arm. "Where's this one been?"

The stocky man followed his gaze to the newly docked steamboat. "The *Dynasty*? Don't rightly know. Most of the time she travels Louisville way. But once a month they take her on a short jaunt upstream."

Stew cast a glance at the docked boat and the spattering of crew members milling about the deck. "Is this the boat that left a couple nights back?"

Mick wiped sweat from his brow. "Yep. Only one fool enough to head out in the dead of night. Must be why they don't take passengers."

"Why no passengers?" Stew hoped he wasn't pressing too hard, but he needed to find out all he could.

Mick shrugged. "Don't know that either. But then, I don't ask questions." He leaned toward Stew, voice lowered. "I learned a long time ago, if you wanna keep your job, it don't pay to get too curious."

Stew gave a slow nod. "I'll remember that."

With a quick wink, Mick continued on, whistling as he went.

Stew did his best to look busy the rest of the afternoon, all the while mulling over Mick's words and itching for a chance to have a look around the *Dynasty*. Why would the steamboat be singled out for a shorter route each month and pass up the added revenue from passengers? And why leave in the night? The odd routine was enough to garner suspicion. He'd lay low until dark and see if he could find out more. Isaac would be eager to hear from him, but he couldn't risk being found out. Especially now that he was onto something.

After their trip, the crew of the *Dynasty* would likely be eager for a night on the town. All he had to do was bide his time and wait till they left and then have a look down in the cargo hull. Afterward, he'd check with Esther. Hopefully she'd know something.

Memories of her hounded him. Last night's encounter had threatened to undo him—the way her eyes glistened in the moonlight, her lilting voice, the softness of her arms beneath his fingers. It had taken all his willpower not to pull her in his embrace. It tortured him to think of having to see her again.

Would it all be for nothing?

If he had any sense, he'd forget the whole thing and head back to Scout and his job at the Circle J. But his conscience wouldn't let him. Isaac was counting on him. He had no one else to turn to. There was no use asking the Lord's help. He obviously didn't have time for the likes of him. Nor Isaac and Abigail. Despite their faith, the Lord had paid no heed to their pleas. Instead, they'd suffered bruises, broken ribs, separation, and loss of freedom. He couldn't let Benji and Abigail spend the rest of their days enslaved. It tore him apart to think of it. If finding them meant discomfort and inconvenience on his part, so be it.

He only wished it didn't involve having his heart ripped apart each time he saw Esther.

ESTHER GLANCED at the clock on the mantel for the dozenth time. Half-past eight. Most likely William and Mother wouldn't retire for another hour or so. After dining out, she'd declined Lawrence's invitation to the theater, claiming she needed to rest up from the barrage of activities surrounding their engagement. To her surprise, he'd made no argument, escorting her home over an hour ago and departing without so much as a backward glance.

Another glimpse at the clock convinced her she was far too preoccupied. Why did time seem to stand still when she needed it to pass? Stew hadn't given her much time. She'd have only a short window of opportunity to check out her stepfather's dealings before he arrived. Her mouth twisted in thought. Perhaps, if she took to her bed early, Mother and William would do the same.

It was worth a try.

Setting her stitching aside, she feigned a yawn. "I believe I'll retire. I'm a bit fatigued from all the activity of late." In truth, she was more tired from her late-night rendezvous with Stew. His disturbing revelation, coupled by his alluring presence, had left her more than a bit frazzled and lightheaded.

Her mother peered over at her. "You do appear a mite peaked. Sleep well, dear."

"Goodnight." Esther stood and made her way toward the doorway.

William mumbled a "goodnight" as she passed, too intent on his pipe and newspaper to glance her way. His bushy sideburns trailed down his cheeks, and his graying hair formed a halo around the shiny spot atop his head. A twinge of remorse pricked her at the thought of the despicable act she'd agreed to do. Though William had not seemed much like a father to her, he'd been nothing less than kind and accepting to both her and Mother. Betraying his trust seemed a high price to pay if her little ruse was found out.

Humid air wafted out at her as she opened the door to her room. Stepping inside, she clicked the door closed behind her. With soft steps, she crossed to the window, raising it slightly to allow a soft breeze to flow through. She reached to turn her gaslight low to give the appearance of being asleep until William and her mother had gone to bed.

Esther released a wide yawn. Tired as she was, she'd have a hard time staying awake long enough for the opportunity to sneak into William's study. If anyone but Stew had asked her to do such an underhanded deed, she would have adamantly refused. The very notion that William could be involved in the abduction and sale of innocent men, women, and children turned her stomach. Surely Stew was mistaken. And she intended to prove so this very night.

Rather than don her nightgown, she slipped off her boots and lay down on the bed fully clothed. As she settled onto the mattress, every muscle screamed for rest. She closed her eyes, sinking her head deeper into the feather pillow. How she longed to sleep and forget all this foolishness. Forget Stew had ever come.

And most of all, forget how her heart yearned to be near him.

Yet, she'd given her word. Even so, if she could convince herself there wasn't a shred of truth to his accusations, she'd not go through with it. But she knew Stew. Outside of her father, a more honest man never lived. He'd not have placed her in such peril had he not deemed it necessary. In a matter of hours, he'd be here seeking answers. Seeking the truth.

How she wished, instead, he'd come to steal her away and claim her for his own.

What baffled her was how he'd managed to come across such a scheme? Who were these colored friends of his who'd been abducted? And what had he meant when he'd said his reason for coming no longer existed?

Her chest tightened. Had *she* been his reason for coming? Had he followed her here hoping she'd return with him to the prairie? When he'd stood outside the ballroom window, had he witnessed Lawrence announce their engagement? If so, he'd have been deeply hurt. Perhaps even devastated.

And yet, he was still here. Why?

Blinking back tears, she folded her hands and peered out the window into the starlit night. "Lord, I know You've brought Stew here for a reason, whether it be to aid his friends or for my sake. Watch over him and guide his way. Bring the truth to light in regards to the whereabouts of his friends. It hurts to have him here, knowing my commitments lie with another. Forgive me for my divided heart, Lord. If You have a different path for my life than the one I'm following, make it known to me. Above all else, help Stew come to a fuller knowledge of You. Amen."

THE NIGHT AIR WAS STILL, though sounds of the city echoed along the riverbank. Nearly an hour had passed since Stew had witnessed any sort of activity on the decks of the *Dynasty*. He inched his way closer, keeping to the shadows. If he were to make his midnight meeting with Esther, he could wait no longer.

A nervous twinge shot through him as he crept up the thick, wooden plank. To be found out now would be disastrous not only for his friends, but him as well. No telling what would become of him if he were discovered snooping about. As he reached the deck floor, he paused, alert to every sound. Soft light filtered from inside the pilot's compartment window above. Stew craned his neck for a look, but neither saw nor heard anything. More than likely, a lantern had been kept burning for easier access into the dark cabin. Although, it was possible someone had stayed aboard to ward off unwanted visitors.

Like him.

The moon disappeared behind a cloud, complicating his already slow progress. Though he welcomed the added concealment, the darkness increased his chances of knocking into something and alerting whomever might be lurking about. Assuming the layout was similar to that of the *Ohio Belle's*, he inched his way along the lower deck until he reached what he hoped was the cargo hull.

He breathed a sigh of relief as the moon's glow brightened, allowing him enough light to find the door latch. Taking hold, he gave it a quick tug. It creaked slightly, and he stilled, his heart pounding in his ears. When nothing happened, he opened it further. The pungent odor of urine and feces wafted out at him, and he held his breath, cringing.

Heaviness pulled at his chest as he descended the ladder. No doubt the compartment had carried more than supplies to its recent destination. Whether from the putrid smell or the thought of Abigail, Benji, and others being trapped in such a wretched compartment, he nearly lost what little supper he'd eaten. Didn't these men have any morals at all? Or were they so consumed with greed they cared nothing about ripping families apart and forcing them to spend the rest of their days enslaved?

It sickened him to think Esther's stepfather might have something to do with such grisly business. He hoped for Esther's sake, and her mother's, he didn't. No amount of money could account for the ruination of people's freedom and livelihood. Did these men not realize blacks were people too with families and hopes and dreams of their own?

Darkness enveloped him as he made his way down the steps, the stench growing stronger as he neared the bottom. A squishing noise sounded as his boots met with the floorboards. He ventured a step forward uncertain what he was looking for—a tuft of hair, a torn piece of clothing, a shoe—anything tangible that would prove to Esther he was telling the truth.

A sliver of moonlight found its way in, reflecting off a shiny object to his far left. Drawing a shallow breath, Stew strained to make out what it might be. As he started toward it, his boot kicked against something. He bent down and swept his hand over the grimy floor until it touched a hard object.

Metal clanked as he picked it up, and his blood turned cold. Swallowing down his disgust, he ran his hands over the circular object. Shackles. Proof enough that what he and Isaac feared was true. No doubt about it. Abigail and Benji, along with others, had been transported upriver to be sold as slaves.

Heat burned in Stew's chest. He had to find out where they'd been taken and who was ultimately responsible. He wouldn't rest until he did. He gave the shackles a couple of hard yanks, but they refused to budge. Fearful the noise would alert someone to his whereabouts, he set them gently on the floor. Esther, and anyone else for that matter, would simply have to take him at his word. If she found something incriminating where her stepfather was concerned, she'd likely be shattered. If not, he only hoped she wouldn't take offense at his accusations and disbelieve his story altogether.

Muffled voices above set his heart to pounding. From within the cargo hull, it was difficult to tell how far away they were. Would he have enough time to climb out and slip into the shadows? He had no choice but to try. With careful steps, he upped the ladder, pausing to listen before raising his head above the door.

The voices sounded hushed, distant, enough so he dared to emerge. With careful steps, he snuck his way across the main deck and hid behind the paddle box. He was close enough now he could make out most of the men's hushed conversation.

"You sure the boss is comin'?" one of them asked.

His companion's tone was gruffer, deeper. "Stop your frettin', Willy. He'll be here."

Their voices sounded vaguely familiar. Stew ventured a peek from behind his hiding place, but could see only the backs of their heads down to their shoulders, one taller than the other. They stood just to the left of the plank, leaving him no way to escape. Unless he cared to slip in the river for a late-night swim.

"Where's he been lately anyway? Haven't seen him around much."

"Busy with his lady friend. Where else?" replied the gruff-sounding man.

The larger man turned enough so that Stew could see his profile. He seethed inwardly as recognition washed through him. Snoot and his buddy. He should have known. Waiting to collect their slave pay, no doubt.

The shorter man, Willy, let out a "humph". "That's just like him, living it up while we handle the dirty work."

"You know the boss. If he isn't barking orders or turning a profit, he's not happy."

It took a moment for Snoot's words to sink in. Lady friend? Surely they weren't referring to Esther's stepfather. Had he been wrong in assuming Leifer was the boss? But if not him, who?

"Here he comes now."

At Snoot's announcement, Stew turned his attention to the approaching carriage. It rolled to a stop a few yards in front of the men. They edged forward, but not enough to allow Stew the chance to down the ramp and slip away. He strained for a look inside the coach, but gleaned only a shadowy outline of a man. Judging by the carriage's stylish appearance, whoever it was must be well-to-do.

Getting rich at the expense of others, no doubt.

The three conversed in low tones, too soft for Stew to overhear. He needed to find out who this fellow was and put an end to his despicable practices. The question was how? He had to get closer, find some way to distinguish his buggy or, better yet, follow him and learn where he lived. A near impossibility given his present situation.

He scrubbed a hand over his face. If he could only find a way to sneak off the boat. A barrel rested just to the left of the plank. At first opportunity, he slunk over to it and crouched behind it. The position allowed him a better vantage point to see and hear more of the conversation. Phrases like "the next batch of Negroes" "do what you have to" and "you're paid for your trouble" were enough to convince Stew the man in the carriage was indeed the mastermind behind the operation.

Venturing a look from behind the barrel, he could make out a small portion of the man's face, a sizeable hat atop his head. The more he strained to see, the more obscured his view became. At last, the conversation hit a lull, and Snoot shifted, allowing Stew a better glimpse of the man in the carriage. His eyes widened, disbelief gnawing at his gut.

It couldn't be. But it was.

Chapter Thirty-Four

ESTHER TIPTOED down the hallway toward her stepfather's study, lantern in hand, the wick turned low so as not to awaken her mother and stepfather. She'd waited as long as she dared. A floorboard creaked under her bare feet, and she cringed, frozen in place. When everything remained quiet, she edged forward until she came to William's study. She reached for the latch then paused, a wave of guilt washing over her. She shouldn't be snooping through her stepfather's things. But, two incentives begged her to continue —the hope of proving William innocent of any wrongdoing and her regard for Stew.

With unsteady fingers, she turned the latch. The dark room seemed large and foreign to her, its thick curtained windows shutting out even the glow of the moon. Rarely had she even stepped inside the room. Not that she wasn't welcome. There'd simply been no need. It was William's place to conduct business or retreat to when he wished time to himself. Esther much preferred the brightness of the sitting room or the enticement of the library.

Crossing the room, she set the lantern on the desk and turned its wick to draw more light. A stack of papers rested at either end of the desk, a quill and ink bottle at its center. The edges of the papers were neatly aligned, not a single edge out of place. The desktop itself appeared spotless. She hadn't realized how meticulous William was. It would require great care to leave everything just as she'd found it.

Sliding onto the cushioned chair, she picked up one of the piles of papers and started riffling through each page. What exactly was she looking for? Stew had asked her to seek out anything odd or unusual. She knew nothing of the shipping industry. How was she to decipher if something was awry? She finished off the stack with a relieved huff. Nothing stood out at her. Neither did she find anything alarming in the second pile. All were purchase notices, shipping orders, or supply lists. Not a one out of the ordinary as far as she could tell.

She opened both drawers, finding similar papers inside from years past. Nothing incriminating or disturbing. She took a moment to ensure the papers were replaced as found and the drawers properly shut. With a satisfied breath, she gave the piles on the desk one final straightening. There. She'd done what Stew asked and found nothing.

She stood and clasped the lantern and then paused, brow knit. Come to think of it, there was one oddity. There seemed to be a complete lack of financial statements. No sort of record of profits lost or gained whatsoever. Raising the lantern, she perused the room for some other possible storage place. Nothing. Only two upholstered chairs, a footstool, and a large painting of what appeared to be one of William's predecessors.

Could there be a hidden compartment? Striding over to the painting, she gently pulled on first one side, then the other. With the second tug, the painting gave just a bit. Her mouth twisted as she gave the frame another yank. The painting swung open, revealing an iron door hidden behind it. Lifting a shaky hand, she pulled at the lever. Just as she'd feared.

Locked.

Whatever her stepfather kept inside would remain a secret.

Swinging the picture frame back around, Esther released a frustrated breath. She'd hoped to dispel every shred of doubt regarding William's innocence. What she'd found wasn't much, but she feared the hidden safe and the missing financial records were enough to keep Stew's suspicions alive.

STEW SANK BACK into the shadows, a cold chill sweeping over him. Esther's fiancé was the boss? *He* was the one responsible for Abigail and Benji's abduction? His eyes crimped, a renewed sense of urgency coursing through him. Somehow he had to get word to Esther and warn her.

The question was, would she believe him?

The carriage driver smacked the reins on the horses' rumps, drawing Stew's attention back to the street. As the carriage pulled forward, he caught another glimpse of Del Ray, and his stomach clenched. If he had reason to dislike the man before, he had a dozen more reasons now. The carriage rounded a building and vanished into the night, leaving Stew to mull over what he'd just learned and Snoot and his friend, Willy, to pocket their earnings.

Snoot slapped Willy on the arm. "Told ya he'd come through."

"He's asking for trouble where that gal's concerned. If the old man finds out what's going on, we're all in for it." Willy's hushed, cynical voice carried in Stew's direction.

"He won't find out. The boss is too smart for that. Besides, once he's married her, what's Leifer gonna do?" Devious laughter poured from both men.

Stew balled his fists. It was all he could do to keep from running down and pounding their heads together or tracking Del Ray down and ripping him apart. He had to find a way off of here. Esther needed to know the truth about the man she'd agreed to marry.

Their laughter died away as their boot steps trailed into the night. Now was his chance. He waited another long moment to ensure they were out of earshot then stepped from behind the barrel and onto the plank. He'd almost reached the bottom when a voice from the pilot house called out. "Who's there? Stop, you!"

Stew leaped off the plank and into the shadows, slipping in the loose dirt below. Pain shot through his bad leg as he landed, and he rolled onto his side. Pulling himself to his feet, he drew a jagged breath. He should have known better. Footsteps pounded on the deck above, edging closer. Most likely, he'd never outrun the fellow. But if he stayed where he was, he didn't stand a chance.

He limped up the incline, heart pounding. If he could make it to one of the buildings, he might be able to elude the fellow. The sound of running pulled him to a stop. Two dim figures raced toward him from the street. Veering to his left, he sought refuge behind a pile of lumber outside a darkened shed.

"Where'd he go?"

"Over there, by that building."

Stew's heart sank. There was no mistaking the men's voices. Evidently Snoot and Willy had heard their shipmate's shout and circled back. He slunk lower, grateful when a passing cloud darkened the moon. Footsteps neared his hiding place then traipsed past.

He held still, waiting, praying.

Moments passed. When all seemed quiet, he ventured a glance around then eased from his hiding place. Standing, he blew out a soft breath. Much too close for comfort. The forgotten light in the pilot house had nearly been his undoing.

With careful steps, he ventured forward, intent on making his way across town to meet with Esther. By now it must be close to eleven, if not later. He still had time to make it. No thanks to his brutish friends.

A rustling sound from behind brought him to a standstill. Before he could turn, strong arms encircled him, pinning his arms to his sides. "I got him."

Stew wriggled one arm free and jabbed the man he recognized as Snoot in the ribcage with his elbow. For Isaac.

With a loud groan, Snoot doubled over, hands gripping his belly. Stew darted away, only to have Willy skitter in front of him, a puzzled expression spilling over his face. "Hey, ain't you that new fella? Now I know where I've—"

Before he could finish, Stew lunged forward, knocking him to the ground with a blow to the jaw. "That's for Abigail and Benji."

Something smacked against the back of Stew's neck and pain sliced through him. He turned to see Snoot poised over him, a board in his hands. Stew ducked as he swung it at him then landed another punch to the burly man's gut. With an angry growl, Snoot drew a hand to his side and spun to face Stew.

Willy staggered to his feet, rubbing a hand over his jaw. "He's that fella from the other night."

A spark of recognition ignited in Snoot's eyes. "Then he knows too much." He lunged toward Stew, raising the board for another swing.

Stew dodged, but not enough. The board clipped him on the shoulder, knocking him to his knees. Dropping his crude weapon, Snoot fell on him, fists flailing. Stew held him at bay with a powerful blow to the cheek. Anger flared in his opponent's eyes and then a taunting grin crept onto his face.

Stew sensed, more than heard, Willy come up behind him. Something hard bashed him on the head. He fell to the ground, his vision blurring. As darkness enveloped him, one word fell from his lips. "Esther."

WHERE WAS STEW?

Esther paced back and forth outside the house, her angst mounting. Last night he'd been a few minutes late. Tonight she'd been waiting well over an hour. Questions pummeled her mind.

Had his plans changed? If so, why hadn't he sent word? What could be detaining him?

She stopped pacing and stared down into the street, her irritation blossoming into anger, then melting into concern. How long must she wait? Would he come at all? Worse yet, had something happened to him?

A knot formed in the pit of her stomach. Whoever was behind this slave operation wouldn't take kindly to Stew poking around. She leaned against the house, her heart at her throat. *Please, Lord, be with him.*

The moon hid behind a cloud, spreading a blanket of darkness over the yard, stealing what little hope she had left.

PART IV
AWAKENINGS

Chapter Thirty-Five

STEW AWOKE, head throbbing. What had happened? His eyelids flickered open and shut as he became aware of breathing that was not his own. He caught a glimpse of a man he'd never seen before staring down at him. Unsettled by the stranger's appearance, Stew snapped his eyes wider. The man was enormous, with yellowed teeth and a misshapen nose.

Stew's gaze swept past the man to the rafters of what appeared to be a small shanty. Where was he?

The man grunted and motioned to someone behind him, and a woman's voice called. "Be he awake?"

The creak of a rocking chair sounded from across the room followed by the shuffling of shoes on the floor. Stew attempted to rise, but fell back as though his muscles were weighted. He let out a fearsome cough, spitting up something that smelled and tasted of river water. Every breath seemed a struggle.

"Lay still, young man. You're in no condition to move about." The voice was kind, motherly.

Pain surged through Stew's head and neck as he shifted his gaze in the direction of the voice. Beside him stood a silvery-haired woman no more than five feet tall, her sea-green eyes clouded with age. "Where am I?"

She placed a wrinkled hand on his arm, its veins showing beneath thinning skin. "Someplace safe."

Someplace safe? He cringed, realizing he was at the mercy of these people, whoever they were. Last he recalled, he'd been bashed on the head while fighting off Snoot and Willy. His gaze darted to the giant of a man and then back to the woman. "Who are you?"

"Rest now. There'll be time for questions later."

Whether it be due to the woman's soothing tone or fatigue, he closed his eyes. When he woke again, the scent of fresh-baked bread and some sort of fried meat filled his senses. The pain in his head had lessened, allowing him a fuller view of the small shack. Though tidy in appearance, the one-room home was modest, if not depleted. He raised his head in search of his hosts, but glimpsed only the old woman at the hearth. Daylight streamed through a curtained window to the right of the fireplace. Apparently, he'd been asleep a long while.

Seeming to sense he'd awakened, the woman turned, a cheery smile spreading over her face. She ambled over to him, slow of step. "I was in hopes the scent of food would rouse you. How ya feeling, young man?"

"I've had better days." Stew threw back the thin blanket covering him and eased up on his elbow. He glanced down at his bare chest and felt of his damp trousers. Had he fallen in the river? He stared over at the woman, forehead creased. "How'd my clothes get wet?"

She arched a brow. "You don't know?"

Stew shook his head.

"No, I don't suppose you would know, seein' as you'd been knocked silly," she mumbled under her breath. Offering no further explanation, she gestured over her shoulder to where his shirt lay stretched across the back of a chair. "Your shirt's about dry. I thought it best to let ya keep your britches."

Stew pulled the cover back over him, trying to make sense of her meandering words. A sudden thought drained the blood from his cheeks. Isaac's money had been in his shirt pocket, along with the freedom papers. Had he lost them, his only means of getting Abigail and Benji back?

"If you're frettin' over your belongings, your papers are drying there on the mantel."

His eyes searched the shelf over the stone fireplace. "Was there a money pouch as well?"

The woman joggled her head side to side, her expression earnest. "Didn't see any pouch."

Stew eyed her, wondering if she'd pocketed the money for herself. He reached in his damp pants pocket, a surge of relief rippling through him when he found his own stagecoach money intact. If she'd wanted to rob him, she'd have taken that as well.

He settled back on the pillow, thankful to at least have the precious freedom papers and his fare home. Snoot and Willy must've been in an awful hurry to get rid of him not to search all his pockets.

The woman leaned closer, her wrinkled face pleasant. "Are ya hungry?"

Now that she'd mentioned it, the savory smells and mention of food brought to mind just how famished he was. Yet, uncertain of the woman and her giant of a son, he cautioned himself not to appear too eager. "A mite."

She wagged her finger at him. "Stay put. I'll bring you some victuals." Ambling over to the table, she took up one of three empty plates and began to fill it, calling to him over her shoulder. "Toby and I'll eat when he gets in, but seeing as ya missed break-fast, I hate to make ya wait."

Stew watched her every move, curious how such a tiny woman

could have given birth to such enormous offspring. To be truthful, he was a bit relieved her intimidating son wasn't around. Easing himself to a sitting position, Stew cleared the phlegm from his throat, hoping for some answers. "I'm a bit fuzzy on what happened. Can you clue me in as to how I got here? And where *here* is?"

"Toby fished ya out of the river and brought ya here." She grinned at him over her shoulder as if she'd informed him he needed to wash up before eating. "And *here* is Kentucky."

Stew's mouth drooped open, and he snapped it shut. "No offense, ma'am, but your responses leave me with more questions than answers."

"The name's Annie. And I've a few ponderings of my own where you're concerned." With careful steps, she brought the plate of bread, hominy, and fried meat over, along with his shirt, and held them out to him. She tilted her head to the side, an inquisitive look in her eyes. "What name do ya go by, lad?"

"Stew. Stewart Brant." Setting the plate on his lap, he slipped on his shirt.

Annie smiled. "Well, Mr. Brant, I hope ya like frog legs. It's them that saved your life. Them, my boy, and the good Lord."

Stew stared at the plate of food, then at the curious woman who seemed to talk nonsense.

She chuckled and pulled a chair up beside the cot. "I can see you're hankerin' for more of an explanation." With a deep breath, she settled down onto the chair, her short legs barely reaching the floor. "My boy was out hunting frogs late last night. Toby doesn't speak but, near as I can figure, some fellows in a rowboat tossed ya in the river and left ya for dead. Soon as they left, he fetched ya out. I 'spect you'll have to figure for yerself how ya got in such a predicament."

Stew coughed and gave a slow nod. At last, the woman was making sense. Snoot and Willy must have knocked him unconscious, rowed him downstream, and thrown him in the river with the intent of making it his permanent resting place. He knew why he'd been waylaid, but was hesitant to tell Annie. Given that she and her son lived in Kentucky, it was likely they would disapprove of him aiding colored folks. Thankfully, it appeared she'd not unfolded the papers to learn what they contained

He raised one of the frog legs to his mouth only to have Annie reach over and pull his hand away, her grip surprisingly strong. "I don't know your upbringing, Mr. Brant, but you'll not be eating in this house until grace is spoken. After all, you've much to be grateful for."

Stew scoffed. "For being bashed on the head and left to drown in the river?" It wasn't like him to voice his misgivings about God so openly, but with all he'd been through, it felt good to bare his soul.

Annie leaned back in her chair, lifting her gaze to the rafters. "Forgive him, Lord. I'm certain he didn't mean any disrespect." She dropped her gaze to Stew, her eyes narrowing. "There's two ways of looking at your situation, Mr. Brant. You can dwell on being thrown in the river, or praise the good Lord for sending someone to fetch ya out."

Stew set the frog leg down, his mouth twisting. She had a point. "Yes, ma'am. I suppose you're right."

She crossed her arms and gave a brisk nod as though pleased with his answer. "Well, then, go on. Say the blessing before your food gets cold."

Stew bowed his head. "Many thanks, Lord, for Miss Annie and her son's kindness for sharing their victuals and seein' to it I didn't drown. Amen."

Her head lifted, and she peered over at him, her eyes searching his. "By the sounds of that prayer, it seems you and the Lord aren't on the best of terms."

She had that right. For months now, every attempt Stew had made to move forward in life had gone awry. His prayers had gotten him nowhere. Now, he'd given up—on himself, on Esther, on God. "I reckon you could say that."

"Ah, your heart has been wounded somehow."

Stew wet his lips, pushing the untouched plate of food aside. "I need to go." He started to rise, then fell back, lightheaded.

Annie placed her hands on his shoulders. "You'll go nowhere until you're able."

He swiped a hand over his face. "You don't understand. People are depending on me."

"I may not know your circumstances, but I feel certain the Lord brought you here for healing. Both body and soul." She pushed the plate toward him. "Now eat. You'll need your strength."

He hesitated then took a bite of meat. What else could he do? For the moment, he was in no shape to travel. And where would he go? Abigail and Benji were lost to him. He hadn't a clue how to find them. And if he returned to warn Esther, more than likely she wouldn't believe him.

Annie's eyes probed his. "What's truly troubling you, Stew? What is this thing that's come between you and the Lord? Tell me."

He sighed, feeling a bit like Jonah. On the run from God. But rather than being tossed overboard and swallowed by a fish to get him back on course, he'd been plucked out of the river to be set aright by a pint-sized woman who seemed to glimpse into his very soul.

Wiping crumbs from his lips, he leaned back on the pillow and told her everything—from his reason for coming to Cincinnati, to his encounter with Isaac, to his anger at God for letting everything in his life fall apart.

THE HORSE'S hooves clipped along the cobblestone street, the rhythm like that of a ticking clock, reminding Esther of the hours that had passed since she was to have met Stew. She twisted her neck side to side, glancing out first one side of the carriage then the other in search of him. Though the chances of spotting him were next to none, she prayed, somehow, she would catch a glimpse of him.

Weary from her sleepless night, she blinked back tired tears, heaviness pulling at her chest. Stew would never go back on his word without due cause. Something must have happened. But what? He'd given her so little to go on. How would she ever find him?

All she knew was his friend's name was Isaac. More than likely he and his family lived in the southwest section of town known as the Fourth Ward, or "little Africa" as some referred to it. But what good did knowing that do? There must be dozens of colored men there by that name. And how could she, a white female, travel the area alone asking questions? They'd consider her touched in the head at best, and at worst grow suspicious or even hostile.

As the carriage neared the riverfront, Esther leaned her head out the window and called to the driver. "Stop here, Leland." The carriage rolled to a stop, and Esther waited for Leland to climb down and open her door. Stepping onto the street, she took another glance around. She had no idea what she was doing or where she was going. She simply had to try something. "Wait here for me."

The white-haired carriage driver bowed as she strode past. "Yes, Miss Esther."

The cobblestone gave way to hardened dirt as Esther started down the incline of the public landing at the corner of Broadway and Giffin. If she couldn't find Stew, perhaps, if she made herself visible, he would find her. At least she prayed so.

A cooling breeze swept across the water, tousling loose strands of hair along her cheeks as she strolled closer to the riverfront. If nothing more, the trip to the scenic Ohio would help ease the tension brewing inside her. Here, for a few precious moments, she would try to forget her troubles and drink in the peaceful beauty of the river.

"Esther!"

She startled, her heart racing at the sound of the man's voice calling her name. For a brief moment, thoughts of Stew crowded out any other possibility. But as she turned, her heart sank when she saw Lawrence waving to her instead.

A puzzled expression crept over his face as he dashed over to her. "This is unexpected. Whatever are you doing here?"

Caught off guard, Esther struggled to answer. "I…"

With a chuckle, he took her gloved hand in his. "Are you so eager to see me you've come here unescorted?"

Not wishing him to know her true purpose, she gestured over her shoulder. "Leland drove me in the carriage at my request."

"Ah! Then it's fortunate I spied you roaming about. Come, I'll accompany you home."

Reluctantly, she slid her arm through his, a knot balling in her stomach. With Lawrence alongside her, how could she expect Stew to show himself? If he were even around. She was beginning to wonder if he'd left the city altogether.

Or had something befallen him or his friends? Stew would never leave without knowing the full truth.

Lawrence tightened his hold on her arm, pulling her from her thoughts. "What is it that has you so preoccupied? You have me wondering if it was me you came to see after all."

She moistened her lips, hoping to sound convincing. "It's just…I have something weighing on my mind."

He paused, his dark eyes perusing hers. "What is it, my dear? Surely you can tell me."

Esther hesitated. Could she? How she wished Stew was here to confide in instead. But, perhaps Lawrence could provide her with information in regards to William that she could pass onto Stew, should he ever appear. Venturing a glance around, she tugged Lawrence away from those who might overhear. "It concerns William."

"What about him?"

She leaned in close, keeping her voice low. "Have you ever

known him to do anything uncouth in regards to his business affairs?"

Lawrence knit his brow. "Such as?"

Esther brushed a stray strand of hair from her cheek. How could she put this without arousing suspicion? "Have you known him to seek to make a profit at the expense of others?"

His lips curved upward, and he threw back his head in laughter. "My dear, William is a businessman, same as I am. We make a living off the expense of others."

She shook her head, further softening her voice. "No. I'm referring to profits gained by smuggling free blacks across state lines to be sold as slaves."

Lawrence's face grew taut, his eyes piercing into her. "Who told you this?"

Her heart drummed in her ears. She couldn't tell him the truth and risk putting Stew in jeopardy. She'd have to think of something else. "I—I've heard rumors that make me suspect some of his workers are involved."

"How could you possibly know about his workers?" He smoothed his mustache which could only mean she'd somehow irked him.

His impudent tone made her blood run cold. Something told her it was best to drop the whole matter. "I'm sure I must be mistaken. Sorry to have bothered you with such inane gossip."

A devious glint shone in his eyes and his expression brightened. "Not to worry, my dear. You were right to come to me. I'll look into the situation, and if there's anything amiss, I'll take care of it."

With a nod, she looked away, feeling twice as dreadful as before she'd mentioned it. Something *was* amiss, and she couldn't help but think she'd just made matters worse.

Chapter Thirty-Six

"So, you think the Lord gives little thought to the poor and down-trodden. People like you, me, and Toby, and your friends Isaac and Abigail. You're convinced He favors the attractive and well-to-do folks, aye?"

Annie's pointed question took Stew off guard. He swallowed, crossing his arms over his chest. "That's been my experience of late."

For a long moment, she stared at him, a hint of sadness in her blue-green eyes. Then, without a word, she stood and crossed the room, pausing beside her rocking chair. A Bible rested on its caned seat. Picking it up, she held it to her chest then turned toward Stew. "Now I know for certain you're not well acquainted with the Lord." She strode toward him, chin held high. "The God I serve pays no heed to whether we're rich or poor, plain or beautiful, maimed or whole. It was Him who created each of us."

Heat crept up Stew's neck and onto his face, the truth of Annie's words slicing through him. Hers was a genuine faith, one that reached the very core of her being, so unlike his own shallow relationship with the Lord.

She took a seat beside him, poking a knobby finger to her

chest. "It's what's inside here that counts." Thumbing her way through the pages, she came to a passage near the middle of the Bible, her lips moving silently as she found her desired place. She held up a finger as if testing the wind. "You listen here."

"And great multitudes came unto Jesus, having with them those that were lame, blind, dumb, maimed, and many others, and cast them down at Jesus' feet: and He healed them: Insomuch that the multitude wondered, when they saw the dumb to speak, the maimed to be whole, the lame to walk, and the blind to see; and they glorified God."

She looked up at him, her eyes boring into him. "Does that sound like a Savior who favors the rich and powerful?"

Without waiting for a response, she flipped through more pages and forged ahead. "And here's how I know the Lord understands and cares for the lowly. Isaiah described Jesus as 'a man of sorrows, and acquainted with grief; he was despised, and we esteemed him not'."

She closed her eyes, no longer reading the verses, but pulling the words from the recesses of her mind. "Surely he hath borne our griefs, and carried our sorrows: yet we did esteem him stricken, smitten of God, and afflicted. But he was wounded for our trans-gressions; he was bruised for our iniquities: the chastisement of our peace was upon him; and with his stripes we are healed."

Silence fell between them as if the moment had somehow become hallowed, the potency of scripture winding its way through Stew's very being. He hung his head. How wrong he'd been. He was the one who'd failed, not the Lord. Jesus understood better than anyone what it meant to suffer. Stew had expected God to cater to his every whim without being sincere in his faith. God didn't want Stew's empty prayers or praise given out of habit or obligation.

All He wanted was his heart.

A warm hand touched Stew's arm, and he glanced over at Annie, her eyes soft, gentle. "The Lord spared you for a reason, Stew. I believe He brought you here to fulfill His purposes, not your own. It was your intention to find your girl and take her back home. All you've seen are the troubles that have gotten in the way. But the Lord sees what we can't. Perhaps He has something more in mind for you."

Stew thought back on all that had happened since he'd arrived in Cincinnati. Maybe it wasn't a coincidence he'd happened upon Isaac when he did. Aiding him had led Stew to discover the truth about Lawrence Del Ray. Even being tossed in the river had landed him here with Annie where he was being strengthened both physically and spiritually. He'd deemed his unanswered prayers and difficulties as obstacles, yet it seemed the Lord was using them to woo him back to Him. He gave a slight cough. "You may be right."

Her eyes sparkled. "Just look how the Lord put you right where you needed to be to help your friends."

Stew's stomach clenched. "But I've not helped anyone, as yet. Not really. Esther knows nothing of the danger she's in, and Abigail and Benji are off somewhere being sold as slaves."

A wry grin crept onto Annie's lips. "The Lord has taken care of that too. You'll likely find your friends a few miles south of here at a town called Greenhurst. It's a holding place for slaves before they're transported farther south to be auctioned."

Stew riffled through his thoughts. "How do you know?"

Annie stood and tossed him a wink. "No one pays an old woman any mind. Living along the river, I see and hear things not meant to be seen or heard. Now, get some rest. You'll need your strength if you're to leave by morning. We've a pony and cart out back you can use for travel."

Stew's lips spread in a wide grin. "Annie, I could kiss you."

The aged woman swiped a hand through the air and chuckled. "Save your kisses for your lady friend."

Stew's smile faded. "Esther. She'll be wondering about me. I need to warn her about Del Ray. No telling what he might do if he finds out someone's been snooping around."

Annie tilted her head and shrugged. "Then I reckon you've a choice to make. Go after your friends or look after your girl. What do ya sense the Lord telling you to do?"

Stew raked a hand through his hair, warring within. How he longed to return to Esther, to protect her from Del Ray and his plot to marry her and take over Leifer Shipping. But if he waited, Abigail and Benji would be lost.

He blew out a breath. There was no choice to make. He'd promised Isaac he'd do all he could to bring Abigail and Benji back. Esther was in no immediate danger. At least, not that he knew of. It was time to put his own selfish wishes aside and do what God was calling him to do.

And entrust the outcome to the Lord.

ESTHER PAUSED FROM HER NEEDLEPOINT, her gaze flicking to her stepfather. He seemed perfectly calm, natural, while her insides churned with uncertainty. Could he really be so greedy as to undertake such a diabolical scheme—stealing people from their homes and transporting them where they could be sold as slaves? The very thought made her shiver.

With each glance, her suspicion swelled. How she longed to boldly confront him on the issue, but try as she may, she couldn't bring herself to do it. If she were wrong, both he and Mother would be devastated by the accusation. And if she were right? No telling what would happen.

"Is something troubling you, dear? You seem preoccupied of late."

Mother's words penetrated Esther's thoughts. Realizing her stare had stalled on William, she snapped her head away and returned to her needlepoint. "I'm fine, Mother."

She turned to see Mother scrutinizing her with raised brows.

"Have you and Mr. Del Ray quarreled? I noticed he's not called on you again this evening."

It did seem odd. Since she'd spoken to Lawrence yesterday morning, he'd made himself scarce. It wasn't like him to miss calling two nights in a row without so much as a word. Had both men in her life gone missing? She shook her head. "Perhaps he has other more pressing engagements to attend to."

Another glance at William ensured he hadn't the least bit of interest in the conversation. Instead, he continued to puff on his pipe and stare into his newspaper, seemingly unaware of her angst. She shifted in her chair and returned to her work, a bit disgruntled by the whole ordeal. First, Stew makes accusations against her stepfather, then up and disappears. And when she shares her misgivings with Lawrence, he responds in a rather odd way and falls strangely silent.

Something wasn't right, and it was time to find out what.

She poked her needle into the fabric and set it on her lap with a sigh. Sitting up straighter in her chair, she turned to face her stepfather. "Last I spoke with Lawrence he seemed disturbed by some rumors regarding Leifer Shipping."

The comment produced little response from William who mumbled something under his breath and returned to his paper.

Mother lowered her sewing. "What sort of rumors?"

Esther cleared her throat, heart pounding. "Something in regards to its involvement in a slave smuggling ring."

This time William's reaction was noteworthy. He lowered his pipe and paper, brow furrowed. "Hogwash."

"William would never tolerate such," piped her mother, a hint of irritation in her voice.

Exactly what Esther had told Stew. Her stomach reeled. Had she been wrong to bring it up? After all, she had nothing of consequence to base such an accusation on. She'd merely wished to gauge William's response. Yet, instead of guilt or suspicion, his expression sparked of outrage.

He folded his paper and slapped it down on the stand table. "Where did you hear such nonsense?"

Esther dropped her gaze to the floorboards. The very thought of Stew left her a bit lightheaded. "The source is a reliable one, I assure you."

William stood and paced back and forth, hands clasped behind his back.

Mother winced. "Don't excite yourself, William. Remember your heart."

Ignoring her plea, he paused and turned to face Esther. "Does Lawrence know of this?"

"Yes. I mentioned it to him yesterday morning. He said he'd look into it." She gnawed at her lip, her breaths shallow. "Please tell me you have nothing to do with this."

He grimaced. "Of course I don't. Surely you know me better than that."

The knot in her stomach loosened slightly. She believed him. And yet, one question remained. One she needed to know the answer to. She took a deep breath, praying he wouldn't hate her for her boldness. "Then why do you keep your financial records hidden away?"

He studied her in silence for a long moment, his expression fluctuating between hurt and resolve. At last, his chin lifted. "I don't know why you would suspect me of such, but I've hidden nothing. Lawrence keeps the company's financial records, not I."

The blood drained from Esther's face, her mind churning. "Lawrence keeps the accounts?"

William nodded. "With the additional boats and passengers, not to mention my delicate health, he insisted it was too stressful and complicated for my liking. I was relieved to have him take it over."

Moisture pooled in Esther's eyes as she crossed the room to stand beside him. "Forgive me, William. I never truly thought you could be involved in such debasement, and yet I doubted you. I'm sorry."

He touched a hand to her cheek, his expression softening. "I don't suppose I've given you much cause not to doubt me. Since I married your mother, I've been little more than a stranger to you. Certainly not a father. I'd say we're both in need of forgiveness."

She nodded, a slight smile edging onto her lips. "I'm willing if you are."

A sniffle sounded behind them, and Esther turned to see her mother dabbing her eyes with a handkerchief. William strolled over and placed an arm around her shoulders. "No need to weep, Clara. All is well."

Esther's throat hitched. All might be well here, but what of Stew and his friends? Knowing Lawrence possessed unbridled control over Leifer Shipping gave her cause for concern. Was he the one running the smuggling operation? Had she inadvertently supplied him with information he could use to their disadvantage? Had he played a part in Stew's disappearance? The very fact that Lawrence had made himself scarce worried her.

She could only pray Stew was safe and Lawrence wasn't plotting something sinister.

Chapter Thirty-Seven

STEW STEPPED from Annie's dim cabin, squinting against the morning light. Still a bit woozy from his whack on the head, he took his time downing the porch steps. Dense trees and undergrowth surrounded the small clearing. At the far end of the yard stood a rickety barn, a small bay pony hitched to a cart at its front. Toby stood beside it, running a hand over the pony's neck, his large frame dwarfing the animal like a cat hovering over a mouse. Yet, his touch was gentle, and the pony unafraid.

"Hold up there, young man."

At Annie's summons, Stew paused and turned. She ambled down the steps, a worn hat and a small sack in her hands. "You'll need something to shade your head and some nourishment along the way. The road to Greenhurst can be long and lonely."

"Much obliged." Stew took them from her, venturing another look around. Other than the narrow trail leading through the grove of trees, the homestead seemed in total isolation, the Ohio bordering to the north, hills and timber to the south, west, and east. "How'd you manage to make your home so far out?"

Her expression turned thoughtful. "My husband, Thomas,

thought it best we live apart from people. A few years back, Toby frightened a young girl in the settlement and the townspeople asked us to leave." She cast a loving glance at her son. "Toby didn't mean any harm. You can see he's gentle as a kitten, but folks don't understand people who are…different. So, when Thomas passed on a couple years back, Toby and I stayed on. It's a good life, really. I travel into town from time to time for supplies and visit with those who'll have me. The Lord looks after us."

A smile lit her face as she peered at the hat in Stew's hand. "That was my Thomas's. It may not be purty, but it'll keep the sun off your face."

With a nod, Stew set the hat gently on his head. "It will at that." He clutched the food sack tighter. "Thanks, Annie. Thanks for everything."

She patted his arm. "The Lord bless your journey. My prayers go with you."

He tipped the broad-brimmed hat and started across the yard.

Annie followed after him, her short legs struggling to keep up. "Once you've found and freed your friends, return here, and Toby will ferry you across the river."

Stew gave a soft snicker, slowing his pace. "You mean if I find them."

"Don't you fret. The Lord will see to it you find 'em."

Stew paused beside the cart, head bowed. "I wish I shared your confidence."

Annie clasped his arm, and he turned to face her. Her aged eyes sparked of hope as she peered up at him. "You must have faith. To doubt is to be tossed to and fro like a boat on the water. The Lord is eager to help those who unselfishly do His bidding. Pray, believing He will answer."

Her words coiled their way around his heart, squeezing out his doubt. It was time to stop dabbling in the Lord's affairs and start entrusting his whole life to Him. With a reassuring nod, Stew hoisted himself onto the seat. Taking the reins from Toby, he smiled over at him. "Thanks for your help."

Toby grunted and flashed a toothy smile. Stepping away from the pony, he lumbered toward his mother, his intimidating size less threatening now that Stew knew his gentle nature. The pair had lived as outcasts and yet they seemed to thrive on faith and love. Even knowing them for such a short time, he understood better what it meant to be poor by the world's standards, and yet rich in what mattered most. Like the scripture he'd read, their treasures were heavenly ones.

Annie pointed toward the narrow trail. "Keep to the path and then veer to the right when you come to a fork in the road. After a good piece, you'll see a sign for Greenhurst."

With a nod, Stew slapped the reins across the pony's back and clicked his cheek. The bay lunged forward, jerking the cart into motion.

"Godspeed to you!" Annie called after him.

Stew waved, then turned to steer the pony along the worn trail. As he rounded a bend, the humble homestead disappeared behind the jumble of trees and foliage. Birds chattered in the branches above, giving him some semblance of company. The abundance of ruts and rocks made a smooth ride impossible. With every jolt of the cart, Stew longed to be astride Scout. How he missed his horse. What an unexpected turn of events had taken place since they'd parted ways. Would Scout forgive him for leaving him holed up so long in the livery?

Stew sighed. Things hadn't gone as planned with him and Esther either. Was she safe? Had Del Ray found out about him sneaking around and done something rash to put Esther or her family in danger? The very thought made Stew's blood boil.

If only he could warn her not to have any more to do with the fellow. Yet, he couldn't. Not now anyway. He slid a hand down his face. Dwelling on the situation would only get him worked up again.

You must have faith, Annie's words played over in his head.

He took a deep breath. What other choice was there? It would be days before he would make it back to her. He was needed here. Trusting the Lord seemed his best and only option. *Look after Esther, Lord. Help her see Del Ray's true nature. She's in Your hands, same as I am. And I reckon that's where we most need to be, whatever the outcome.*

A rush of wind stirred in the treetops, pulling his attention to the heavens. As he peered into the morning sky, a calming presence washed over him, bringing him a sense of hope and renewed courage. Whatever the future held—for him, for Esther, for Abigail and Benji—for the first time in a long while, he had a keen awareness that he'd not have to face it alone.

IN ANSWER to the vibrant knock, James's steady footfall trailed to the front door. Esther's heart raced, certain she knew who was calling, but eager to be mistaken. She supposed it was inevitable Lawrence would come. The two nights he'd neglected to call had her curious what he was up to. If her suspicions were correct, she'd soon learn the reason. Mustering her courage, she brushed aside the impulse to retreat into her room.

She kept her eyes trained out the sitting room window, anticipating the lively click of Lawrence's shoes in the hall. Instead, James approached, pausing just inside the door. "Excuse me, Miss Esther, but Mr. Del Ray begs a word with you in private on the front lawn."

She cast a cautious glance at William, and he started to rise. "I'll speak to him. I've a few answers to seek."

Esther shook her head. "No. I'll go. It's best he's unaware I've spoken to you."

With a consenting nod, her stepfather settled back in his chair.

Standing, Esther smoothed her dress, doing her best to stymie her nerves. Though she wasn't certain of Lawrence's involvement in the abductions, the very notion that he might have something to do with Stew or his friends' disappearance left her a bit queasy. With a steadying breath, she strolled from the room, catching a glimpse of Lawrence waiting just inside the door.

"Will that be all, miss?"

"Yes, James. Thank you."

With a bow, James turned to leave. Esther pasted on a smile as she started toward Lawrence. He strolled toward her, his expression more somber than usual. Instead of his usual pleasantries, he arched a brow, his voice barely above a whisper. "Come outside, my dear. There's something I need to discuss with you." Not allowing her time to respond, he placed a hand to the small of her back and ushered her onto the lawn.

A bit disgruntled, Esther turned toward him. "What is this all about?"

He blew out a breath, taking her hand in his. "My apologies for the secrecy, but I've been delving into your suspicions regarding William, and I fear I have grave tidings."

She knit her brow. "What do you mean?"

He leaned closer, his voice but a whisper. "I fear your suspicions toward William, though misguided, are not altogether unfounded. I have evidence he has been smuggling not slaves, but stolen merchandise."

She pulled her hand away, her pulse quickening. "I don't believe it. What evidence?"

"There are discrepancies in the accounting records which cannot be overlooked."

She eyed him wearily. Dare she tell him what she knew, that her stepfather had no dealings with the financial records? No. It would be best to play along with his little ruse and find out what he was up to. "How do you know he's to blame?"

He shook his head as though in pity. "It shames me to tell you, but a couple of workers admitted to aiding him in his deceit."

The conniving look in his eyes was all she needed to convince her that his words bore no truth. Yet, how should she respond? He was her fiancé. To reveal a lack of trust would surely invoke his anger. She bowed her head. "I see. I didn't realize William was so strapped for funds that he would stoop to stealing."

Lawrence placed a finger under her chin, and she lifted her eyes to meet his gaze. "That's just it, my dear. He's obviously unfit to continue ownership of Leifer Shipping. We must confront him, but not until we're married."

Her eyes narrowed. "Why is that?"

"Don't you see? You being his only heir, it will be much simpler to gain possession of the company if we are wed. That's why we must hasten to marry." He brushed the back of his hand along her cheek. "I wish to spare you living here any longer, darling. We must forego our previous plans and wed privately at the end of the week."

She pulled away, her heart hammering. "I couldn't. I…"

He placed a finger to her lips to silence her. "It isn't as I would choose either, my dear, but it's for the best. Say nothing of what I've told you. I'll come for you in a couple of days."

With that, he turned and trotted toward his carriage, leaving her dumbfounded and speechless. She balled her fists, heat rising in her cheeks. If she were reluctant to marry him before, she was much more so now. She'd not believed a word he'd spoken, and yet she'd said nothing to the contrary. When would she find courage to voice what was in her heart, instead of letting others dictate how she lived her life?

How she ached for Stew. With him, she'd had the freedom to be her true self. Yet, the longer he was missing, the more fearful she became she'd not see him again. She strolled along the side of the house, pausing outside the ballroom window. Tears stung her eyes as she stepped to the place she'd last seen him, a whispered prayer on her lips.

"Lord, I don't know the whole truth of what's happened, but this I do know—I love Stew and with all my heart I pray he's safe. But whether I see him again in this life or not, I entrust my future to You. A future I pray will not include being the wife of Lawrence Del Ray."

Chapter Thirty-Eight

Hours of travel had stolen much of Stew's resolve. A sign bearing the name Greenhurst rejuvenated him. As he drove the cart through the small river-town, his every sense heightened. He wasn't sure what he was looking for. Whoever was in charge of the illegal slave operation on this side of the river would be doing his best to keep it under wraps. The town was sparse and spread out, its occupants far from welcoming with their scowling faces and averted gazes.

Stew panned the surroundings, eager to glimpse something out of the ordinary. The place was little more than a cluster of rundown buildings and a spattering of people, a handful of slaves intermingled. He tapped the reins down on the pony's back, keeping an eye out for Abigail and Benji. More than likely, they'd be hidden away somewhere, but one could hope. He only prayed he wasn't too late.

Annie had referred to the town as a holding place for slaves to be shipped farther south and sold at auction. If that were the case, there'd be some sort of holding cell, most likely down by the river. Up ahead, the Ohio sparkled in the afternoon sun. Only two buildings rested along its edge. One looked to be some sort of storage shed, The one farther down, toward a batch of timber, was merely a large shack. The shed was astir with activity, its open front bursting with barrels and supplies. Not a likely holding cell for illegal slaves.

His gaze flitted to the far shack, and he spied two men stationed at its front, two others loitering about. A knot balled in Stew's stomach as he veered the pony toward it. Farther from town and at the river's edge, the secluded spot seemed the perfect place to harbor slaves, as well as free men being masqueraded as slaves. On this side of the river, one would never know the difference.

Stew reached to ensure the free papers still rested in his pocket, along with his fare money home. All he had left. He cast a wary glance at the wooden shack, unable to see between the planks at what or *who* was inside. Pulling the weary pony to a stop, he sized up the men out front. Their scraggly appearance and disgruntled features didn't bode well for them being any sort of upstanding citizens. He hopped from the cart and glanced down at his wrinkled shirt and trousers. Likely, he wouldn't give off the best of impressions himself. Certainly not someone of culture or standing. Would they take him seriously?

He drew a deep breath and sauntered toward them. As he neared, the ganglier one stepped toward him rifle in hand, his wiry beard concealing much of his somber face. "What's your business here, mister?"

"I need to speak to the man in charge."

The man turned to his companion who raised a brow and shrugged. Returning his attention to Stew, the guard knit his bushy eyebrows and gestured to his left. "That would be Dooley over there."

Stew followed his gaze to a slender, well-dressed man rummaging through an open crate. Clean-shaven and not much older than Stew, Dooley appeared to be doing well for himself. With a nod, Stew turned and started toward him. At his approach, Dooley glanced his way, a curious glint in his eye. He brushed his hands together and stepped toward Stew, taking him in head to toe.

"If you're looking for work, I'm afraid I've all the laborers I need."

With a shake of his head, Stew gestured over his shoulder. "Not looking for work. I'd like to have a look in that shack, if you don't mind."

The man's eyes narrowed. "Why's that?"

Stew didn't intend to mince words. He'd grown tired of these people's games. "I'm looking for a couple friends of mine, a woman named Abigail Simmons and her son, Benji who were abducted from their home in Cincinnati. I have papers verifying their freedom." He pulled the folded free papers from his pocket, still a bit damp from his "fall" in the river.

Dooley stared at him long and hard. "Friends, huh?"

Stew held the papers out to him, meeting his gaze. "Yep."

With a smirk, Dooley snatched them from him and unfolded them. Looking them over, he gave a loud snicker, then tossed them back at Stew. "Worthless. Like your so called friends."

Stew caught the papers as they flitted downward. Clasping them in both hands, he stared at them with widened eyes. Instead of clear wording, dark ink blotches streaked the damp pages, Abigail's name barely visible at the bottom of one. His heart sank. He should have realized the once water-soaked papers would be rendered illegible from his douse in the river. "Believe me. These declared Abigail and Benjamin Simmons free."

"Well, they don't now." The man's sneer ensured he had no intention of taking Stew's word on the matter. Even if the papers had been readable, he had the notion Dooley would sooner have ripped them in half than honor them. The only thing that spoke to his kind was money.

Stew's mind reeled. He still had the money he'd saved back for his and Esther's fare home. He dug deeper in his pants pocket, knowing before he pulled it out it wouldn't be enough. Yet, it was all he had. He held it out to Dooley. "Here's forty-eight dollars. It's yours if I find 'em inside that building."

Dooley pushed Stew's hand away. "Keep your trifle of money. If I did have 'em, which I ain't sayin' I do, they're worth ten times that at auction."

Stew grabbed Dooley by the shirt. "They're free, I tell ya,"

Dooley let out a yell, and hurried footsteps sounded behind Stew. Strong arms pulled him back. When he tried to wriggle free, a second man landed him a blow to the gut. Stew doubled over, breathless, wondering how many more poundings he could take.

"Get him out of here." Dooley's gravelly voice oozed with disdain.

The men tightened their grip on Stew's arms and drug him backward up the embankment. Shoving him to the ground, the pair stood over him, guns pointed at his chest. "I suggest you move on, fella, before you regret it," threatened the guard with the beard.

Nodding, Stew pulled himself up, his body sore and bruised. They'd won for now, but one thing was certain. He wasn't going anywhere until he found out if Abigail and Benji were locked in that shack.

"I can't marry you, Lawrence." The words rolled from Esther's lips with practiced ease. She stared at herself in the mirror then sank back on her bed, wondering if she would have the courage to speak the words in person. She could sound confident and forceful holed up here in her bedroom, but finding her voice in Lawrence's commanding presence was another matter altogether.

More than once she'd considered sharing his accusations with Mother and William, and yet she knew how upset they would be. Instead, she'd decided to shoulder the burden alone. If she refused to marry Lawrence, perhaps he would give up the notion of trying to take over her stepfather's business. Mother was certain to question her refusal. If so, she would have no choice but to share the truth, that Lawrence's intentions were selfish ones. Somehow knowing greed and power had initiated his marriage proposal made spurning it easier. He'd never really loved her.

At least not in the way she loved Stew.

Tears stung her eyes. Would she ever see him again? Two days had passed, and still her prayers for his return went unanswered. Every hour that ticked by further ravaged her hopes. Setting her looking glass on her dresser, she doused the lantern. With a sigh, she slipped under the covers, tears dampening her cheeks. Scripture said to pray in faith and not waver. She was trying, but oh, how hard it was not to lose heart when hope seemed so dim.

She drew in a jagged breath and dried her eyes. Stew wouldn't want her to be sad. He'd tell her to be strong the way she'd been when she'd tended his rattlesnake bite. She set her jaw, staring at the darkened ceiling. With the Lord's help, she would be strong. For Stew and for herself.

And when Lawrence returned...she'd be ready.

Chapter Thirty-Nine

STEW WOKE from what must have been a couple hours of sleep. The night was black as pitch, the moon and stars veiled behind a thick layer of clouds. Unless he missed his guess, it was well past midnight. He crouched behind a tree, staring into the darkness. From his hiding place, he could barely make out the outline of the shack several yards up ahead. An occasional voice assured him the guards were still in place. All else was quiet, but for the chatter of insects and the splash of the water against the riverbank.

He rubbed a hand over the bump at the back of his head. He seemed to have a way of getting himself into fixes. Just how did he intend to get past those thugs? Years of night duty tending cattle had conditioned him to maneuvering in the dark. Experience told him the guards would be less alert in the wee morning hours. If he were going to help Abigail and Benji escape, now would be the time.

A sudden breeze stirred in the treetops, reminding him of the One who was in control. He bowed his head in silent prayer. *Lord, up until now my prayers have been selfish ones. But now, my thoughts are for my friends, Isaac, Abigail and little Benji. They've done nothing to deserve the situation they're in. They need my help. They need Your help. Please, Lord, show me what to do.*

A strong gust of wind swept through the trees, lifting Stew's hat from his head. He reached to hold it in place, a bit perplexed. It wasn't uncommon for a breeze to roll in off the river, but this blast had come out of nowhere. Almost as if the Lord had sent it. If nothing else, the added noise would help conceal his approach.

He edged closer, suddenly aware of a clapping sound in the direction of the shack, like wood banging on wood. Movement to the side of the building caused him to duck behind a tree. He waited, listening. The tapping grew louder and steadier in the swelling breeze. As Stew ventured another look, a smile tugged at his lips. A loose plank. Without the wind, he'd never have found it. Was God answering his prayer?

With careful steps, he ventured out into the open and made his way to the side of the building. Placing a hand on the loose plank, he eased it up and peered into the darkened hold. His innards churned as the stench of urine wafted out at him. Anger burned in his chest at the thought of Abigail and Benji wallowing in such filth. Were they among those inside?

Eerie silence poured from within, with only an occasional clank of a chain or scraping sound to confirm its occupants were indeed prisoners. This time of night, many were probably asleep. If he called for Abigail and Benji, he risked startling them awake or alerting the guards. He attempted to slip in through the hole, yet as slender as he was, the opening was too narrow. The slightest noise could prove detrimental.

With a prayer on his lips, he tugged at the boards on either side of the loose plank. His hopes soared when the one to the right gave ever so slightly. Movement stirred within as he gently pried it loose, thankful the stiff breeze helped mask the sound when it pulled free. He eased his leg through the opening and paused when his foot struck something solid. The object moved away, allowing him to continue. When he found a foothold, he slipped inside.

Though too dark to see even six inches in front of him, he sensed he was far from alone. Squatting down, he ventured the slightest of whispers. "Don't be afraid. I've come to help."

All stirring ceased, and for a moment he feared he'd made a mistake. At last, a man's deep voice answered back in a soft murmur. "Who are you?"

"A friend. I'm looking for Abigail and Benji Simmons."

"Mis'er Stew? Is that you?" A woman's hushed voice squeaked behind him.

Stew pivoted, peering into the darkness. "Abigail?"

"Over here."

He dropped to his knees, quiet whimpers pulling him forward. As he neared, he felt a hand grope for his, and he latched onto it. "Are you all right? Is Benji with you?"

"Yes'r. He's here sleepin'. Oh, Mis'er Stew. You is truly a Godsend. How's my Isaac?"

Stew's throat hitched. In her dire situation her first thought was still for her husband. "He's fine. Concerned. Right now, let's work at getting you out of here."

Her hold on his hand tightened. "But how? I is chained to a post."

He clenched his jaw. That *was* a problem. "How many are in here?"

"Twenty or more. They plan t' ship us out come mornin'."

"Then there's no time to lose." Stew blew out a breath. "There are two armed guards out front. I need some sort of distraction so I can slip around and catch them unaware."

"Don't you fret. We'll give 'em a distraction all right."

Stew's pulse quickened. If something went awry, he'd be putting not only his own life in danger, but everyone's in here as well. "Give me a few minutes to work my way around."

She squeezed his hand before releasing it. "God be with you."

On hands and knees, Stew inched his way through the awakening captives to the opening. As he slipped outside, he drew in a breath, the fresh air filling his lungs and calming his jittery spirit. Edging his way to the front corner of the shack, he ventured a peek at the guards. They looked half asleep, one leaning against the building, the other propped against some sort of crate. Though half tempted to rush them, Stew decided his chances of downing both without getting shot were greater if he waited.

He held back, listening to a cricket chirp in a nearby shrub as he awaited some sort of promised distraction. A woman's sharp voice pierced the night air, bringing the guards to life. The one nearest the shack tapped the butt of his rifle against the plank door. "Quiet down in there."

Other disgruntled voices stirred within, growing louder as though a heated argument was brewing. "I said, quiet down."

His plea met with still more heightened voices. One of the men spewed a loud curse and moved to unlock the door. The other guard stirred from his spot and stepped up behind the first. Rifle in hand, the guard in front eased the door open. "What goes on in here?"

Stew crouched higher on his haunches. Now was his chance. With soft steps, he sneaked up behind the guard closest to him and covered his mouth with his hand. A sharp jab of Stew's knee in the man's back sent him crumpling to the ground with a moan. The other guard turned, and Stew hurled a fierce punch to his jaw before the man knew what struck him. He fell back, hitting his head against the building and dropping in a heap. With a quick glance around, Stew tossed their rifles into the darkness then searched their pockets. His fingers latched onto a small piece of metal, and he lifted it out.

Rushing inside, he called softly to Abigail.

"Over here."

Working his way toward her, he handed her the key to the shackles. As he did, small hands fastened onto him. "Mis'er Stew?"

Benji's quivering voice tugged at Stew's heartstrings. When

they'd first met, the boy had hidden. Now the youngster clung to him as though his very life depended on it. Stew brushed a hand down the young boy's back "Let's get you and your ma out of here. Your pa's waiting for you."

Free of her shackles, Abigail handed Stew the key. He placed it in the palm of the man closest to him, and raised his voice for all to hear. "Quickly. Unshackle yourselves and run to freedom."

Excited mumbles rippled through the group of captives as Stew lifted Benji in one arm and took Abigail's hand in his. Soft starlight filtered through the open door, guiding their way toward it. Before stepping outside, he ventured a look around. The guards lay motionless where they'd fallen. Tugging Abigail forward, Stew broke into a run toward the timber. With heavy breaths, they wound their way through the undergrowth and into the shelter of the trees. Neither Abigail nor Benji asked any questions, their trust in him a comfort.

A shot rang out behind them. Then another. Then curses and confused shouts. Stew quickened his pace, doing his best to shield Benji from the spray of branches in their path. He'd hidden the pony cart in a clearing some distance from the shack. If they could make it there, they'd have every chance of a safe getaway. To their left and right, other freed captives sprinted past unhindered. Another shot sounded from behind, followed by an ear-piercing scream.

Stew's chest squeezed. Some would find freedom this night. Others would not.

Stew breathed a sigh as they came to the clearing where he'd left the cart. A pony's soft nicker beckoned them closer, stirring hope in Stew's heart. He slid Benji into the cart and lifted Abigail in beside him. "Lie down," he urged. Without a word, they flattened themselves on the floor of the cart, and he covered them with a thick blanket. Hopefully the one guard hadn't gotten a good look at him before he'd punched him. He'd take no chances. No matter how exhausted, he would push through until they'd reached Annie's cabin.

Taking a seat at the front, he tapped the reins across the pony's rump, sending him into a quick walk. As they cleared the timber and veered onto the worn path, Stew drew a strident breath. His knuckles ached, his muscles were tense, his body fatigued, yet his spirit soared. He'd found Abigail and Benji, and they were on their way home.

Without a doubt, the Lord had fought for them. Stew could almost feel Annie's prayers spurring them to freedom. He could only pray the Lord would fight for him again when it came to Esther and Lawrence Del Ray.

DAYBREAK WAS DAWNING as Stew reined the pony into Annie and Toby's secluded yard. With only a couple of hours sleep, his eyelids drooped heavy. He glanced down at the lumpy blanket behind him. Abigail and Benji had made nary a sound the entire trip. They must be terrified to remain under the thick cover so long in the humid summer air.

Annie peered at him from the porch, a smile spreading over her face. She dropped her broom and sauntered to meet them. Without any urging from Stew, the pony picked up speed and headed straight for the barn area as though eager to return to his life of leisure. The meager animal was no Scout, but had done well for himself, nonetheless.

Toby laid his ax aside and took hold of the pony's bridle, stroking a large hand down the animal's face. The pony rubbed his head against him, and the oversized man responded with a toothy grin. The pair seemed to share an unlikely bond. Large and small finding unspoken friendship with each other.

"Has the Lord granted you success?" A breathless Annie shuffled up beside them, craning her neck for a look inside the cart.

"See for yourself." Grinning, Stew eased back the blanket.

Widened eyes stared up at them, and Annie clasped her hands together, her face lighting like a Christmas tree decked with candles. "The Lord be praised!"

Benji clung to Abigail, hiding his face in her lap. The horrific experience had obviously taken its toll on the boy.

Stew tapped him on the shoulder. "It's all right, Benji. You're among friends here."

A slight smile edged out the frightened look on Abigail's face. She nudged the boy up. "We's safe, son. Mis'er Stew's gonna take us home to Papa."

The boy's head lifted, a smidgen of hope stirring in his eyes as his gaze fastened on Stew. "When?"

He tossed the boy a wink. "Soon." Though Stew hated to admit it, their journey to freedom was far from over. They still had the trip across the Ohio and a lack of free papers to contend with. And right now, he was too tired to think how to manage either.

"Can't we go now, Mis'er Stew?"

Seeming to sense Stew's fatigue, Annie placed a wrinkled hand on his arm. She leaned over the side of the cart, addressing Benji in a gentle voice. "Don't you fret, child. Us and the good Lord will see you home." Then, turning to Abigail, she added. "We'll need to wait for nightfall t' ferry you across the river. In the meantime, let's get you folks inside. I've biscuits, gravy, and a pot of hot coffee awaitin'."

She winked at Stew. "After that, you'll have a chance to catch some shuteye."

Stew nodded, not knowing which sounded better, the meal or the sleep. He was as eager as Benji to cross the river to freedom, but Annie seemed to know what she was doing. And if he'd learned one thing on this difficult journey, it was to trust.

Chapter Forty

THE RIVER BECKONED, each slap of water against the bank uttering freedom. From the underbrush, Stew awaited Toby's signal. The last glimmer of sunlight had faded, and a spattering of stars shined overhead. Benji leaned in close to Stew, his body atremble. Placing an arm around the boy's shoulders, Stew gave him a reassuring wink. He and his mother had been through so much. Stew could only pray their nightmare would soon be over.

At the all clear signal from Toby, Stew led Abigail and Benji to the rowboat and helped them in. Toby loosened the rope that held the boat in place and gave it a shove with his foot. The back of the small vessel dipped deeper in the water as he climbed in. The giant of a man seemed amazingly agile for his size. Stew eased closer to the front to better distribute the weight, it taking all three smaller passengers to offset Toby's abundance.

Taking up the oars, Toby turned the boat slowly about until the city of Cincinnati loomed ahead of them. Like beacons calling them home, the gas street lights flickered in the distance. With long, even strokes, he propelled them forward. No one spoke or even moved. Stew tensed when an occasional voice carried from across the Ohio side of the river. Would Toby know a safe place to moor the boat?

The three-quarter moon glowed amber as it topped the eastern horizon. They'd timed their trip across by Annie's specifications, waiting just long enough for darkness to settle, but before the light of the moon would shine down on them. Though she'd not said as much, Stew gathered he and the Simmons' weren't the first wayward souls Annie and Toby had ferried to freedom.

When they were almost across, Toby stopped rowing and allowed the current to carry them downstream. Using one of the oars as a rudder, little by little he steered them closer to the bank away from the crux of the city. A short time later, they came to a smooth landing along the riverbank. Clearly, he knew what he was doing.

Stew hopped from the rowboat and tugged it until the bow was aground. Careful not to slosh the water too loudly, he lifted Benji from the boat and started for shore, Abigail at his heels. Setting the boy down, he turned for a final look at the gentle giant who had transported them across. Though Toby had no voice, his broad smile spoke satisfaction.

He made no attempt to exit the boat, but instead motioned for Stew to give it a shove. With a mighty push, the boat broke free and drifted silently onto the water. Stew raised a hand in unspoken gratitude, and Toby responded with a generous wave. Both he and Annie had been a blessing. Without their help, Stew would have returned to Isaac empty-handed with the news that Abigail and Benji were lost to him. Through Annie, God had given Stew a truer glimpse of the extent of His love, and for that he would forever be grateful.

A small hand slipped into Stew's, and he felt a tug on his arm. Shiny, dark eyes stared up at him, urging him forward. Abigail stood at a distance, gesturing for them to follow. On this final leg of the journey, it was her turn to lead. With quick strides they climbed the embankment and started along the darkened street toward home, their eagerness to reunite with Isaac, no doubt, spurring them on.

They gave the few people still milling about a wide berth, keeping to the shadows. Though once again on free sod, they had no papers with which to prove their freedom. If they should happen upon the wrong person, such a position was an endangerment.

Stew had lost track of time, but judging by the number of blackened houses, several had taken to their beds. His mind churned. Would yet another night pass without him knowing Esther and her family's fate? As much as he longed to see Isaac reunited with his family, he was even more eager to learn how things fared with Esther—and if there was still a chance for them.

Nearly three days had passed since he'd asked her to meet him. What must she think of him not showing? Was she worried? Irritated? Relieved? He'd dealt her quite a blow telling her what he had about her stepfather. Not having the opportunity to admit he'd been wrong unsettled him.

Lantern light shone through the window of a dilapidated shack up ahead. Abigail slowed her pace, a smile spreading over her face. She bent to give Benji a hug. "We's home."

With a giggle, Benji darted forward and pounded on the door. "Papa, Papa! Open up. It's Benji!"

A chair toppled within, followed by hurried footsteps. With the lift of the latch and a furious pull, the door swung open, revealing Isaac's stocky frame. He let out a joyful wail and thrust out his arms. Benji lunged forward and hugged his father around the waist. Abigail flew into his arms, pressing her lips to his cheek.

Happy tears streamed down Isaac's face as he leaned to plant a kiss atop the boy's head. He winced slightly at the movement, obviously still in pain from his cracked ribs. Warmed by the scene, Stew edged closer. A brilliant smile spread over Isaac's face as he glanced his way. The look of gratitude in his friend's eyes was indeed a treasure no earthly thing could equal.

Releasing his hold on Abigail, Isaac thrust out a hand. "I'm forever indebted to you, Mis'er Stew. There is no words to express my gratitude."

Stew gripped his hand. "None needed. Just seeing you together is thanks enough."

With an appreciative nod, Isaac ushered his family inside. Turning, he motioned for Stew to follow. "Come, my friend. Tonight is a time of celebration to the Lord."

Stew placed a hand on Isaac's shoulder. "The celebrating belongs to you. I have some pressing, unfinished business to attend to."

"Your lady friend?"

Stew nodded. "Yes. I need to warn her of what's happened."

Clapping him on the back, Isaac smiled. "Then go you should. And may the Lord go with you."

Stew hung his head, reluctant to put a damper on his friend's celebration. "There's…one more thing you need to know."

"What is it?"

Stew cleared his throat, regretful of what he had to say. "The freedom papers were destroyed and your money taken. I'm sorry."

Isaac's smile faded, his gaze trailing downward. "Then they're still in danger."

Stew's chest clenched. Buying one's freedom was costly. Isaac and Abigail's life savings had already been lost. It would take years to save up enough to replace the papers. Until then, Abigail and Benji's freedom would be in jeopardy. Reaching in his pocket, Stew pulled out his stagecoach money. Somehow he'd manage to find a way home, even if he had to walk. "Here. I know it's not near enough, but it's all I have."

With a shake of his head, Isaac closed Stew's hand over the thin wad of bills and nudged it away. "Keep your money, my friend. You've given enough already. The Lord is faithful. He'll provide."

Grudgingly, Stew slipped the money back in his pocket.

"God be with you."

Stew leaned into Isaac's hug, and at the same time, felt a tug on his pant leg. He glanced to see young Benji's chocolaty eyes staring up at him. "Thank you, Mis'er Brant."

He reached to tousle the boy's hair, a wave of joy washing through him. He'd earned the boy's trust, and in turn had gained a better understanding of God's love for him. From here on, he'd entrust his future to the Lord.

Starting with the unpleasant task ahead of him.

"A MOST SATISFYING MEAL, MRS. LEIFER."

Mother smiled. "Thank you, Mr. Del Ray. I'll pass your compliment onto Cook."

Esther set her fork aside, her appetite waning. The burden of uncertainty she carried threatened to undo her. She flicked her gaze to Lawrence who seemed strangely at ease in comparison to her own turbulent state. His request to join them for a late evening meal left her wondering just what he had planned. How effortlessly he masked his true intentions. If he'd not confided his accusations to her, she'd be hard-pressed to suspect the slightest discrepancy in his character. But his blatant lies regarding her stepfather left her ill-at-ease.

Lawrence met her gaze, his dark eyes probing hers. "Not hungry, my dear?"

She folded her hands in her lap, her tone a tad stauncher than normal. "Not particularly."

He smoothed his mustache, his stare lingering longer than necessary. "Well then, may I suggest we retire to the sitting room? I have some news of interest to share with all of you."

"My, but that sounds intriguing." Mother wiped the corners of her mouth with her napkin and scooted her chair from the table.

Taking up his pipe, William shined it on his shirt. "Doesn't it though?"

Esther cut a glance at her stepfather who arched a brow, seeming more attune to the situation than her mother.

Lawrence moved to slide Esther's chair from under her as she stood. Willing herself not to appear uneasy, she stared straight ahead, taking the arm he offered her. She would play along with his charade until he made his intentions known.

Her heartbeat quickened as Lawrence guided her to the settee and took a seat beside her. She'd rehearsed her response a hundred times over the past twenty-four hours. If he refused to accept the annulment of their engagement, she would divulge the secret lies he'd imposed upon her regarding William. She drew in a breath, closing her eyes in silent prayer.

Courage, Lord.

When everyone was seated, Lawrence rubbed his hands together. "Now for the happy news." Flashing his most dashing smile at Esther, he reached for her hand. "Esther and I have decided to forego a formal wedding. It's our wish to marry as soon as tomorrow."

Esther pulled her hand away, cheeks ablaze. She'd not anticipated he'd act so quickly.

Her mother's mouth dropped, shock rippling over her face as she turned to Esther. "Is this true?"

Before she could respond, Lawrence called out, "I know, we'd planned for a large wedding, but we feel a simpler one is in order. I've made all the necessary arrangements. We're to be wed tomorrow at…"

"No!" Esther's bold declaration stopped Lawrence in mid-sentence. Her stomach lurched. A refusal was destined to initiate a string of objections. With Stew lost to her, she had no other suiter, no noteworthy reason not to go through with the marriage, save her distrust and lack of affection for Lawrence. But would her mother and stepfather understand?

"What's that?" Lawrence's vexed tone and pointed stare sapped her confidence.

"I…" She swallowed, her heartbeat drumming in her ears. This was the moment for which she'd prepared, and yet the words caught in her throat, finally spilling out in a whisper. "I can't marry you."

Her mother's sudden intake of breath sounded loud against the stillness. "What?"

Lawrence's eyes narrowed. He leaned toward Esther, putting his mouth to her ear. "Be careful what you say, my dear. Either you'll marry me, or I'll take what I want by force."

Esther wrung her hands, certain he would make good his threat. Moisture pooled in her eyes. Refusing to marry him would likely bring financial ruin on William and her mother. And yet, she refused to cower to his demands. She had but one choice. Expose Lawrence for the devilish fiend he was.

Grant me strength, Lord.

Perching herself on the edge of the settee, she turned her gaze on her stepfather. "He has in mind to marry me with the sole purpose of taking over your shipping industry."

With a look of distain, Lawrence fastened his hand on her arm and whispered, "My dear, you've just sealed your fate. I'd hoped to have you of your own free will, but it appears I'll be forced to use you as a bartering chip."

Yanking her arm from his grasp, she stood and joined her rather bewildered mother.

Lawrence glanced at William, his expression growing animated. "I'm afraid Esther has a rather skewed view of our business dealings, William. She's obviously misconstrued my intentions."

Her stepfather glowered at him, not seeming to share the sentiment. "On the contrary, I've known Esther to be a shrewd judge of character."

Esther's chin tipped upward, her respect for William mounting. Lawrence arched a brow. "Then you leave me no choice." He stood, reaching a hand in his vest pocket. Striding over to William, he handed him what appeared to be a legal document. "I took the opportunity of having a lawyer draw up these papers. All you need do is sign at the bottom."

William glanced over the document. "What's this?"

A smug grin crossed Lawrence's lips. "Simply put, it transfers ownership of Leifer shipping from you to me."

With a disgruntled scowl, William wagged his head side to side. "Are you so greedy you can't wait until I'm gone to inherit the company?"

Lawrence dipped the quill in the bottle of ink and thrust it at William. "I'm afraid I am."

Mother let out a wail, and Esther placed calming hands on her shoulders. "Don't do it, William."

"I haven't the slightest notion to," he replied, taking the paper in both hands as if to tear it in two.

Lawrence raised a hand to stop him. "I wouldn't do that if I were you. You forget. I hold the financial records, and there appears to be some discrepancies which, I'm afraid, you can't account for."

William's mouth flinched, his face reddening. "Why you…"

"Stop! Come back here!" James's frantic voice sounded in the hallway, diverting everyone's attention to the doorway. It wasn't like the butler to become so agitated.

Bold boot steps approached, never once slowing amid James's repeated demands. Esther detected a slight limp in the gaited steps, and her heartbeat quickened. She peered toward the doorway in eager anticipation, gasping as Stew bolted into the room. "Stew," she whispered under her breath, raising a hand to her mouth. His clothes were smudged and wrinkled, his hair askew, and his eyes bloodshot, yet never had she seen a more glorious sight.

Without missing a step, Stew crossed the room, his gaze fixed on Lawrence.

Edging back, he looked Stew up and down with a sneer. "Who are you?"

Before Lawrence could so much as shield his face, Stew landed a hard blow to his jaw, hurling him backward. Pulling him to his feet, Stew was about to deliver another jab when Mother called out, "Please, Mr. Brant. No more violence."

Stew paused and lowered his fist, slipping a glance in first her direction, then Esther's. "Are you all right?"

Esther gave a slight nod, tears of joy welling in her eyes.

The fury in Stew's pale blue eyes died away, and he loosened his hold on Lawrence's shirt, giving him a shove backwards.

Lawrence steadied himself against the settee, rubbing a hand over his jaw. "How dare you accost me. I'll alert the authorities and have you arrested.

Stew crossed his arms over his chest. "Go ahead. You'll save me the trouble. But it won't be me they take into custody."

"Whatever are you babbling about?"

Stew stepped closer, his tall frame towering over Lawrence. "Once I tell them about your illegal slave racket, they'll waste no time putting you behind bars."

Lawrence's eyes flickered then narrowed. "You've nothing on me. No proof of wrongdoing whatsoever."

"That may be, but I know of a couple of no-good deck hands by the name of Snoot and Willy who are likely to talk to save their skins."

Lawrence paled, every muscle in his face seeming to droop. For the first time since Esther had known him, he had nothing to say.

As Stew turned an uncertain gaze on Esther, every fiber of her being melted. Myriad questions churned in her mind, but she pushed them away. It made no difference where he'd been these past few days or why he'd left her stranded without a word. The Lord had brought him back to her. That was all that mattered.

With three quick strides, she was at his side, wrapping her arms around his waist, head pressed to his chest. And as his arms encircled her, for the first time in many years, she hadn't the slightest care what those around thought or expected.

She'd, at last, followed her heart.

Chapter Forty-One

"I CAN SEE there's no use trying to persuade you to stay."

At her mother's words, Esther squeezed Stew's hand, smiling up at him. "I'm afraid our hearts are set on returning to Illinois."

Stew returned her smile, warmed by her touch and the certainty in her tone. After Lawrence had been cuffed and whisked away against his own heated protests, Stew and Esther had taken a long, moonlit stroll, during which time they'd agreed wholeheartedly to return to the prairie and take up where they'd left off.

He still didn't know what Esther saw in a broken-down, penniless cowboy like himself, but the Lord had shown him everyone was of value in His eyes. Maybe she saw something deep inside him, qualities he himself didn't know he possessed until he'd made this trip. "Chad's been more than patient with me being gone. If it's not too much of a hardship, we'd like to head out on the morning stage."

Mrs. Leifer heaved a sigh. "I suppose I never should have interfered. Though, I'm not so sure I approve of you traveling unchaperoned."

"But, we won't be. There'll be others on the stage and at the inns." Esther cast Stew another brilliant smile. "Besides, you've nothing to fear from Stew. With him, I'm in the best of care."

Stew's face flamed. Though he had to agree, he thought it best not to mention the final leg of the journey in which they'd be riding double atop Scout. And during which time, they'd be quite unchaperoned. "I'll look after her, ma'am."

The response seemed to satisfy for Clara's expression softened. "I was wrong about you, Mr. Brant. Forgive my rudeness."

The words were balm for Stew's soul, ones long in coming. "No offense taken, ma'am. I'm happy things worked out." In truth, though his heart was full, it remained a bit heavy where Isaac, Abigail, and Benji were concerned. Their freedom was shaky, at best.

William clapped him on the arm. "We're indebted to you, my boy. You've spared us terrible hardship, not to mention saving Esther from a fiendish marriage. How can we repay you? Name your price. Whatever you say, it will be granted."

A dozen possibilities pummeled Stew's mind. This was his chance to get ahead, to give Esther the abundant life she deserved. He could use some ready cash to fix up the old cabin and homestead Chad had lent him. Or better yet, purchase his own cabin and land. But he shook his head, not wishing to line his pockets with someone else's money. "I appreciate the offer, Mr. Leifer, but it isn't necessary to reward me for something God had a hand in. Having Esther back is reward enough for me."

Whether due to him allotting credit to God or his heartfelt comment, moisture pooled in Esther's eyes. She leaned into him, and Stew slid his arm around her shoulders. When he'd come here, this was all he'd hoped for. All he'd wanted. Little did he know the Lord had so much more in store. He'd been so self-centered, so shallow in his faith. All that had changed when God had gotten a hold on his heart.

When he'd looked beyond himself to the needs of others.

A thought struck him, and he smiled. Could be the Lord wasn't done yet. Straightening, he turned to face Esther's stepfather. "On second thought, there is one thing I'd ask of you."

STEW RAN a hand down Scout's neck. Other than being reunited with Esther, he'd never been so happy to see anyone. The horse whinnied and nuzzled against him.

"I do believe he missed you."

A slight grin edged onto Stew's lips at Esther's words. "That makes two of us. I never intended to leave him here so long."

Esther rubbed a hand down Scout's face as Stew set the blanket on his back. "I suppose that's my fault."

"Maybe." Her mouth twisted, and he winked at her, sliding the back of his hand down her cheek. "But I'd do it all again in a heartbeat."

He meant it too. Every bruise, every blow to the head, every agonizing minute that had brought him to this point had been well worth it.

Esther blushed, her hazel eyes fastened on his. "You frightened me half to death, you know, disappearing the way you did. I thought I'd lost you."

The memory of that night still haunted Stew. He'd come so close to death, and yet God had saved him. In more ways than one. "For a while, I thought I was a goner, but the Lord saw fit to spare me. The people who found me, Annie and Toby, taught me a lot about who God is. That He takes no stock in a person's status or appearance. What's important is whether our hearts are right with Him." He lifted the saddle onto Scout's back then paused. "I was about the least likely person God could have chosen to do His bidding, and yet He used me in ways I never dreamed possible. Sort of like David in the Bible being plucked out of the pasture to lead Israel."

Esther smiled. "Then I take it you put my Bible to good use."

"I did at that." He pulled the worn Bible from his saddlebag, having stopped to retrieve his knapsack on his way to deliver the news to Isaac and Abigail that William Leifer had agreed to purchase new freedom papers. His smile deepened. "Thought of you each time I opened it."

At his words, Esther's grinned and she stood on her tiptoes to kiss his cheek. "I love you, Stewart Brant, and I'm not afraid or ashamed to say so."

His heart drummed in his chest as he brushed a hand down her oval face. Her words were genuine and from the heart, ones he'd yearned to hear, but never dared to hope for. Pulling her to him, he leaned over and did what he'd longed to do since he'd first laid eyes on her outside the Avery cabin—took her in his arms and pressed his lips to hers.

ESTHER CLUNG to the back of Stew, swaying to the rhythm of his horse's easy gait. The stagecoach ride had been far less confining and dreary with Stew at her side. Now, as they rode together over the familiar prairie landscape, she found herself wishing the journey would never end. Even in the July heat, she loved the feel of being next to Stew. He sat tall and straight in the saddle, one hand holding the reins, the other caressing her fingers.

She'd known all along, he was special, even more so now that he'd come to a deeper relationship with the Lord. How grateful she was to have her mother's blessing and, more importantly, the Lord's. God had been faithful in answering her prayers. Against all odds, He had incited Stew to follow her to a place he must have dreaded going and, in the process, used him to aid others, all the while wooing Stew back to Him. She shuddered to think what would have happened if he hadn't come.

She'd changed as well, learning to stand up for what was right, instead of catering to the opinions or expectations of others. Only

God could fashion beauty out of such volatile circumstances. Stretching her neck, she placed her mouth close to Stew's ear. "That was a wonderful thing you did for your friends."

Stew shifted his head to the side, allowing her a glimpse of his handsome profile. "William's the one putting up the money. I only suggested it."

"It wasn't William who risked his life to bring them back."

"Even so, I'm real grateful. It's much more gratifying to know they'll be safe than to have taken a reward."

Esther smiled to herself. The man was humble to a fault. She hadn't the heart to tell him the man she married would gain a sizeable dowry. Before they'd left, William had insisted she bring a handsome sum to live on, for herself and Stew. Though she hadn't yet figured out how to get around his manly pride, she'd find a way to benefit him. He'd given so much of himself. It was time he learned to receive.

"There she is. The Circle J."

At Stew's words, Esther craned her neck to see past his broad shoulder to the pastures and small homestead beyond. Before leaving Cincinnati, she'd sent a telegram notifying Chad and Charlotte they were coming. Funny. She never had sent word of her engagement to Lawrence. Somehow she hadn't been able to bring herself to do it. Now, her heart thrilled at the prospect of one day announcing her engagement to Stew.

She caught a glimpse of Charlotte and the children headed around the side of the cabin. Rubie let out a string of barks, drawing their attention. A squeal sounded from Rachel, and she ran toward them, her crimson hair flying out behind her. "Aunt Esther! Uncle Stew!"

With a tap of his heels, Stew spurred Scout faster. They were home, and whatever the future held, Esther had every confidence she and Stew would face it together, the Lord at their side.

Epilogue

September 10, 1859

STEW PUSHED the door to the cabin open with his foot, Esther cradled in his arms. He carried her inside, pausing to drink in her beauty. She removed the wreath of wildflowers from about her head and let her golden hair flow free. Love radiated in her eyes as she stared up at him. She was his cherished bride, the richest blessing the Lord could bestow. One he would not take for granted.

He gave her a long and loving kiss then set her feet gently on the floor of their fully furnished home. In the weeks prior to their wedding, friends and neighbors had gathered to chink and daub the neglected cabin walls. Where the money for the fine furnishings—the finished bed, the corner cabinet, the wash stand, the polished silverware—had come from, Esther refused to divulge. "The Lord provides," she would answer, her smile telling what her words would not.

As he gazed into her rich, hazel eyes, all the heartaches from his past were forgotten. The journey the Lord had taken him on had been a difficult one, but so worthwhile. For all the hardships that had come his way, he was grateful for they had provided him a faith that was strong and real.

Pulling Esther into a warm embrace, he rested his chin atop her head, knowing he'd found the truest of treasures—a wife who loved him for the man he was on the inside and a faith that was sure to span a lifetime.

THE END

About the Author

Cynthia Roemer is an award-winning inspirational author with a heart for scattering seeds of hope into the lives of readers. Raised in the cornfields of rural Illinois, Cynthia enjoys spinning tales set in the backdrop of the 1800s prairie. Her Prairie Sky Series consists of Amazon Best-Seller, *Under This Same Sky*, *Under Prairie Skies*, and *Under Moonlit Skies.* She is a member of American Christian Fiction Writers and writes from her family farm in central Illinois where she resides with her husband and their two sons. Visit Cynthia online at: www.cynthiaroemer.com

f facebook.com/AuthorCynthiaRoemer

🐦 twitter.com/cynthiaroemer

Discussion Questions

1. When Stewart Brant arrives at the Circle J Ranch, he feels he has little to show for himself compared to his friend Chad Avery. Why is it a bad idea to compare our lives with others?

2. His attraction to Esther Stanton is immediate, and yet he is reluctant to pursue a relationship with her at first due to heartbreak in his past. Why do you think he struggled to get past the hurt even after three years had passed? Do you think his lax view of faith played a part in holding onto his pain?

3. Esther had what sounded like the perfect beau awaiting her when she returned home to Cincinnati—suave, handsome, wealthy, attentive—and yet she preferred Stew's company. What was it about Stew that drew Esther? How can one's inner qualities supersede outer appearances?

4. When Stew saves Rachel and becomes a sort of hero around the Avery household, how does he respond? There is a fine balance between humility and low self-esteem. Which do you feel best describes Stew?

5. Esther's main issue in the story is her lack of ability to know her own mind and follow what the Lord wants for her instead of bowing to the expectations of others. Why is it often so difficult to look to the Lord for affirmation rather than people? How should you gage when it's best not to be overly concerned with what others think?

6. Though Stew is from a slave state, he states he doesn't believe the Lord meant for one person to own another. How do his actions bear this belief out? How do Isaac and Abigail benefit from his fairness?

7. Despite her misgivings, Esther yields to her mother and Lawrence Del Ray's expectations. Why is it sometimes easier to give into the pressures of others than to do what we feel is best? God used her willingness to honor her parents to bring Stew into a deeper relationship with Him. How does our obedience to God affect those around us?

8. Annie plays a key role in helping Stew understand his value in God's eyes. What was it about her that stirred him to have a renewed heart for the Lord? Toby and Annie saved Stew from certain death by pulling him from the river. How else were they instrumental in saving him?

9. Isaac makes the comment that if a free black is taken no one would be fool enough to go after him and yet Stew does. How does Stew's willingness to help affect Isaac and his family? How was Stew's faith in God strengthened as he sensed the Lord fighting for him?

10. In the end, Clara Leifer realizes she has misjudged Stew. Why do you think she was prejudiced against him? Do you think she was right in wanting an affluent life for her daughter or should she have remained silent

and let Esther make her own decisions? How does God
work good even out of our mistakes?

Author's Note

As I considered the setting and plot for *Under Moonlit Skies*, some of which transpired in Cincinnati in 1859, I began to wonder how free blacks had been treated in the north just prior to the Civil War. The deeper I delved into my research, the more I realized how challenging life was for so called "free blacks". As tensions flared in the late 1850s, African Americans began to lose the rights they had at one time enjoyed.

Situated just across the Ohio River from the slave state of Kentucky, historic Cincinnati provided a perfect backdrop for tension and conflict within the storyline of *Under Moonlit Skies*. Though the characters in my novel are fictional, the threat for loss of freedom for blacks was very real.

With all the research involved in this diverse story, I would say this has been my most challenging novel to write thus far. But since I love research and learning about the past, it was a joyous challenge indeed!

As Stew undergoes a spiritual journey from one of selfish desires to selflessness and submission, God uses his encounters with Isaac, Abigail, and Annie to provide a glimpse of what He truly values—a person's heart.

I pray you are blessed by Stew and Esther's story in *Under Moonlit Skies*. If you have yet to read the first two books in the series, I encourage you to delve into Becky Hollister's story in *Under This Same Sky* and also Esther's sister Charlotte's story in *Under Prairie Skies*. Blessings as you read!

If you enjoy my Prairie Sky Series, I would so appreciate you posting reviews on Amazon, Goodreads, B & N, BookBub, and social media. The kind words of readers are the best endorsement an author can receive.

I welcome you to visit my website (www.cynthiaroemer.com) and subscribe to my Author Newsletter where you'll receive inside information into my novels, as well as giveaway opportunities and updates.

God bless you, dear reader. Thank you for taking the opportunity to journey back in time with me and discover some of God's truths.

Also by Cynthia Roemer

Becky Hollister wants nothing more than to live out her days on the prairie, building a life for herself alongside her future husband. But when a tornado rips through her parents' farm, killing her mother and sister, she must leave the only home she's ever known and the man she's begun to love to accompany her injured father to St. Louis.

Catapulted into a world of unknowns, Becky finds solace in corresponding with Matthew Brody, the handsome pastor back home. But when word comes that he is all but engaged to someone else, she must call upon her faith to decipher her future.

Unsettled by the news that her estranged cousin and uncle are returning home after a year away, Charlotte Stanton goes to ready their cabin and finds a handsome stranger has taken up residence. Convinced he's a squatter, she throws him off the property before learning his full identity. Little does she know, their paths were destined to cross again.

Quiet and ruggedly handsome, Chad Avery's uncanny ability to see through Charlotte's feisty exterior and expose her inner weaknesses both infuriates and intrigues her. When a tragic accident incites her family to move east, Charlotte stays behind in hopes of becoming better acquainted with the elusive cattleman. Yet Chad's unwillingness to divulge his hidden past, along with his vow not to love again, threatens to keep them apart forever.

  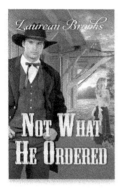

If you enjoy historical romance, Mantle Rock Publishing has many titles waiting for your enjoyment.

CPSIA information can be obtained
at www.ICGtesting.com
Printed in the USA
LVHW011541170520
655738LV00005B/134